THE LION AND THE WITCH

LYNN BRANCH

To all who have found the courage to step beyond tradition and walk their own path.

CONTENTS

PROLOGUE

ENID

ERIS TWIRLED HER SWORD, already a master at fifteen. She was weightless on her feet, dancing around like she was made of air as she sparred with Father. He beamed at her footwork, keeping his grin as he attempted to outmaneuver her and failed. I dreaded my turn. Sword practice was worse than arithmetic, and I hated arithmetic.

I sighed. It was overly dramatic, causing my mother to peek over the top of her book. Her amber eyes studied me beneath thick lashes, and she tucked a strand of her buttery hair behind her ear.

"What's wrong, little dove?"

I tossed my hand up. "Eris is so good. Everyone already talks about how she'll be an amazing Alpha. I'm not a good fighter, and that means I'm a bad wolf."

Mother frowned and opened her mouth to reply, but Father's voice boomed across the exercise field.

"Enid, chin up. It's your turn!"

I sighed again, and Mother offered me a tenderhearted smile. "You're such a good girl, Enid, always doing as you're asked without complaint."

I nodded and trudged over to the sparring circle. As expected, I was still better at arithmetic than I was at sword practice. Always slow on the block and weak of the wrist. Father bested me several times.

"Light on your feet, Enid. Footwork! Where is your footwork? Sword at the ready. At the ready! Do not drop that sword down. Punch into the block; don't absorb it. Steady, quick blows when you are attacking! Move your feet. Your feet!"

When we finished, he said, "You are improving leaps and bounds every day, dove. Very good."

"What? I'm awful." I looked up into his round face and watched his forest-green eyes crinkle with a smile.

"You worked hard. That's all I ask of you, and all that matters."

"Are you busy or can we go again, Father?" Eris asked, stepping up beside me and taking the wooden sword from my hand.

His smile broadened. "Aye. And I'm not going easy on you this time!"

I shuffled back to Mother with tears in my eyes. She took my hand, and we walked in silence towards the library. Thad, Mother's personal guard, followed closely behind; the gentle, quiet shadow that was always with us.

Mother and I loved the library. The librarian always had a puzzle set out for us. We would work on it, sometimes for hours, until we finished it. Other times, we played chess. I hadn't beaten her yet. Someday I would.

I chose the puzzle table while Mother returned her now-finished book to the counter. The pieces presented two easy matches right away, and I smiled, clicking them into place.

Mother sat down and studied the puzzle, watching me find three more in quick succession.

"Enid," she said, pulling my eyes up to hers. "I don't like when you insult yourself by comparing your worth to others, especially Eris. Everyone is special in their own way."

I ran my finger over the small notch of the puzzle piece in my hand. "But Eris is so strong."

"She is older than you and has years more practice. That girl picked up a sword when she was a toddler and never put it down again. That's why we have a rule about no weapons at the supper table!" Mother laughed, shaking her head. "Eris' passion lies in being an Alpha. It's what's expected of her. She is a strong-willed woman and is going to make an excellent ruler someday."

"So I've heard," I said dryly. It felt like that was all anyone ever talked about.

Mother chuckled and grabbed a few strands of my hair, braiding it. "Well, I'm not a good fighter. Why do you think I need Thad?" I snickered, glancing at him, and he winked. Mother continued, her brow knitting with solemnity. "Maybe you should count yourself lucky."

"Why?"

"Eris' destiny has been chosen for her already. You are free to walk your own path. I think you're more like me, my lovey dovey. Your passion lies in art and beauty. We appreciate the small things. The sweet beauty of watching the tiny seedlings in the garden find their roots and blossom into flowers. The grace of the spider as she weaves her intricate web." Her eyes filled with tears. "Sometimes I think you're much too lovely for this dark world."

My cheeks warmed. There was no one in the world I'd rather be like than my mother. Maybe I was getting too big for it, but I wiggled into her lap and hugged her. She'd been in the stables. Her scratchy wool sweater still held the musk of her horses, and it mixed with her woodsy scent, the tinge of sharp pine tickling my nose.

"As you grow older, I hope you remember one thing."

"What, Mother?"

"Compassion is not weakness. Never, ever be ashamed of having a gentle heart."

She stroked my hair and hummed one of our lullabies while we both quietly clicked pieces of the puzzle into place. I hummed along, feeling better.

When she finished the song she added, with a soft curl at the edge of her lips, "I have a feeling, my sweet girl, that you will be the most special of all."

CHAPTER ONE

LEO

I SIGHED, GLANCING AT the clock. In thirty more minutes, I could finish for the day without Gideon getting pissed at me for leaving early. After I had turned nineteen and graduated in the spring, I moved right into my position as Gamma.

It didn't matter that I hated it. It didn't matter that it did not interest me.

I loved my oldest brother. Gideon was a great Alpha, but he didn't understand me, and he didn't care to try. Gamma was basically a glorified secretary for him and my other brother, Finn. A supposed honor bestowed upon me for the simple reason of being the youngest brother.

I wanted to travel a little. Play my music. See the world and experience things outside of the pack. Gold Moon was all I had ever known. I craved more.

Finn was a little better, at least. He sympathized that I didn't enjoy my job, but he still insisted it was my duty. It was a blessing that I should be thankful to have. Many others would be happy to serve the pack in such an honorable way.

Easy for them both to say. They were in their twenties before they had to start in their official positions.

I closed the folder I'd been staring at for the last two hours. An investment portfolio that I didn't care about. I had read the same page three times, and none of it registered.

The top drawer of my desk squeaked as I pulled it open and retrieved my sketchbook. I flipped to my latest drawing, studying it and then using my pencil to soften the edges. It was Enid, of course, because I was the biggest fucking creep alive and drew her ninety-nine percent of the time.

She was my muse, as corny as it sounded. I'd loved her since the moment we'd met. Enid was the only person on the entire planet who understood my soul. I sighed at my weeping-heart drama. With Enid, I was a walking cliché.

I'd never made a move, romantically, because I was terrified of losing her as a friend. More so, it was common knowledge that falling in love before finding your true mate was a fool's errand.

She was turning nineteen this month, on Samhain, and I was a wreck, having a meltdown every other day at the thought of her finding her mate. Or of finding mine, and it not being her. My birthday had been right after the turn of the year, and the relief I felt when I paired with no one was shameful. It was so bad that I'd entertained taboo thoughts. Maybe I would reject my mate in favor of Enid.

'You will not,' my wolf, Bleiz, snapped in his deep, warbling baritone. *'Rejecting your mate to follow the Green Witch around like her lap dog would be reprehensible.'*

'I know.' I rubbed my hand down my face, wondering again who her mate could be.

'Maybe it will be us, and I won't have to listen to your constant pining all the time anymore. Goddess spare me, I am so tired of bearing witness to this melodrama that is your life.'

'Doubt she is. The Moon Goddess must have someone special planned for Enid.'

'Do not venture to know the thoughts of a goddess and do not regard yourself so lowly. Enid is a powerful being, but that does not automatically count you out as her mate.'

'I wish I believed you.'

Bleiz sighed, exasperated, and stayed quiet, not having the patience to argue this with me again.

I'd watched in horror as Daro, *Mr. Unicorn Charisma*, had moved in and swept her off her feet a few months ago. The graphite tip of my pencil snapped off from the pressure I applied, and I sighed, turning it to the eraser to fix what I'd just done. I shouldn't be upset. It wasn't his fault that he was bold enough to make a move, and that I had permanently shackled myself into the friend zone.

I liked Daro. He was a nice guy, and we had hung out quite a bit, the three of us together. Then, suddenly, he broke the silent agreement I thought he and I had brokered, and they were dating, and it was weird. Third-wheel status wasn't awesome, especially when you were in love with one of the other wheels.

There was a heavy thump on my balcony, and the right side of my mouth lifted. I closed my sketchbook and pushed my chair back, reaching for the door and unlocking it. We'd learned quickly, my brothers and I, to lock our balconies. Cass was not shy about letting himself in. It didn't matter whether you were there or not. If you weren't, he would reorganize your entire office, answer your phone, and make himself at home. I didn't mind any of those things, but I always locked my door, worried he'd open the top right drawer and find the sketchbook.

After a moment, Cass entered, dressed in his usual white shirt and black jeans. No shoes, much to my oldest brother's exasperation.

"Fine evening, Little Lion," he said around the cigarette in his mouth.

He always called me that. Maybe because of my name, or my hair. I hadn't cut it in a long time, and it was past my shoulders now. Gideon hated it, so I kept it that way.

"Cass. What's up, man?"

"I'm going to Pike's. You wanna come?"

"You know I'm not old enough to go to a bar yet."

He shrugged. "So? You're the Alpha's brother. What are they gonna do?"

"Tell him. Then we'll both be in trouble."

His chin jutted out, his lips pulling down at the sides. "Yeah, I better be careful. He's already testy with me because he had to bail me out last night."

"Another fight? Goddess, Cass."

"The other guy started it." He chuckled under his breath. "I ended it, though."

"Can't you stay away from the mated women?"

"It's not my fault! They can't stay away from me! What am I supposed to do when they proposition me?"

"Say no?"

He blinked as if he didn't understand and blew a puff of flame on the end of his cigarette, shaking his head.

When Cass had first started hanging around, I hated his guts because Enid seemed to have a crush on him. After being around him for a while, I realized that was just Cass. All you had to do was walk down the street with this guy, and you could literally smell the arousal he elicited from women. It was weird and gross.

Obviously, women with true mates didn't feel that way. The true mate bond was too strong. Chosen mates were where the dragon regularly found himself in trouble.

"Gideon says if I don't quit inciting fights, I'm going to be banished from socializing in the packlands," he said, chuckling. "I don't think he'll do it. He loves me too much."

I shook my head, laughing with him. "Yes, he will do it, Cass. If you haven't noticed, he doesn't like fun."

He tilted his head in acknowledgment of the statement, taking a long drag on his cigarette. "Well, I know for a fact that you were at Pike's two Saturdays ago."

"That's different. My band was playing a set that night."

Two of my friends from school and I had started playing casually, and it had turned into something. Some rock, some metal, and everything in between. Our drummer, Theo, had picked the name *Sordid Insanity*, and we'd gone with it. We'd won the talent show at school our senior year, and now we played at small venues. We weren't terrible. People seemed to like us. Cass, for one, loved our music. He loved all music, though. Being locked in a dungeon for two centuries had that effect, I supposed.

'I hope you don't think you're clocking out yet.' It was Finn's voice in my head.

'Why? What now?' I asked, sighing aloud.

'There's a group of vampires in the northwestern territory. Gideon wants us to take care of them.'

'Can't you take another warrior?'

'Stop being a baby. I'll see you there, Gamma.'

I blew out my lips in a raspberry and stood.

"What?" Cass asked.

"Vamps crossed the border again. Finn's making me go with him."

He perked up, grinning. "Can I come?"

'Can Cass come?' I linked Finn.

There was a pause before Finn sighed. *'Yeah, I guess Casanova can come. If he promises to leave a couple for the rest of us to kill. He takes all the fun out of battle. I'm getting rusty because I never get to fight for real anymore.'*

I smirked. "He says you can come if you leave some for him this time."

Cass was already undressing, lifting the white t-shirt over his head. "Then I suggest he hustle."

'He says you'd better hurry and get there then.'

Finn growled but didn't answer. I stood, loosening my tie and heading to the door. Cass went back out on the balcony, ready to shift to his dragon.

"Northwestern forest," I told him as I was grabbing the doorknob.

He looked over his shoulder as wings sprouted from his back. "You want a ride?"

"Nope."

I'd done that once. Never again. Crux was not a gracious mount. He reveled in your fear.

Cass was laughing as he shifted, his voice deepening to a growl. "See you there."

I turned and gave him a faux salute, watching him flap his wings and disappear into the darkening night.

ENID

This kiss was growing more intense, and a pang of anxiety blossomed in my chest. His hand traveled down my chest and pushed up my shirt, feeling under my bra and grabbing my breast. It felt good, and I hummed deep in my throat at the contact. I shouldn't have. This was supposed to just be a fun, casual thing, but I felt all the time that Daro wanted it to be more than that.

Taking that hum as a signal to continue, his hand moved down my tummy to my thigh. When he started to push up under my skirt, I broke the kiss, placing my hand on his and stopping him.

"Wait," I whispered, feeling guilty as the familiar look of disappointment crossed his features. His pastel eyes studied me, trying to find a way to convince me otherwise.

After a lengthy pursuit where I could only say no nicely so many times, I had finally agreed to a date with Daro. It had snowballed into another, and then another, until we were considered an item, apparently. It had gone well enough these last few months. Daro was simply fun to be around. He always had been. I enjoyed kissing him, but he was growing impatient with me and my hesitation to go past that. Things were different—unicorns were different—in their free-loving culture of polyamorous relationships. Promiscuity was accepted and expected.

"Wolves wait for their mate," I said. "You know that."

He sighed and rolled away, sitting at the edge of the bed. "We've attended the same high school, and I know for a fact that's not always true. There are plenty of wolves that... experiment with sexuality before they are mated to the same person forever. It's good to experience things, Enid. We don't have to go all the way, you know?"

As I often did, I used my sister as an excuse. "Eris would kill us both."

"I'm just in love with you, Enid," he said, turning back around and cuddling me to his chest. My mouth fell open, but he saved me from having to answer. "It's okay. You don't have to say it back. I just do love you. I have since I first saw you at the Dragon's Keep." He kissed me, and said against my lips, "I want you."

"Falling in love with a wolf before their nineteenth birthday has broken many hearts, Daro."

His hand drifted under my sweater, his fingers toying with my navel. "Well, I can't help it. You're so beautiful and powerful."

Part of me wanted to give in. I liked him. How I was, being part witch, I didn't even know if I'd have a wolf or, coincidentally, a mate.

My breath was shaky. His body felt good against mine, and my raging hormones stirred in my blood. So why, when I was with him, did I always think of another?

Leo. Stupid Leo, who I was stupidly obsessed with, although he'd never given me a single romantic indication. We were best friends. Soulmates in that way, but he'd never shown an interest otherwise.

I sighed and nudged his hand out from under my sweater. "I'm sorry, Daro. I'm just not ready."

Daro nodded. I knew he'd never push me any farther than I wanted to go, but his bright blue eyes searched mine, looking for an answer to my hesitation. When he didn't find one, he glanced at his phone.

"It's okay, I've got practice, anyway." We had both graduated in the spring, but Daro was helping with the football team this year.

I snatched my phone and turned it my way. "Oh, gods. So do I. River is going to skin me for being late again."

Daro leaned down and kissed me again. "See you at dinner?"

I nodded, and he smiled before he left. It was forced. The water witch in me, the empath, could sense his disappointment like a heavy blanket on the room.

I sprang up, fixing my clothing, and doused myself in sweet floral perfume. I had made it myself using rose essence. The stairs were faster than the elevator at a run, and I sprinted through the pack house, trying not to knock over any of the busy staff. Out in the back garden, River and Rhia waited. Rhia reclined on a bench, but River was pacing, and when she saw me, she folded her arms over her chest.

"Nice of you to show up. You're ten minutes late."

"Sorry. I'm ready."

"This is the third time this week. Where were you?"

"Studying," I said, and the lie was so pathetic that Rhia chuckled.

I didn't see him, but River's familiar, Gaon, a giant monarch butterfly, was floating around behind my head. I winced when he coasted past me, back to River, and landed on her shoulder. She leaned toward him, as if he were speaking to her, and her brows lifted.

"Studying the sexuality of unicorns?" she asked, and Rhia blew out a raspberry, then laughed.

River shook her head, her lips drawn in a tight line. "It's not funny. Enid, we have talked about these distractions. Chess league. Art club. Community theater. Now Daro. You have no time for them. Your water craft is shaky at best, and you are terrible with fire. We have work to do. Be serious."

"I am serious!"

"You should not be dating. You do not have time for it! Love is so messy. It distracts you, and it makes you emotional. You know how the fire feeds on that."

"Well, you're in love."

"One, I am not a fire witch, and two, I am in love because I have to be." River lifted her long sleeve and presented her witch's tattoo, a sacred mark that denoted her goddess-chosen bond to Rhia. "Life was easier when I was alone."

"Rude," Rhia muttered.

River sighed. "You know what I mean. Love is weakness. She needs to focus."

"I'm sorry that I wanted to kiss a boy and feel like a normal teenager for five seconds!"

"See," River said, looking at her wife. "Emotional."

"Just don't be late anymore, child," Rhia said, shrugging. "Hades is always on time, so that means you can be, too."

I glanced over at the fountain. My black cat familiar, Hades, was lounging in the sun. He lifted his head and yawned.

"Thanks a lot," I muttered to him, and he stood, running his back under River's hand. He agreed with her.

River scratched his chin. "See? Hades understands that every minute of training counts."

I trudged to my spot. "Then why are we still talking? Let's get started."

River dug her bare toes into the earth. "Fine with me." She manipulated the ground into targets. "Let's see some fire. And try not to let your emotions burn down the entire forest."

River was hard on me during the drills, forcing me to use fire without the aid of the other elements. I was terrible with it, struggling to get it to do as I wished. Fire was defiant, set on its own path and unwilling to listen. When we got to sparring, my frustration was peaking. River was exceptional. She had hundreds of years to hone her craft. In the blink of an eye, she sent a spattering of small dirt clods spinning in my direction. I panicked, raising my hands and releasing a torrential stream of fire. My eyes widened. I had only succeeded in turning the sandy dirt into shards of glass, which still careened towards me at high speed.

I screamed, protecting my face, and a burst of wind nearly sent me off my feet. The glass shards flew to my side, breaking against the ground and trees. I looked at Rhia, who shook her head, lowering her hand that had just saved me from some nasty wounds.

River dusted her robes off. "Practice again tomorrow."

"What? It's supposed to be my one day off!"

"Maybe you should be on time," she said, and flashed away before I could argue.

"She hates me," I muttered, scooping Hades into my arms.

Rhia walked over and put her hand on my shoulder. "I promise she does not. I know you are under tremendous stress with the world on your shoulders, but so are we. We have been chosen as your mentors by the forces that be. Your success is our success, and your failures are ours, too. If the mission is unsuccessful, we feel it is more our fault than yours. The dragon threat hides in the shadows, waiting. It is more than that, too."

"The crone," I said, having been lectured many times. My mentors suspected an old dark witch had freed the dragons and was now in their employ.

"Yes, Morga and her daughters are just as dangerous as any dragon. River knows better than anyone her power. That's why she pushes you so hard."

Dark witches often held the upper hand in duels, their advantage born of forbidden magic. They burned soul stones to amplify their elemental power, gaining an unnatural edge. The price of such evil was steep. Over time, their hearts grew black, and their youth and beauty withered away.

I looked at my feet. "I'm sorry, Rhia."

"I hold no anger toward you, child. But we must be ready. All of us."

It's all I'd heard for the past three years. "I know."

"Be on time tomorrow."

"I will be."

I trudged back to my room and showered, watching the dirt from the blows I'd taken swirl down the drain. When I got out and checked my phone, there was a text from Daro.

> *It's stroganoff tonight. Your favorite. See you at dinner.*

I frowned, sighing.

> *Sorry. I don't feel well. See you tomorrow, okay?*

I tossed the phone onto my bed after I sent the reply. I wasn't in the mood for food or for Daro. He would know I had had a bad training day, and if I tried to talk about it, he'd just give me some rah-rah speech. Positivity was good, but it wasn't what I wanted. Sometimes I just wanted to complain and have someone listen.

Even though I knew it made me a shitty, desperate person, I stood and put on my pajamas, walking down the hall and knocking a secret little tune on Leo's door to let him know it was me. If it were one of his brothers, he'd sit perfectly still, remaining silent until they left. It was something I'd been witness to, both of us trying not to laugh while Finn talked to the door, letting us know he knew we were in there.

When Leo didn't answer, I typed in his code and the door unlocked. I had his permission to enter whenever I wanted. The bathroom door was open, empty, and the room was dark, confirming he wasn't there.

Trying to forget the day, I sighed and sat down in the gaming chair. The familiar ding of the gaming console sounded as it booted up. Pushing the headset over my ears, I found the game we'd been playing lately. When I heard a familiar yowl at the door, I got back up and opened it.

Hades grumbled, and I said, "I'm sorry, I couldn't hear the scratching."

He strutted in and lingered by the chair for me to sit so he could take his spot on my shoulders.

To my cat, I said, "I'll just wait for Leo."

Like I had for years.

Chapter Two

LEO

I DIDN'T HAVE TO do much. I killed a vampire and then watched Finn and Cass compete. Cass won. He killed twenty-three. Finn killed seventeen.

Finn, never a good loser, was talking a bunch of shit to Cass, who stood there grinning with his hands on his naked hips. Shifters weren't a shy species, but Cass took it to another level, proud of his nude form.

Finn would never admit it, but it was a good thing Cass came with us or we would've had to call for backup. There were a lot more than we expected. Over forty vampires. That was a sizable group to breach the walls.

'Leo? Why won't Finn answer me?' Gideon asked through the link.

'He's pissed off that Cass killed more vampires than him.'

I didn't have to be with him to know my oldest brother was rolling his eyes and rubbing his temples. *'Well, can you give me the report, then?'*

'We killed them all, but there were over forty this time.'

'Not good. The attacks are coming more frequently. They're more aggressive, too. They're planning something. I know it. They're testing us.'

'I guess we just wait and see,' I said, deflecting the serious conversation.

I didn't enjoy thinking about it. I hated that Enid was who she was, and how dangerous her life had already been and was still destined to be. Even though I had never seen her fight, I knew she was a badass witch. Finn told me she was far more terrifying than any dragon, but to me, she was just Enid. Soft-hearted and lovely. I'd never known anyone before her who would capture a weary bumblebee and feed it sugar water out of their palm until the rejuvenated insect was ready to fly home.

'*Get back safely,*' Gideon said, '*and let me know if you run into any problems.*'

'*Will do.*'

Cass taunted Finn. "Well, I'm just saying, Beta. Don't issue challenges you can't possibly win. Why must you always disappoint yourself?"

"Yeah, fuck you, Toothless."

"Fuck you, too." Cass clapped his hands and grinned. "Well, gentlemen, I've still got a full night ahead of me."

"What, you haven't slept with every available woman in the pack yet?" Finn asked, rolling his eyes.

Cass shrugged, chuckling. "Apparently not. I keep finding new ones. Or they find me, I should say."

"Oh, shut up," Finn grumbled, and Cass snickered again. I joined him, treasuring any moment that someone annoyed my middle brother.

Finn had been quite a player before he found Kat, his true mate. But he didn't hold a candle to Cass. The dragon was the definition of emotionally unavailable. He never slept with a woman more than once.

Cass was a silly guy, but the longer I knew him, the more I peeked behind that facade. There was a wicked bloodlust in him, as with all dragons. You could see it when he was fighting. He'd just torn twenty-three vampires to pieces, and he'd enjoyed it.

He shifted and took off, the wind from his wings stirring the surrounding trees. Finn and I shifted back to our wolves and ran to the pack house together. When we were back in human form, he threw me a pair of shorts from his duffle.

I held them up with two fingers. "What are these? Women's?"

They were tiny and made of a spandex material. I was a big guy. Finn was snickering, slipping into a nice-sized pair of gym shorts.

"Whoops, did I grab the wrong pair?" he asked, unable to stop himself from grinning. "And you know the rule. No wolves in the house. Mom wouldn't like it."

"Seriously, Finn? Gods, is this stupid shit going to last forever? Is there ever going to come a day when you tire of torturing me?"

"Oh, Baby Brother. If I ever stop messing with you, it means I don't love you anymore." He ruffled my hair even though I was two inches taller than him.

So, no. I would have to endure this torture forever.

I pushed his hand away, growling.

He lifted his brows and shoved my shoulder, laughing. "Do something about it then, Gamma."

'I agree,' Bleiz hissed, hating the way Finn pushed us around. *'You are bigger. If you want this teasing to stop, then stop it.'*

I prodded Finn's open wound. "What, Cass embarrasses you, so you have to take it out on me?"

That earned me an annoyed growl in return, making me feel better.

I looked at the spandex, and Finn watched to see what I would do, his eyes boasting a familiar and annoying mischievous glint. I thought I should just walk to my room naked. That would show him. He knew I wouldn't, though, and I begrudgingly squeezed into them.

It was worse than I had expected. With the way they squished everything, it was almost more lewd than nudity. Adjusting my junk, I asked, "Why me? Why don't you bother Gideon?"

He shrugged. "Because he wouldn't let me. He'd kick my ass. Plus, I figure Cass has that covered."

He was right. Cass's chaos pushed Gideon to the edge daily.

We walked together through the house. The staff either averted their eyes away from me or covered their mouths to hide their smiles.

"Goddess, I hate you so much," I said, my cheeks burning as Finn pressed all the buttons on the elevator to drag this out for as long as possible.

When the elevator stopped on the housing floor, I pushed out a deep breath. My relief was short-lived. When we stepped off into the hallway, Finn snickered.

"Good luck, Brother," he said, beaming.

A girl, Christine, who had been pursuing me relentlessly for, like, two months was standing by my door. My face erupted with heat, and I looked down at the tiny shorts.

"No way. Finn, please. Please, let me come to your room and get something else to wear," I whispered, begging. "Or hide!"

I was holding his arm, but he twisted free, laughing.

My eyes widened when he started shouting, "Alright, good night to you, too!"

"Shut up!"

It was too late. Christine looked our way, and her eyes lit up. Then she tilted her head, eyeing my outfit. Finn abandoned me, walking in the other direction toward his room.

'Finn, I swear, one of these days.'

'Bring it,' he snapped at the challenge. *'I'm waiting, Little Brother.'*

I sighed and started towards my room, trying to hold my hands casually in front of my crotch.

"C-Christine? What are you doing here?"

'How many ways can I nicely reject someone before they take the hint?' I asked Bleiz.

'You are Gamma. Be wary of people trying to use you for your position.'

'Not Christine, though. She's nice.'

Christine was one of Enid's oldest friends. We'd all hung out over the years, and she'd never given me any sign that she was interested in me. Then, suddenly, over the last two months, her unwanted attention was a daily thing. Texts, calls, and now here she was, standing outside my bedroom.

She pressed herself against me. "I thought I would come check if you're busy." There was that, too. She had always been nice, but recently she'd morphed into this overtly sexual being that I didn't know how to handle.

She was wearing a low-cut shirt and pushed her breasts at me, making my face blaze with heat. I wasn't interested, but that didn't mean she wasn't attractive. She had wide, bright eyes. They were a nice color, a deep chocolate brown, and her fawn-brown hair was long and straight, but she always curled it. A dusting of freckles dotted her nose and cheeks, completing her soft, round features.

"Uh. Well, I was... There were. We were. Some vampires in the forest."

"So, you aren't busy now?"

She stepped forward, pushing up against me and running her hands up my bare chest.

"Uh. I am. There's sweat. On me. I need to shower, so..."

She giggled and said, "Then I'll shower with you," as my door opened.

I jumped back from Christine. "Enid!"

Enid's face flushed a deep scarlet. "Oh, I'm sorry." Her lip was split, and she had bags under her eyes. A bad day of training that she probably wanted to talk about.

"Enid. I—this is not what it looks like."

She shook her head. "I didn't know you had company. I should go."

Christine pushed past her, letting herself into my room. "Yeah, that'd be awesome, thanks."

Enid blinked, her brow furrowing and her chin jutting out like it did when she was trying not to get emotional. My eyes flicked between them. Weren't they friends? What did I miss?

Enid didn't look at me as she hurried past me down the hall. Hades followed at her heel, glaring at me as he stalked by.

Everything was happening so fast, and I was just standing there like an idiot in my spandex.

"Enid, wait! Is everything alright?"

She smashed the code into her door as if she hated the keypad. "I'll just see you tomorrow, Leo."

"Fuck!" I said to myself, watching her disappear into her room.

CHAPTER THREE

LEO

I TOOK A STEP after her, wanting to follow Enid and tell her nothing was going on here. Why, though? My heart pinched. She liked Daro. She'd been with him today. I'd smelled his scent intermingling with her shampoo when she walked by me.

I looked at my door, not wanting to go in there. But I couldn't stand here in women's spandex all night, so I put in the code and shuffled inside.

"Look, Christine."

She was right there, rushing me like a tornado of horniness. Her lips pressed to mine, and she molded her body into me.

I was thinking of Enid and Daro. It hurt. My heart had carried a constant, jealous ache these last months. It would be nice to escape it. When Christine pressed her lips harder, I didn't stop her. I put my hands on her waist, closing my eyes. She tasted like strawberry lip balm.

Christine walked me towards the bed, and I sat down when the mattress caught the back of my knees. She straddled my lap, taking my hands and pushing them up her shirt and under her bra. My face was so hot it might melt off, but I tried to be cool, like I'd done this before. I cupped her breasts, and she moaned into my mouth.

When she rolled her hips, grinding against my hard length that stretched the spandex, I uttered, "Gods," as no woman had ever touched me like this before.

She slid out of my lap onto her knees. I was breathing hard, my brow knitted with bewilderment about what she was doing. She grabbed the top of the shorts and pulled them. I realized what she wanted and grabbed her hands, stopping her. Making out was one thing, but it was customary to wait for your mate for anything past that. Christine certainly seemed like someone who would have been taught that.

"Woah. Um, Christine, are you okay?"

She looked up at me, confused. Enid's face lingered in my mind, and my gut twisted with guilt. Like I'd betrayed her, even though she wasn't mine to betray.

"You just seem different, and I was wondering if something happened?"

"I'm fine," Christine snapped, rolling her eyes. "I'd be better if you'd just relax."

"I was supposed to go talk to the Alpha," I lied, trying to slide away from her. "So I probably should go, uh, do that."

She grinned a strange smile and yanked at the spandex again. "Don't worry. I can be fast."

My eyebrows shot up. Holy Hades, this girl was desperate.

I tried not to make it awkward. "Uh, he's pissed, so I should hurry. So you should probably go."

"Oh, okay." She pouted, sticking her lip out. "But we should go out sometime?"

"Uh, yeah. I mean maybe, I guess."

"I'll text you."

I was sure she would.

"Okay."

After she left my room, I pressed the heels of my hands into my eyes and groaned.

ENID

I made it back to my room and shut the door behind me, trying to take deep breaths. I didn't know Leo and Christine had a thing. She had been distant and downright rude to me for a couple of months.

Gods, had it been going on for a couple of months and I didn't know?

"I'm an idiot," I whispered, sliding down to sit on my floor with my head in my hands.

Intense jealousy bubbled in my chest, and I wiped at the tears forming in my eyes. Why her? What made her better than me? Christine wasn't his type. At least I didn't think she was. She'd been a cheerleader and a class representative. She'd played on the varsity volleyball team. They won the championship last year. If anything, she would be Daro's type.

Maybe that was what Leo liked.

If so, then obviously I wasn't his type. The only thing I was a champion of was the community chess tournament. Two years in a row, but who was counting? Maybe I could've been good at volleyball, but I didn't have time for sports with my training.

"Leo likes Christine?" I asked my empty room. "*Christine?*" I repeated, putting my hands out. "What?"

Hades meowed, and I said, "I know, right? It's weird!"

He chortled and went to his window, curling into his bed and licking between the toe pads on his front paw. Rain pattered on the glass behind him, growing in intensity as my emotions bubbled.

I just couldn't see it. Leo was the opposite of what Christine was. He wore black every day and was so uninterested in sports or school that Gideon had to bribe him to get him to stop skipping classes. He cared about music and art.

"And Christine, apparently," I said aloud, laying my head back against my door.

Hades meowed, and I glared at him. "I know opposites attract, but... no! Not Leo and Christine! It just doesn't jibe, okay?"

He made a low sound in his chest, using his paw to wipe his ear.

"I know I'm the one that dated someone else first!" I snapped, a bolt of lightning cracking across the dark sky behind him.

Hades stopped and looked at me, his pink tongue poking out of his mouth.

"Shut up." I stood, smoothing my pajama top. "Whatever, it doesn't matter. I don't even care if they're together."

Hades grumbled again.

"What? You can't call me a liar! You still haven't fessed up to that dead mouse in my bed two weeks ago!"

He chortled, chewing at his claw.

"Oh, don't even. That mouse did not die of natural causes, and you know it!"

He rolled over, facing the window, and stuck his back leg straight up in the air, licking himself and ignoring me.

"How did she do it?" I asked, my hands on my hips.

Leo's vibe was aloof, even harsh. Many girls had tried and failed to crack the code, including me. I didn't think he was aware, but he was quite attractive. His hair was long, a dirty strawberry blonde, and a little unkempt. He ran his hand back through it when he was stressed and always put his hands in his pockets when he was embarrassed. Did Christine know that about him? His habits? I imagined not! I knew him, not her.

In his early years, he'd been a little chubby and awkward, but he'd blossomed during his senior year. He grew taller, and his body evened out. His face grew sharper, his jaw defining. Leo wasn't cut like Adonis, as were most warriors, but I liked it. It made him seem real. Those other girls liked what they saw now, but I liked him when he was chubby and awkward!

Hades meowed again, and my mouth dropped open. "What do you mean I have baggage?"

He rolled on his back, scratching himself on his bed.

"So that's it, you think? The Green Witch is too much for him. Christine has a carefree, normal life, and I've got... well, what I've got."

Hades looked at me, his green eyes sympathetic.

I sighed, going to the bathroom. My eyes filled with tears again as I aggressively brushed my teeth and wondered what they were doing in his room right now.

I wrinkled my nose when I smelled something burning, and I opened my hand. "Ugh! Darn it." I'd charred the bamboo toothbrush in the shape of my fingers. "Stupid fire."

Like I had any right to be jealous. I was dating someone else. It shouldn't matter if he also wanted to date. How selfish could I be? I'm going to date other people, but he can't?

I slumped on my bed, and Hades sauntered over, cuddling into me and purring. I ran my hand through his fur as tears welled up and fell. The rain was heavy now, tap-dancing its song on the roof. This was a new development that I'd only recently noticed. It rained whenever I was sad, and I hadn't the slightest clue how to control it.

What I really should do is tell Leo how I feel. But what if I did, and he didn't feel the same? It would ruin our friendship. I couldn't handle that. My friendship with Leo and my relationship with my sister were my anchors, keeping me buoyed in the storm that was my life.

I sighed, thinking of Daro. He was amazing, and here I was, crying about another guy who was into someone else.

"I suck, don't I?" I asked Hades, but he was asleep in my lap, purring softly.

I couldn't calm my mind, so I dug the old grimoire out from my nightstand. The Alchemist's Codex. A detailed spellbook of all things alchemy. Within minutes, my eyes were drooping at the dry, technical terminology.

Chapter Four

Enid

I T WAS THE WEEKEND, but I still had to wake up early thanks to my extra practice session. For the shifter warriors, it was their most intense combat training day. Finn, as Beta, was in charge of the workouts, and from what I understood, he ran a pretty tight ship. I knew Leo would begrudgingly be attending.

For me, it was an entire morning of elemental mastery with River and Rhia. After yesterday, I wanted to prove I was serious about my role, so I was twenty minutes early.

Unfortunately, last night was heavy on my mind, stealing my focus. I stared at the target in front of me. We were working with fire again, a precision drill. There were twelve holes, each the size of a quarter, and I had to shoot small fire projectiles through each one without burning the paper they were cut into.

Fire had been the third element to manifest for me, but it was the hardest one to master. Each element had its own personality. Their own whims.

Earth was strong and steady. My oldest and easiest friend.

Air was soft and playful but had a wild side that could easily get out of control.

Water was smooth and graceful. It was easy to manipulate because it followed a set number of rules. I wasn't the best with it yet because it was the newest, only appearing a few months ago.

Fire was the most unpredictable and violent. A destructive force, it did not like to be tamed. All the elements were powered by the witch's emotions, but fire was the most reactive by far. I had to be in complete control of myself, or it would take advantage. River said that fire witches were cold and emotionally shut off, a symptom of restraining their element.

I was certainly not in control of myself as I summoned the flames to my right hand. They sat at my fingertips and waited for my instructions, acting like they were going to listen. I concentrated, trying to compress them into smaller, more compact projectiles.

They didn't like that and fought me desperately, flickering wildly. Fire always craved freedom. It wanted to burn. The hotter, the better.

I concentrated harder, my frown deepening. *Don't be rude*, I scolded the flames and pushed the first one toward the target. It flew quickly to its destination, passing through the intended hole cleanly. I'd had to manipulate it the whole way, using air to help me hold it in form.

"I saw that," River scolded in her steady voice, her hands clasped at her waist. "No wind, young lady. This is a flame only exercise."

"I don't understand why I have to learn fire magic, anyway. Dragons are immune."

River frowned at me. "You are the Pythonissam Viridi. It is your duty to learn all four of the elements. Whether you think it'll be useful matters not. Plus, they are only immune to witches' fire in their second form."

Arguing with River was like arguing with stone.

A trickle of sweat rolled down my temple, and I looked at the flames, begging them to do as I asked. They didn't, and I grew more frustrated. As my emotions heightened, the flames grew bigger. I launched one, and it burned a hole the size of a baseball in its intended spot. I sighed.

River took a deep breath and let it out slowly. "Breathe, Enid. Do not try to control the flame."

I took a deep breath, copying her. "How can I control something without trying to control it?"

"You cannot *control* destruction," Rhia said behind me. "Only be-friend it."

"Okay." I closed my eyes, thinking calming thoughts. Hades purring. The bubble of a friendly brook. Leo strumming his guitar and singing to me. The flames calmed as I reigned in my frustration.

"Please do as I ask, friend," I said to the fire, and it flickered like it would listen.

I got ready to fire again when the image of Christine pressed up against Leo pushed to the front of my mind. Just as I let the flame go, it took full advantage of the discord. Fueled by my jealousy, anger, and hurt, it was a huge fireball by the time it reached the target; approximately the size of a washing machine. It blew through every target, incinerating the entire exercise in one fell swoop.

"Oh, Goddess! Enid!" River cried, throwing up her hands.

The fire was determined to spread, but River pulled dirt from the Earth and started choking it, putting it out. I helped her, a blush prickling beneath my cheeks.

Rhia was laughing. "Well, that is one way to end the exercise."

River glared at her wife. If you hadn't spent a lot of time with them, you would think Rhia would be the tougher of the two. It turns out, air is softer than earth.

"Don't encourage her, Rhia! Enid, what was that? It seems like you are slipping backwards instead of improving."

"I'm sorry! I lost control of my emotions for just a second," I said, holding up my fingers an inch apart.

"And what plagues your mind now, child?"

Knowing lying to them never got me anywhere, I mumbled, "Boy problems."

"Boy problems? Boy prob—gods! You can't have problems, Enid! You have to focus."

Rhia stood and put her hand on my shoulder. "River. She is eighteen years old. You can't expect her to be in control all the time. She is so young. It's normal. She's had a poor couple of days. Fire craft takes years to—"

"She doesn't have years! She doesn't have the luxury of being normal, because she's not," River snapped, looking at me. "We are running out of time, Enid."

My heart sank, both at the reminder of my dreaded uniqueness, and at the ominous warning. "What do you mean?"

River's eyes turned to Rhia. "I know you feel it, too. The earth hums with anticipation. Our enemy is preparing to make their final play for the artifact."

Rhia nodded. "The winds warn of it." She sighed and offered me a sympathetic smile, her dark eyes crinkling at the edges. "You can do this, Enid. We believe in you." Her falcon, Reinier, clacked his beak from her shoulder, agreeing, and Hades meowed his encouragement.

River went over and grabbed another target, setting it up for me. "No, you *must* do it. Now take ten steps back and try again."

LEO

I snoozed my alarm for the fifth time, rolling over in bed.

'Sorry to disturb your beauty rest, but you're late,' Finn hissed in my head. *'Again!'*

I didn't answer.

'I know you can hear me. Do you know how bad it looks when our Gamma is late for training every Saturday?'

I said nothing and blocked him. A few minutes later my ears vaguely registered the code being typed on my door. My groggy eyes tried to open. I heard it before I felt it, a slosh and the shuffle of ice. Freezing water spilled over my face, and I sucked in a sharp breath, sitting up.

"Finn! You asshole! How'd you get my code? I should—"

I stopped. It wasn't the brother I expected.

"You're late." Gideon tossed the cup onto my bed and turned on his heel.

When I arrived at the gym, everyone else was already there. Even Cass was there, fighting three young warriors at once. They were laughing but determined to beat him. Their efforts were trivial. They'd probably celebrate if they even laid a hand on him.

Finn and Gideon glared at me during my entire trek across the gym.

"Sorry, not sorry," I said to Finn. "I had a shitty night because of you."

Gideon glanced at him with an arched eyebrow.

Finn shook his head. "No excuses. Now warm up."

He exacted revenge for my tardiness for the next three hours. He made me run more than usual, lift more than usual, and then spar with Cass. Which always sucked.

When we were finally done, I checked my phone. Twelve texts from Christine? Great, I'd given her new hope. I also had a text from Marcus Pike, the owner of Pike's bar.

> *Hey short notice, but I had an act cancel last minute for tonight. Think you guys can help me out? Same time as last time?*

I linked Theo and Ethan before I texted back. They both were excited to play again.

> *Yeah, we'll be there.*

I looked up and found Cass. "Hey, we're playing Pike's again tonight."

Cass beamed, but Gideon glared at him. "You'd better stay out of trouble, Cass. I will leave you in jail next time."

"No, you won't. You're my best friend."

Gideon frowned, taking more offense than I expected. "We are not best friends!"

"Oh, come on, who's your best friend if it isn't me?"

"Finn is certainly my best friend."

"Finn is a terrible choice for a best friend."

"What?" Finn asked. "Why?"

Cass snorted, and smoke puffed out of his nostrils. "What do you mean, why? Look at you."

Finn looked down at himself. "What's that supposed to mean?"

"Oh, I think you know, Finn."

Finn's mouth dropped open, and he threw out his arms, but Cass only laughed, offering no explanation.

"He's messing with you," Gideon said, shaking his head. "Let's eat."

We all walked to the dining hall, and I looked for Enid once we passed the threshold. She wasn't there yet, but Daro was in our regular spot. He was chatting with Kat. She held her and Finn's toddler, Odin, on her lap.

After the battle of Diamond Moon, our pack had been flooded with pups whose parents had been killed. Kat and Finn decided they had to do what they could to help. They adopted a four-year-old girl named Sierra. Eris and Kat had rescued her after the vampire horde killed her mother. They also adopted the baby boy that Gideon's best friend, Rudy, and his mate Beth had died saving. His car seat had the name Odin written on it, so they kept it.

"Hey," I said to them, sitting in my spot.

That left an empty seat between Daro and me so Enid could sit. That was how it had been for the last three years.

Finn sat on the other side of Sierra, who was on Kat's right. She was seven now and hugged him tightly around the neck.

"Look!" she told him, holding up a drawing of their family.

Like Kat and I, Sierra loved to hang out in the art room.

Finn studied it for several long seconds. "It's very good. You caught my handsome jaw perfectly."

Kat laughed, and I rolled my eyes.

"No!" A small yell sounded from across the table, drawing everyone's attention. Meals were madness these days with all these kids.

"Henry." Eris held up the spoon, trying again.

His arms were crossed across his chest, and he pursed his lips, glaring at the spoon. Peas, his bane. Well, not just peas, but anything that was the color green. Broccoli, beans, and salad were all unacceptable as well.

"I want meat!" Henry said, growling like the little wolf he was.

Ceres sat on Eris' other side, judging her twin brother with a look of distaste while she ate everything on her plate.

Gideon took the open seat next to Henry.

Eris reasoned, "Henry, you have to eat peas if you want to grow big and strong like daddy."

"No! I want to grow big like Leo!" Henry said, grinning at me.

Finn barked out a laugh, and Gideon scoffed. I smirked. Henry was now my new favorite. Eris looked at me, pleading with her eyes.

I got the gist. "Oh. Yeah, I eat a lot of peas for sure." I took a bite of my own for emphasis. "Mm, love those peas."

"Fine," Henry said, taking a bite and making an exaggerated gagging sound as he swallowed them.

Eris sighed and turned back to her own food.

Cass was the last one to show up, walking in with Enid and drawing a lot of female attention, as usual. He sat on my left, and to my relief, Enid sat on my right in her usual spot. She wasn't mad enough about last night to move seats, at least. Everyone continued with the meal, chatting casually.

Enid didn't look or talk to me, choosing instead to focus completely on Kat and Daro. He had his arm around her waist, holding her close to him, and I thought I might pull a Henry and barf up my peas.

"Little Witch," Cass said, pulling Enid's attention our way. She looked past me at him. "Did Leo tell you he's playing at Pike's tonight?"

"Really?" she asked, finally addressing me. Her smile was genuine. She'd been the one who'd convinced me to share my music in the first place, talking me into playing one of my songs in the school talent show. "They must have liked you guys if they asked you back."

I nodded, shrugging. "Yeah, I guess. Someone else canceled, though. I mean, it's not a big deal."

Cass clicked his tongue. "It certainly is a big deal. You should come, Little Witch. You and Daro both. It will be fun."

"Cass." Gideon rubbed his temples. "I know I'm not listening to you inviting minors to a bar. Please tell me that is not what I'm hearing. Especially not Enid. She cannot be at the bar."

"Not to drink, you grumpy old man!" Cass said, patting me on the back. "To support their friend."

"You're the old man," Gideon grumbled, taking another bite and returning to the conversation he was having with Eris.

Everyone finished eating until it was just Daro, Enid, Cass, and I left.

Enid and Daro got up to leave, and Daro smiled at me. "Good luck tonight, man."

Enid nodded. "Yeah. Congratulations again, Leo. I really wish I—we—could go to your show."

"Then you should go," Cass replied before I could say anything.

She glanced around. "You heard Gideon. He would be so mad."

"He won't even know. You guys just show up and watch Leo's set and then leave. No big deal."

I scoffed. "Yes, he will definitely know."

He shrugged. "Well, I live my life along with the philosophy that it's better to ask forgiveness than permission. Seize the day."

"Well then, you are nailing it, dude," Daro said, laughing.

Cass arched his brow. "Thank you, dude. Now, I'm just saying, Little Witch, you're the most powerful being on the planet. You can do whatever you want, and you should. You work so hard. Have some fun. Marcus will let you in if I ask him to. I'm his best customer."

That I certainly believed. Pikes had done some renovations lately, probably fully funded by Cass's alcoholism.

Enid had a glint in her eye that reminded me of the day when we'd taken a car without permission, and I'd driven her to the dragon's keep so she could help save Eris.

She blurted, "I'm in. I'll do it."

I glanced at Daro. He was as stunned as I was, but he was grinning. Enid was usually such a rule follower. A levelheaded, responsible young adult. I couldn't believe it.

"I'm in, too," Daro whispered, glancing around to make sure no one heard us.

Chapter Five

Enid

"OH, GODS, WHAT AM I doing?" I asked myself in the mirror.

Hades was lying on the rug and meowed crossly, laying his chin on his paws.

"I'm sorry. You can't come. We've talked about this. I'm going in disguise."

For once, I just wanted to be another girl. Someone else besides the Green Witch. River had said it today. I didn't have the luxury of being normal, and she was right.

Enid always had to be sensible. It was not possible for Enid to have boy problems, or live a normal life, or make any mistakes. Enid was *always* in control. Enid always did as she was told.

Maybe, this once, I could just be someone else.

I looked down at the colored contacts I'd ordered a while ago. This wasn't the first time I'd thought about altering my looks to make myself less noticeable. They were a dark cerulean blue, and I hoped they would be opaque enough to hide the bright fluorescent green of my natural eyes.

I grabbed the small can off my sink. It looked like hairspray, but it was a temporary hair color spray. The color was "Ruthless Red." With the Samhain celebrations right around the corner, it had been easy to find. My hair was past my mid-back, so I'd gotten three cans just in case.

I had already showered and dried my hair, like the instructions said to do, and I had a trash bag on like a poncho over my clothes so it wouldn't stain.

I went to work, spraying my long wavy hair. My natural color was almost white, so it was working better than I expected. When I finished, I giggled in the mirror. The red was a brighter, more cherry color than I was prepared for, but I could handle it.

The contacts were last, and after several minutes of a sharp learning curve and frustration, they were in. I blinked a thousand times, trying to get them to settle. They were uncomfortable, but it didn't matter when I saw how well they covered my natural color.

"What do you think?" I asked Hades, and he blinked once, got up and left the room.

"You're just mad that you can't come!"

He chattered back like he did at the birds out the window when he wanted to murder them.

"Don't be a sourpuss!"

Hades ignored me, and I smiled at the girl in the mirror. No one would know I was the Pythonissam Viridi. For once. In fact, unless you knew me really well, you most likely wouldn't recognize me.

I heard a quiet knock on my door. Daro was there, glancing up and down the hallways. He looked sharp in an emerald-green, one-button, two-piece suit. The blazer was unbuttoned, and he wore a yellow-gold t-shirt underneath.

He gaped, his mouth open while he tried to find words for me. I giggled, grabbing the front of his shirt and pulling him into my room. We were both old enough to go out, so we didn't really need to be that discreet, but we wanted to avoid questions because I was a notoriously terrible liar.

"Holy shit, Enid, you look totally different!"

"I know," I squeaked, bouncing on my toes. "Gideon will be less likely to find out if I'm not so recognizable."

I offered that explanation instead of the actual truth: *I'm tired of no one seeing the real me, so I don't want to be the Green Witch tonight.*

"It's hot," he said, holding up his fingers and framing me like I was a picture. "Like a hot Jessica Rabbit look. You should color your hair like that all the time." He looked me up and down. "I don't know about the outfit choice, though. It's a little trashy."

I looked down and laughed. I was still wearing the garbage bag.

I pulled him into the bathroom. "You need to check and make sure I got all of my hair before I take it off."

He eyed the hair dye spray, unsure. "Okay, I'll do my best."

There were only a few little spots I'd missed on the back, and he did fine.

I ripped the trash bag off and tossed it into the recycling bin. As an earth witch, I always insisted on the compostable ones because I felt bad about the waste. The pack house had certainly gone greener since I'd been living here, with Gideon sending out truckloads of recyclables to the human world at my request. Now, if I could get him to sell the private jet, I would be happy. That gas-guzzling beast made me sick.

For my outfit, I'd chosen a pair of black high-rise chino shorts accented with two rows of gold-tone buttons up the front. My blouse was an off the shoulder white top with bell sleeves. I was shorter than most shifter ladies, so I wore black ankle boots with a good-sized heel.

Daro whistled, making me blush.

"Seriously," he said, framing me in his fingers again like he was taking another mental snapshot. "Who are you, and what did you do with Enid?"

Having my bare shoulders and neck so exposed felt a little scandalous to me. I was more of a hand-knitted sweaters and pleated skirts type of girl.

"Are you wearing lipstick?" Daro asked.

I frowned. "No, should I put some on?"

"No." He grabbed my waistband and pulled me into him, trapping me with his body against the bathroom wall.

The kiss deepened, and I wrapped my arms around his neck. He ran his hands down my back, over the curves of my shorts, and squeezed while he pushed his hips against me. I could feel that he was hard through our clothes, and my face warmed, a thread of desire unraveling in my lower stomach, but a pang of panic in my chest. The kiss continued until I was breathless, and his hands were trying to untuck my shirt. As always, I just didn't want to go past that.

I broke away, grabbing my phone off the sink and looking at the time. "We've got to go or we'll miss the start."

He huffed, but he was smiling. "Fine, but we're continuing this later, you know?"

LEO

Cass and I sat together at a table, waiting for my set to start. I needed to head backstage soon and get ready. There weren't tons of people here yet, but Cass was starting early, per the norm. Three empty shot glasses sat in front of him, and now he was drinking something on ice. He could drink an enormous amount of alcohol and still somehow not get drunk.

"Cass, you keep drinking like this and you might die," I said, half joking and half not.

"That's the point," he muttered in a singsong, running his finger over the rim of the glass.

I blinked. "What?"

"What? Just kidding."

"Cass... gods. You alright, man?"

"Oh, yeah. Sorry. A little dark humor."

He drained the glass, and the server was right there the next second, flirting with him and setting another drink down in front of him. He'd already slept with her once, so he was masterfully averting her aggressive advances. She was like a dog with a bone, and I was almost embarrassed for her and the way she threw herself at him.

"What do you do to those women in that tower?" I asked, watching her walk away.

He smirked, glancing over at her. "What they want." She got back to the bar, and he fixed me with a serious look. "You should tell her how you feel."

"Who? The server?"

"Our sweet little witch. Tell her you love her already, my gods. It's painful to watch you suffer."

"I don't know what you're talking about."

He rolled his eyes. "How dumb do I look?"

"Do you want me to answer honestly?"

"You'll seriously regret it if you don't," he said, ignoring my joke.

I leaned closer, giving up the idea that I could deflect the conversation. "What if she doesn't feel the same way? It would ruin our friendship."

This was the first time I had ever openly admitted the truth to anyone. I knew people suspected it, especially Finn and Kat, but I had never actually said it out loud.

"I think you'll be pleasantly surprised."

"Really? Why? She likes Daro."

"Daro is wonderful. Daro is also not you. You never know until you try. If you don't try, you'll regret it."

His tone was so dark. "What's up with this mood you're in, Cass?"

"Hm," he said, his brows coming together. "I haven't been sleeping well."

"Hey, Leo! This amp is being weird again!" I looked and saw Ethan waving to me to come backstage.

"You should tell her. Good luck, Little Lion," Cass said, downing the rest of his drink and heading back to the bar.

What he was wishing me luck for, I couldn't be sure.

CHAPTER SIX

ENID

WE DROVE TO PIKE'S even though it was relatively close to the pack house. Daro had asked if I wanted to walk, because I almost always did if the destination was close enough. This time, I'd looked at the shoes I was wearing and opted for the car.

By the time we arrived, a crowd was forming outside. People laughed, holding drinks and lit cigarettes. Pikes was a popular bar, but it certainly wasn't like the bigger clubs we heard stories about in the Fae Kingdom. It was low-key. There weren't any bouncers or lines or anything like that.

Daro took a deep breath. "Cass told us to just walk in like we belonged here."

Acting cool even though my heart raced, I nodded. "Yep."

It surprised me how much of my self-confidence was curled up in his bed at home. Hades and I were rarely apart, and I felt his absence more than I expected.

Daro grabbed my hand and led me inside. I waited for someone to stop us. People glanced our way, but no one said anything. We looked for Cass, heading to the back room where the stage was set up.

I could hear the music but knew it wasn't Leo's band. This was electronic dance music, and *Sordid Insanity* played rock. As I suspected, a DJ was on the stage, and a crowd of people was dancing while several others sat at the tall tables along the walls.

I scanned the crowd and pointed. Cass was at a table with a group around him. There were several shot glasses in front of him, and he was using his breath to light them on fire. The surrounding people cheered him on. They all picked up their shots, blowing out the flames on the alcohol before they took them. Cass lifted his glass and gulped it without blowing the flame out. Everyone around him paused, and then cheered louder when he grinned, blowing out a puff of smoke.

One of the most beautiful wolf shifters I'd ever seen pressed herself against his side and appeared to whisper something in his ear. Cass looked at her with a smirk and then whispered something back to her. I could see her body shudder at whatever he said.

"Cass's life is crazy," Daro said, as we both watched the exchange. "He's like a celebrity. He is like my hero."

Being the only dragon around that didn't want to murder or enslave everyone did kind of make him like a celebrity.

"You want to be like Cass?"

"Look at that! Every guy wants to be Cass at least a little."

Daro and I shuffled over towards them, sticking to the wall. Cass saw us and said something to his little crowd of people. They all headed back towards the bar.

We sat at the table with him, and he beamed, throwing his arms out. "You made it! It shouldn't be too long until our Little Lion roars."

Leo's equipment was set up on stage. His guitar, which he'd taught me to play a few songs on, was leaning on its stand, plugged into an amp. It made my heart blush to think of those times, his arms around me while we played the notes together.

A hand fell on Daro's shoulder. "Now, I know you're not old enough to be here!"

We both jumped, thinking we were caught. Daro laughed when he looked over his shoulder and saw who it was. I recognized him. His name was Dane, and they'd played football together. He'd been a senior the year Daro started here, so he was probably just old enough to be at the bar now.

"Danny, what's up, man?" Daro asked.

Danny held up his hands, showing that they were dry and calloused. "Working my ass off. Been busy on the walls. We finished them last year, but now the maintenance is an everyday thing. Alpha pays well, though, so I'm not complaining."

Gideon had commissioned that all the pack's lands be surrounded by walls. It was an ambitious project, but Finn had planned and executed it with such precision that it was finished within the time slot expected. A lot of the young wolves who had graduated in the last few years had aided in the construction, all learning various trades.

Daro and Danny chatted, and it quickly segued into football.

I looked at Cass and shrugged.

"So," he said, his brows lifting, "that hair."

I blushed. "You hate it?"

"No," he said, taking a quick drink to hide the lie. "And if I did, it wouldn't matter if that's what makes you happy, Little Witch. Life's too short to care what other people think." He paused a second and then added, "Your life, anyway. I'm practically immortal."

I provided my prepared explanation. "I thought maybe Gideon wouldn't find out if I weren't so obvious."

"Right," he deadpanned, dragging out the word. "It's definitely the hair and not your crushing aura that gives you away."

I looked around and saw that people were watching me and sighed. I'd tried in the past to control the power of my aura, and I could somewhat if I sat in a meditative trance and really focused on it.

So much for being someone else.

Cass noticed my mood and tilted his head. "What's wrong?"

Cass was perceptive. Of everything. It was impossible to hide anything from him. I glanced at Daro, who was still in an animated conversation with Danny.

I shrugged. "I don't know. For one night, I hoped I could live a normal life. Not be me, you know?"

His features fell, a deep sadness dragging them down.

"Hey," Danny said, cutting in. "Do you mind if we borrow him for a second?"

I looked behind them and saw two more guys who used to be Daro's teammates.

"Oh. Uh, no. Not at all."

Daro was grinning, already having a great time as Danny dragged him away towards the bar area.

Two people walked close to our table, and I caught a piece of their conversation. "Yeah, here they are. These are the guys I told you about. They're great. The singer is the Alpha's little brother. The Gamma. I had no idea."

When I looked back at the stage, I saw that Leo's band was ready to start. I smiled, biting my bottom lip because I was nervous for him. I had listened to Leo play for years, but this would be the first time I'd actually seen a show besides the talent shows at school.

Cass, whose sadness from earlier had completely disappeared, was whistling through his teeth and clapping.

They made final adjustments, and then Leo stepped up to the mic. I sighed, leaning on my hand. He was wearing a white cut-off t-shirt, black ripped jeans, and black boots. So simple, yet so attractive. I felt like a puddle sitting in that chair, looking up at him on a stage for the first time. His long hair was down, as usual, and I noticed him run his hand through it. People pushed up to the stage, forming a thick crowd.

Leo squinted into the lights. "Hey everyone. We're happy to be back at Pike's. We are *Sordid Insanity,* and I hope you like the show!"

They started into a song, one of their originals that I knew Leo had written. Usually, I was the one who heard all of his music first, and I wondered if that would change now that he had Christine.

The crowd reacted with cheers, enjoying the song, and I joined the clapping. Leo had worked hard on his music for a long time. He had been so shy in his early years that I never expected to see him receive the recognition he deserved.

Cass loved it, bouncing his head to the beat. I watched Leo, not even noticing Ethan on the bass or Theodore on the drums.

After a few minutes, I looked at Cass, who was watching me with lifted brows and stuffing a fry into his face. When did he get food? I blushed, realizing how zoned out I'd been.

"Just tell him," he said, sighing and rolling his eyes.

"Tell who what?"

"Leo! That you're in love with him."

Butterflies stirred excitement in my stomach. "If only I could."

"You can. You see him every day. Watch." He took two fries out of his basket and, with a squeaky voice, moved one up and down, saying to the other fry, "Oh, Leo, you are so handsome with your fancy guitar. I am in love with you. Kiss me," then putting the fries together and making kissy sounds.

"Stop!" I said, grabbing the fries and looking around to see if anyone had noticed his theatrics. "He's my best friend, Cass. I couldn't handle it if our friendship were ruined because he doesn't feel the same."

He put his head back and laughed. Then he put his fingers to his temples and rubbed them, sighing and shaking his head. "Oh, you are killing me. I think you'd be surprised, Little Witch."

I studied him, my heart beating faster. He and Leo were good friends. They hung out all the time. Had Leo said something to him?

"What about Daro?" I whispered, finding him laughing at the bar. Danny was handing him a full shot glass of clear liquid.

Cass wrinkled his nose. "Why are you with him?"

"You don't like him?"

"It's not that. You're not a good pair, though. It feels forced."

I looked down at my hands, picking at my fingernails. "He's great. And he's wanted to date me for so long. I didn't want to keep saying no."

Cass sighed. "If you don't really have feelings for him beyond that, then you're just being cruel, stringing him along like this."

The honest words set in my chest like stone, and I sighed, feeling the slight burn of tears in my eyes. I used my control over water to dry them up, not wanting my makeup to run all over my face. When I glanced up, my eyes went straight to Leo again.

Cass chuckled. "The heart wants what the heart wants."

"I wish I was more like you. You're so confident."

He stared down at his drink, swirling his finger around the rim of the glass. "Trust me, Little Witch, you don't want to be like me."

"Well, what does your heart want?"

"It doesn't matter. My heart lost its chance a long, long time ago." He stared down at his drink and said, almost to himself, "And I can't ever seem to get drunk enough to forget it."

I put my hand on his. "I'm so sorry, Cass."

He swallowed and shook his head, gently taking my hand, which was tiny compared to his, and squeezing it. "Like I said, it was a long time ago. But that's why I can't just sit by and watch you let what you love slip through your fingers."

"Cass. The friendship thing is important, but you know with wolves the actual issue."

"Whether you're true mates."

"If we're not, we'll both be with others. Falling in love before..." I shook my head. "It's just not what we do."

"Would you regret it?"

"What?"

"Loving Leo. Would you regret that if you ended up with another?"

"I don't think so."

"Then why are you feeding me these lame-ass excuses?"

"I-I..." I shrugged, unable to find an answer for him.

His lips curled, and he drank the rest of whatever he was drinking and then signaled to the server. She looked up at him, and he held up three fingers. She seemed to understand what that meant and hurried to the bar. When she brought three more shots to him, he handed her an unreasonably large bill, which made her smile. Cass brought one to his mouth and lit it on fire, then drank it.

We watched Leo sing a slower ballad that stretched his rough voice in the most beautiful way.

"I love you like silk loves the spider,
Woven in instinct, drawn ever tighter.
A thread spun of fire and morning dew,
Binding me tightly, completely to you."

"I'm in love with him," I blurted, looking at Cass.

"Yeah, duh. What are you going to do about it?"

I grinned and then snapped my fingers over one glass, using my magic to light it on fire. He laughed when I took it and drank it myself. Like Cass, I was immune to my own fire and I couldn't be burned. Although my hair could be singed off, which was a bad look. The alcohol itself burned, though. It was my first drink ever, and whatever it was, it was disgusting.

I coughed as if I might die and fought back the urge to throw up.

Cass patted my back. "You might want to start with something a little softer than one fifty-one."

"I'm good," I said around a smoky cough, giving him a thumbs up.

CHAPTER SEVEN

ENID

LEO AND HIS BAND played ten songs: three originals, and seven covers. The crowd loved the show, cheering an ovation to the performers when they were done. Leo was floating on a cloud, grinning and thanking them into the mic, his voice rough from use. He was totally in his element up there.

I had stolen two more shots from Cass before he cut me off, claiming Eris would skewer him with Dragonsbane if she found out. My head was light and spinning from what I'd drunk already, so it was probably a good thing.

Daro had obviously imbibed plenty and was playing pool with his friends, laughing as he swayed, trying to line up a shot.

Now that the band had stopped playing, the lady shifter from before had returned. She didn't even sit at the table, instead strutting up and sitting on Cass's lap. *Good for her*, I thought. She knows what she wants, and she's going for it. Maybe I could be that brazen.

The overt affection she was giving Cass made me feel awkward, so I excused myself and went to find the restroom. A sign indicated it was down a dim hallway next to the stage, and I journeyed into the low light. With the buzz I had going, it felt like a little adventure. There were doors on both sides, and I saw the sign for the men's but not the ladies'.

A door on my left slapped open, and I ran right into the person stepping out, nearly tripping. He caught me, and it was weird how I could tell who it was from the feel of his embrace.

Leo peered at me in the dim light, and I saw his eyebrows lift in surprise. "Holy shit. Enid?"

"Sorry."

He sniffed and eyed me, a little smile curling his lips. "Have you been drinking?"

I blushed but nodded. "It was just a tiny bit, I promise."

He laughed, shaking his head. "Wow. Cass really wants Gideon to kill him."

"It's not Gideon that frightens him," I said, giggling.

Leo chuckled. "Eris?"

I nodded. He hadn't let go of me yet, and I leaned into his warm embrace. His shirt was sweaty from performing, but I didn't care.

For some reason, I blurted, "These shoes really hurt my feet."

He looked down. "I'm sorry. That's why you're taller tonight."

I laughed, nodding.

He grabbed a piece of my hair. "And what's this?"

"Just trying to be inconspicuous, I guess."

"So, you chose cherry red?"

I shrugged, blushing.

"Is it permanent?" he asked, wrinkling his nose.

"No," I gushed. "It will wash out. Why? Do you hate it? I think Cass hates it..."

"No, I don't hate it! It's just I would miss you. Well, you know, not you. I would miss how you look... I like how you look. But both colors look good. You could never look bad. I'm not saying the red looks bad. It looks great. I just prefer the original."

Leo's face had grown progressively redder as he rambled, and he pursed his lips shut, sighing.

I giggled, and he said, "But I really like your outfit."

I looked down to remember what I was wearing, and my eyes went straight down into my cleavage, pressed up between us.

I smirked up at him, raising a brow. "Is that so?"

He looked down, but his eyes snapped right back up. More color flooded his face, and I giggled again.

"Do you need me to hold you?" he asked, motioning to his arms. "Are you okay?"

"I'm okay. I like it, though."

I searched his eyes, seeing a spark of surprise. It grew until there was a heat in his gaze that women could always recognize.

LEO

I couldn't breathe as I stared down at Enid. She was looking at me differently now than she ever had. Studying me through her lowered lashes, she parted her rosy lips. I didn't know how much she'd had to drink, but that had to be it. Right?

'*She certainly desires you right now,*' Bleiz said. '*A very confusing female, this one.*'

My cheeks warmed when he said it, but I knew he was right.

"Leo?"

My arms tightened around her. "What's up?"

A door farther down the hall banged open, and Theo walked out, looking for me. Oblivious to what he'd just interrupted, and to the fact that I wanted to pummel him for it, he asked, "Are you gonna help us with this equipment or what?"

I glared at him. "I'll be there in a second."

He looked at Enid as if he were seeing her for the first time, and then slowly backed up and closed the door again.

My eyes flicked back to hers, but the look had shifted away. She sighed and then whispered, "That was a really great show."

"Oh. The show. Thanks. I'm glad you came."

"Do you know where the girls' bathroom is?"

"Yeah, it's just down there," I said, hitching my thumb toward the end of the hall.

She smiled, but it was forced and gently slid out of my arms.

"Enid? You're not mad at me, are you?"

"For what?"

"That stuff. With Christine. She's—I don't like her. She's been pur- suing me, but I don't want her."

"Oh, that." She shrugged, holding onto the wall as she walked away. "Why would I be mad about that?"

My mood soured even though I had been on cloud nine after the show. It had gone so much better than the last one thanks to the changes Ethan, Theo, and I had made.

However, the hallway scene with Enid poisoned the evening. First, her appearance, which I didn't know if I liked or not. Her clothes, definitely yes. She made knitted sweaters look sexy every day so seeing her in that outfit was killing me. The hair I wasn't sure about, and I hated the contacts.

When she returned from the bathroom, she'd acted like nothing had happened. I wasn't sure if anything had.

Daro's football buddies had gotten him trashed, and he'd sung karaoke for over an hour. It had been funny at first, but now he was looking rough.

"We better get you home," I told Daro, helping him stand up.

He nodded, grinning at me. "I love you, man. You're a good friend."

"At least he's a happy drunk," Cass said, rising from his seat.

I adjusted Daro on my shoulder. "Well, are you going to help me?"

Cass chuckled as if he were surprised I asked. "No, I have other things to do. Literally. Her."

His eyes fell on the girl at the bar, who had made her intentions with Cass very clear already. Several times. And her friend, whom she pointed at as if to ask, "Her too?"

He grinned and gave a thumbs up, saying, "Oh, another. Nice."

I rolled my eyes. "Well, thanks a lot, Casanova."

"I'm not the one who got him drunk. Find that Danny guy to file your complaints with."

"Yeah, what about her?" I looked at Enid, who was bobbing her head to some drunk girl's terrible rendition of "Take Me Home, Country Roads."

Cass shrugged. "She's fine. Poor girl deserves some fun."

His choice of the night sidled up to him again, with her friend in tow. "Are you ready, Candy?" he asked.

She frowned. "It's Cindy."

I snorted a laugh, but Cass didn't miss a beat. "My mistake. You're just so sweet."

She giggled, and I scoffed. This fuckin' guy. Honestly, at this point, he probably could've called her Dave and she still would've gone home with him.

He led them towards the exit, and I heard him ask, "How do you ladies feel about flying?"

"Are you ready?" I asked Enid.

"I flushed my keys down the toilet," Daro slurred, laughing.

My brows lifted. "That sucks. Sober Daro is probably going to regret that one tomorrow. It looks like we're walking then."

The pack house was nearly a mile away, and it was all on an incline. Daro had practically passed out, leaning on me with his eyes closed. Cool. I'll just carry two hundred pounds of deadweight muscle uphill. No big deal.

We walked a little way before Enid abruptly stopped. "Wait."

She sat on someone's fence and unzipped her shoes, set them on the sidewalk, and then started home again.

"Do you want those?" I asked.

She glared at them and then shook her head.

I laughed. "Okay."

"They're so awful," she said, giggling. "Never again."

She tried to help me with Daro for a bit, but I eventually just slung him over my shoulder and carried him. Enid walked in front of me in her socks, stopping every so often to grab a flower that was dying as the days got cooler. She concentrated now on an orange rose and made it bloom, then grinned at it. Which of course made me smile.

River scolded her for it, insisting she let nature follow its cycle as intended, but Enid always kept the flowers in our garden blooming until her birthday. Which was three Saturdays away, on Samhain.

I watched as she floated along, completely entranced by her dance with the flowers.

It made the walk easier, and I was almost sad when the pack house came into view. We snuck to my room, which was down the hall opposite everyone else's.

I set Daro on my bed, but he got up and stumbled to the bathroom. Enid and I cringed when he started retching.

"You'd think he was a dragon," I said. It sounded like he was vomiting fire.

Enid knocked. "Daro? Do you need help?"

"I'm good," he said, laughing from the other side of the door.

Typical of him to still be having a great time while barfing his guts out. Enid giggled, probably thinking the same thing.

We sat on the bed together, and she crawled over to the button on my wall that opened the skylight. I listened to the mechanical whir as the shield retracted.

She lay on half of the bed and pointed. "Look, there's the Big Dipper."

When I was little, I got super into astronomy. My dad would bring a book of the constellations in here and we would sit on my bed and find the ones we could through my skylight. It was one of my best and most special memories of him. That and sword practice. He'd told me once I was better than Finn and Gideon were at that age, but I couldn't know if he was just saying so. Maybe I could've been really good, but I lost interest after he died. Now, I felt connected to him by the stars. And to Enid, having shared our sacred game with her.

She loved to learn, and we would lie here and I would show her the ones I remembered. She always started with, "Look, there's the Big Dipper."

I laid down beside her and scanned the sky. "You remember Cassiopeia? The W."

She searched for a few moments. "There!"

"And right next to it, Cepheus, the one that looks like a house," I said, smiling and pointing. I tried to remember some that were only visible in autumn. "Ah, Pegasus is there."

Enid leaned closer to me, and I tried to draw it with my finger so she could see it. She smelled like roses and lightning.

"I think I see it?" she said, giggling.

Daro stumbled out of the bathroom. "This game again? You guys are such neeeerds!"

As he said it, he fell face down on my giant beanbag. He didn't move again, but I saw his chest was rising and falling, so I knew he was alive.

I pointed out the rest of the constellations I remembered, attempting to fill the heavy silence that was trying to fall between us.

Giving up on finding any more, I shrugged. "I could probably see more outside. That's the problem with the skylight."

We laid there. All I could focus on was how close her body was to mine.

"I've missed this," she whispered.

I sighed. I had been avoiding both her and Daro since they started dating. It sucked too much to be around them.

"Me too."

I miss you, I thought.

I felt her hand searching, and I swallowed when her delicate fingers laced with mine. My heart thundered so loudly I wondered if she could hear it, and I glanced over at Daro, guilt twisting my gut. Her thumb drew circles over mine.

I thought about my conversation with Cass. Should I just tell her now? It felt so wrong with Daro right here.

I ran my hand down my face and braved a glance over at her. Her eyes were closed, a small smile pulling at her lips.

CHAPTER EIGHT

LEO

I WOKE UP FIRST out of the three of us, the open skylight showcasing the pinks and oranges of the rising sun. I snorted a laugh at Daro, who was hugging my beanbag affectionately. A small pool of drool formed where his face pressed against it.

When I laughed, Enid stirred, and I froze. I looked over and saw that she was right next to me. Her hands were wrapped around my upper arm and the side of her face rested gently just above them. She was below the covers, but I laid on top, like always when she slept over. Elation fluttered in my chest, but it was quickly shot down by guilt.

Her hair was a mess of red tendrils spread around her head, and her makeup had smudged under her eyes, but she was still the most beautiful thing I'd ever seen in my life.

I stared at her, greedily accepting this moment of privacy to look at her unabashed. Her soft pink lips drew my attention. Our faces were close. I should just kiss her.

She is dating your friend, I reminded myself.

The conflicting feelings were too much. An unfamiliar heat seemed to appear between us last night, but it was probably the alcohol that drove her.

I eased out of Enid's grasp. When I was free, she frowned in her sleep and turned over to face the other direction.

I was still wearing the same clothes I had on at the bar, so I gently opened one of my drawers and grabbed some jeans and a t-shirt, heading to my bathroom.

To my relief, they were both still asleep when I returned, and I shuffled to the door. When I opened it, Hades bolted in and jumped on my bed to be with Enid.

Sunday was my only proper day off, so I headed to the art room that Finn had built for Kat. I always left a sketchbook there. I trusted Kat. She had already accidentally looked in it once, so I knew she knew what, or who, I was always drawing. I didn't think she'd ever told anyone, though, even Finn.

It was quiet until the door opened and Kat entered, not surprised to see me. I was drawing Enid, of course, in her socks and smiling at an orange rose she'd just brought back to life. Usually, I didn't draw with color, but this one was special.

"Missed you at breakfast," Kat said, a strange smile cracking across her face.

I looked at my phone and realized I had been there for nearly two hours. There were about twenty texts from Christine. I should never have kissed her.

I closed my sketchbook and stretched. "Wow, I didn't realize what time it was."

"I think your brothers are looking for you."

As if on cue, Gideon's voice floated through my mind.

'Leo, can you come to my office?'

I sighed. *'It's Sunday.'*

'Leo.'

'Fine.'

He must have already found out about our being at the bar. Thanks a lot, Cass. I had to go up a floor to his office, and I knocked and then walked in.

He and Finn were there.

I thought maybe I should just start apologizing, but I stayed quiet. It was a good choice because Gideon didn't mention the bar.

"There's an emergency meeting tomorrow. All the packs have been experiencing an uptick in vampire activity."

I nodded, thinking I would get a break from them. "Okay, so you guys are going?"

"No, you and I are going," Gideon said. "It's in Obsidian Moon."

"What? That's almost the farthest pack! You should just take Finn."

My arms went out at my sides, and I knew I was somewhere on the border between arguing and whining, but I didn't care. I did not want to spend all week in podunk Obsidian Moon listening to Alphas talk about vampires and defenses and blah blah blah.

Gideon shook his head. "Finn is staying."

"Why does he get to stay?"

"Because I need him here to watch the pack when I'm traveling."

"I can watch the pack!"

Finn snorted. "If you put in a little more effort on training days, maybe we'd believe you."

I glared at him. I couldn't argue with the truth, though.

"He's right," Gideon said, holding up two fingers. "We have two weapons that can kill dragons. The spear and the bow. You don't seem interested in refining either of those skills, so Finn is staying and you're going. End of discussion."

I clenched my jaw, and he looked at his phone. "The meeting starts tomorrow at eight in the morning, so we're leaving in an hour. You'd better go pack a bag."

I turned on my heel and left. I hated it when they ganged up on me like that.

When I got back to my room, Enid was gone. I stared at the bed where she'd been lying and smiled. I missed her there already.

"Daro?" I asked, shaking him. "You alive, man?"

He groaned and turned over, squinting at me.

"What time is it?"

"Almost ten."

He sat up and groaned again, holding his head.

"Holy shit, I have the worst headache of my life."

"You were pretty drunk last night."

"Yeah, I don't remember much." His face fell. "Did I embarrass myself?"

I smiled, remembering his hour of karaoke.

"Well... it depends on how you feel about singing 'I Don't Give a Damn About My Reputation' at the top of your lungs to the entire bar."

He winced and laughed. "Shit. Was it good?"

"It was certainly entertaining."

"I'm gonna go to my room and sleep the rest of the day. And then I'm gonna go find Danny and kick his ass for getting me so drunk."

I laughed and slapped him on the back, making him groan. "You also flushed your keys down the toilet."

"Awesome," he said dryly, standing and burping into his hand.

After he left, I hurried and showered and then packed my stupid bag for this stupid meeting.

ENID

When I woke up, I found that Hades had taken over the bed, and Leo was gone. I kissed his head, and he purred, glad to be with me again.

Daro was still passed out on the beanbag. My gut twisted. The guilt set in, tying knots in my chest. I knew Cass was right. It was wrong to stay with him, especially after last night. The only thing that kept me from kissing Leo was hurting Daro more. I didn't want to do that to him, or to myself. I wasn't a cheater.

Daro deserved better. Someone who really loved him. I wrapped Hades around my neck and let myself out of the room.

Out in the hall, I froze when I saw someone coming out of Finn and Kat's room. It was Kat, thank the Goddess, and she eyed me before bursting out into laughter.

I blushed, remembering my ridiculous hair. My eyes burned from wearing the contacts all night, and I couldn't wait to get to my bathroom and take them out. They were on an express train to my trash can.

"We missed you at breakfast," Kat said, her smile still broad.

"Yeah, I slept in." My cheeks grew hotter when she arched her brow, looking past me at Leo's room.

Kat sniffed and then glanced around, ushering me to my room. "You'd better go shower before your sister or someone else gets a whiff of that alcohol."

"Thanks, Kat."

I leaned down so Hades could jump onto the bed, and then I stripped my clothes off. When I looked in the bathroom mirror, I covered my mouth, laughing into my hand. My bright red hair was standing up in every direction, and my makeup gave me raccoon eyes, all the black from my mascara flaked and smudged.

"Well, good morning, Bozo," I said to myself, immediately digging the contacts out of my eyes.

When I started showering, it looked like a murder scene as the red washed out of my hair and swirled down the drain. It took a long time, and a couple of different shampoos to get it out. Plus, I was in a deep-thought-shower-world, so I loitered under the water.

My birthday was right around the corner. I knew Leo had to be my true mate. He had to be. If he wasn't, I didn't want one.

"You hear that, Moon Goddess? It's him or no one. I'd rather be a forty-year-old virginal cat lady than have to love someone else!" I declared and then added in a whisper, *"Please, please."*

Eris was probably in her office, and I hoped Kat was, too. I lucked out, finding them sitting together at Eris' desk.

"What's up?" I asked when it looked like they hurried to close the browser window.

Kat said, "Nothing," and Eris said, "Important pack business."

"You're shopping, aren't you?"

They both smiled, their eyes sliding to each other, and said, "Nope!" at the same time.

I sighed, bending to scoop up Hades where he was wrapped around my ankles.

"What's wrong?" Eris asked, her eyebrows furrowing.

"Have either of you ever... broken up with someone? In, like, a nice way?"

Eris shook her head no, which didn't surprise me. To my knowledge, Gideon was her one and only relationship. Kat answered yes, though.

"He's my friend. I don't want to hurt him, you know? I'm sorry."

Tears filled my eyes. I wasn't sure why I was apologizing to them, but I felt so bad for Daro and like such a horrible person.

"It's okay," Eris said, coming around her desk to hug me. "We'll help you figure it out the best we can."

Chapter Nine

Enid

I took a deep breath and knocked on Daro's door. I'd put this off all day yesterday, hiding out in the garden most of the day. It was time. This pit in my stomach wouldn't disappear until I did it. Kat had counseled me thoroughly, and we'd even practiced different scenarios.

Daro opened the door and smiled, making my heart cleave. He had no idea.

"Enid! I've been looking for you."

He reached for me, but I stopped him, crossing my arms. "Can we talk?"

His hands dropped to his sides, and he mumbled, "That sounds bad," but he stepped aside and let me in.

I didn't know what to do. Sit? Stand? I just turned to him, wanting to get it over with. I could see from his fallen face that he already suspected what was coming.

"Look, Daro," I said, trying to keep eye contact but having to look at his forehead. There was a slight bump there where his horn lay dormant. "We've been friends for a long time, and you're one of the most important people on this planet to me. But I can't give you what you deserve. You deserve someone who loves you with their whole heart, and I can't. I've tried. It should be easy to do; you're so amazing and kind." I felt the tears in my eyes, and I whispered, "But I can't."

"Enid…" he said, his mouth falling into a deep frown. "I thought things were going well. We've been good. We have fun! I mean, Enid, I love you."

I cleared my throat. "I know this isn't the way you wanted things to be, but I can't keep leading you on knowing that you're committed to something that I can't commit myself to. My birthday is coming, and I might have a mate."

"But you might not. You're part witch! Enid… come on. Let's just wait until your birthday and see. If you have a mate, then I can accept that."

My cheeks flushed. I didn't expect him to argue so heavily in favor of keeping the relationship. "This is why wolves shouldn't date. It's just pointless."

"It wasn't pointless to me."

My heart sank. "I'm sorry, Daro. That's not what I meant at all! You just deserve better."

"There is no one better!" His tone was snappy, asking, "It's Leo, isn't it?"

I sighed and looked back down at my hands, picking at my cuticles. I told myself I was going to be honest, and I was. "Some of it."

He crossed his arms over his chest. "I thought something was weird at the bar! Did something happen after I passed out? You guys are supposed to be my friends! I thought wolves were loyal!"

"No, of course not! Nothing happened!"

A huge pang of guilt cracked in my chest. I knew he was talking about physical cheating, but emotional cheating was certainly a thing.

"But that's why I need to break up with you," I admitted.

"Because you've wanted to be with him while you're with me?"

Gods, was he going to make me say it out loud or what?

I said nothing, which I guess was answer enough. He sucked in a sharp breath, running his hands over the sides of his head. My water witch kicked in, absorbing his emotions. Shock, disappointment, hurt. I wanted to run out of the room.

"I know you need time. And I know it's cliché, but I would be really sad to lose you as a friend, Daro."

"Yeah, I need time," he said, turning away and lacing his hands behind his head with a sigh. "And I hope you find what you're looking for, Enid. I really tried to give it to you."

When he said nothing else, I opened the door quietly and stepped out.

A little sob escaped my lips, and I turned, hurrying down the hallway. I put in the code on Leo's door and opened it, only to find an empty room.

Frustrated, I linked him. *'Leo?'*

He didn't answer. Leo had his block up a lot, usually ignoring his brothers, and the pack link had a maximum range of a few miles.

I pulled my phone out and texted him.

> **Where are you?**

I saw the three bubbles in the corner indicating he was texting back.

> **At some defense meeting with Gideon in Obsidian Moon. Why?**

My heart sank.

> **Nothing. I just wanted to hang out.**

> **Sorry. Would much rather be doing that, trust me.**

> **No, it's okay. When will you be back?**

> **Gideon says Thursday or Friday depending on how things go. :(**

I sighed. After waiting three plus years to tell him the truth, three or four more days felt like an eternity.

> **Okay, I'll see you when you get back.**

I glanced at the time on my phone and winced, turning on my heel and jogging to the elevator. If I ran the whole way, I would only be a little late for elemental mastery.

LEO

We'd arrived late last night and had gotten up super early for this meeting. Having already gotten in trouble once for doodling in my notebook, I watched my brother as he addressed the room, detailing the attacks on our territory and listening to the other alphas.

I was so bored I thought I might die.

The only other person close to my age here was Glinda, the Alpha of Emerald Moon. She had taken over after Rudy had been killed during the battle of Diamond Moon. I thought her brother would be proud. She took everything seriously—much more seriously than I did—and didn't let these old chauvinistic windbags get her down.

When we were done with the meeting, Gideon and I walked back to the room. My thoughts were with Enid, as always. She had texted me earlier today, and I opened the conversation, reading through it again.

"When are we leaving?"

Gideon was untying his shoe and sighed. "I already answered this question three times today. The answer hasn't changed."

I frowned at him and then looked back at my phone, picking a song I liked and stuffing my earbuds into my ears.

CHAPTER TEN

ENID

THE NEXT THREE DAYS flowed like sap in December, but I received confirmation from Eris that Gideon and Leo would be back that evening. Like I had the other two days, I went and found Eris and Kat with the kids.

Right now, we were at the bathtub in Gideon and Eris' room, giving the boys a bath.

"Giraffe," Henry said.

I concentrated on the water I had suspended in the air and shaped it into the form of a giraffe. He giggled and then I made it walk, which made him squeal in delight.

"Cow," Odin said.

Henry sighed. Odin always said cow. It was his favorite animal.

I shaped the cow and then made it look like it was eating grass. He clapped and bounced up and down. "More!"

"Dinosaur! Rawwwwr!" Henry shouted. I shaped a T-Rex and made it walk and then made a roaring motion with it while I said, "Rawwwwr!"

Eris came in, holding Ceres' hand and leading her to the sink. "Alright, children, we've got jammies and then teeth brushing and then bedtime."

"I want more animals!" Henry yelled.

"Henry, must we argue over everything?"

He giggled. "Yes! A pack of wolves, Aunt Enid! Hunting their *prey*."

My brows lifted at the way he said prey, and I heard my sister chuckle.

I grabbed towels, picking Odin up first to dry him. "I promise I'll be back next bath time, okay?"

"Fine." Henry put his arms up so I could lift him out.

Eris said, "Let's get you to bed, Henry. Aunt Kat will be here shortly for you, Odie."

Henry frowned. "I don't want to sleep. Not yet. I want Daddy to put me to bed."

"Well, I just linked him. He won't be home for thirty more minutes."

I was drying the water around the tub and perked up. "They're almost here?"

Eris' brow lifted. "Yes?"

"Oh, cool," I said, trying to play off my sudden excitement.

Henry said, "Oh. That's okay, Mama. I'll wait in your bed 'til he's home. Come on, Odin!"

Eris sighed and watched Henry and Odin run naked as jaybirds into her bedroom. She called, "No jumping! Henry, do not climb that!"

I snickered. "How was the meeting?"

Eris shrugged. "Pretty standard, I guess. Gideon wants to send some of our warriors to help the smaller packs."

"But you don't?" I asked, reading her tone.

"We need everyone here to protect the artifact. And you."

"But if the other packs need help, we can't just abandon them."

"I know. I just want you safe."

She stroked my hair like she did Ceres' and smiled, choking up a little.

"What's wrong?"

"You just grew up on me so fast. I still think sometimes that you're still that little girl in our cabin out in the woods, and then moments like these just hit me. Watching my own kids grow up is hard enough."

I smiled at her and hugged her again. Eris had cared for me like her own child after our pack, and our parents, had been decimated by the dragon Xeron. She'd been my age when that happened, and I couldn't imagine it.

"I love you, Eris, and I am so thankful to have you."

"I love you, too," she said.

I hurried down the hall to Leo's room to wait for him. No more games. I would just tell him. I would tell him I broke up with Daro and my true feelings for him, and whatever happened, I would deal with it.

Finally deciding was such a relief, and I threw myself onto the bed, giggling. When I did, I heard something fall out of the pillow or mattress and thump on the floor.

I sat up and looked, realizing it was one of Leo's sketchbooks. He was very protective of them. No one ever got to see what was in them, not even me. My cheeks warmed because it had fallen open on the floor.

The sketch was of me and Hades together. I was lying on our favorite garden bench and looking up at Hades, who was perched on the rail and leaning over my face. I touched it to confirm it was pencil because it was so detailed I thought it might be a black-and-white photograph.

"I remember this day," I mumbled, blushing deeper as I picked it up.

I turned the page, and my breath caught. It was me, smiling back over my shoulder in a summer dress that I liked to wear. I turned the page. It was me again. And again. And again.

LEO

The drive at the beginning had been quiet, but a couple of hours ago, Gideon and I had argued about my needing to put more effort in. Needing to train harder. Needing to care about my duty more.

It had been an awkward two hours since, and I couldn't wait to be home. I had my headphones in, but he said something else.

I ripped one earbud out. "What?"

"Is it really that bad? Being my Gamma?"

His face was impassive, but the heavy tone of his voice made my heart shift gears, sinking away from anger.

I sighed. "It's not like that."

"Well, what is it? I don't understand what's so bad about it."

I put my head back against the seat. "How old were you when Dad died?"

"Twenty-three."

"So that makes Finn twenty-ish when he became Beta."

"Yes."

"I graduated high school, and the next day I had to put on a tie and go to work! I didn't get any time to do anything I wanted to do."

"It's not like I was partying, Leo. I was at Dad's side from the day I graduated, even if I wasn't Alpha. What do you want to do that is so important?"

I sighed again. "I don't know. See some of the world before I'm stuck at the pack house for the rest of my life. Play my music for people somewhere besides Pike's. Maybe I want to go to college. I don't know. But I don't get to do any of it because of my *duty*."

College meant going to live in the human world, so people didn't do it often.

I stared out the window, expecting him to tell me how silly it was.

"Leo, I understand your feelings, but you have to realize what a delicate place we're in with the pack."

"I know. The war."

"But I'll consider it if you'll agree to some rules."

I stiffened, thinking I must be hearing things. "What?"

"If you go, you have to pick a subject relevant to your future position as Gamma if you want the pack to pay for it. Because I expect you to come back someday."

"Really?"

He laughed. "Yes, really."

"Thank you! Like, can I start looking? Applying?"

"Yeah," he said, and put his hand on my shoulder. "I just want you to be happy."

When we arrived, I hurried upstairs. I wanted to find Enid, desperate to tell her about potential college.

My door was cracked, and my brow furrowed. I pushed it open and found Enid was already here.

I grinned and started, "Enid!" but I froze when I saw what she was holding.

She held one of my sketchbooks open in her hands. Everything stopped, culminating in heat and pressure that clawed up into my face until I thought the top of my head might blow off. The displayed sketch was a particularly embarrassing one of her I'd drawn this summer. She was in a bikini on the beach at the lake, with Hades wrapped around her ankles. I had spared no detail when remembering the curves of her body.

"What is this?" she asked, tilting her head to study me.

I stared at the sketchbook, wishing it would burst into flames. "Why are you looking at that?"

"It-it fell," she stuttered, waving her hand at the bed.

Her pale brows were knit in the center, and I thought I might vomit. I blurted, "I'm so sorry," and spun away, thankful Finn was exiting the elevator. Shoving past him, I hopped on, my brain trying to catch up with what just happened.

"Hey! What's wrong with you?" he asked, but I jammed the button until the doors closed.

I hurried out of the house and shifted, running to the only place I could think of. The guard tower door rattled on its hinges from the way my fist hammered against the aged wood.

Cass opened it and peered out at me. "Little Lion? Do you need some clothes?"

I ignored his question, shoving past him and going to his kitchen sink. I splashed cold water on my face because I really, really thought I was going to be sick.

"What is it?" Cass asked, tossing me a pair of sweats.

"Well, I told her my feelings! On accident." I plopped into a chair and put my face in my hands.

"And it didn't go well?"

"I don't know. I left before she could say anything."

"About what?"

I recapped the horror of the sketchbook, my drawings, and her finding them.

"So, you didn't wait to see what she had to say?" he asked, sighing and rubbing his temples with his ring fingers.

"She probably thinks I'm a creep. Gods! Why did she have to find that book?" I ran my hands down my face and whispered, "The under the mattress one."

Cass wrinkled his nose and shook his head. "I don't want to know. You should've just told her before this happened. Then you wouldn't look like a weirdo stalker."

"Well, let me just hop in my time machine and go fix it!"

"Just go face the music. You live in the same pack! It's not like you can avoid her forever."

Cass spent the rest of the evening trying to convince me to go back and talk to her, but I refused. He agreed to let me stay there. One night. He said he wouldn't be a party to my stupidity any longer than that.

After he went to bed, I lay on the couch and stared at the ceiling. I would have to face her eventually, but the embarrassment of her seeing those sketches was unparalleled. I'd prefer to wear women's spandex through the pack house every day if it meant today never happened.

I did my best to close my eyes, but I wasn't very successful. The night seemed never-ending, and I was glad when morning came and I could stop trying to sleep.

Cass came down the stairs, and to my surprise, cooked an enormous breakfast. It was one of the best meals I'd eaten in a while.

"I didn't know you could cook," I said, shoveling pancakes into my mouth.

"One must learn if they live alone."

"Well, you're good at it."

"I know. I'm very skilled," he said, smiling and sitting at the table with me.

Good ol' humble Cass.

"What's your plan with the Little Witch?"

I shrugged. I really didn't know.

He sighed but didn't badger me. "Well, I have to go look for a new Samhain costume today. Gideon said I couldn't wear the one I had last year."

I snickered. "I'm not surprised. It was pretty risqué. There're children there, you know?"

"It was a police officer," he said, scoffing. "There's nothing wrong with that."

"A hat, a collar with a tie and a badge, and a pair of bikini underwear doesn't count as a police officer."

He rolled his eyes. "You sound like your brother."

I looked down at my plate. "He's going to let me go to college."

"Really?"

"Yeah. I told him I wanted to, and he said I could go. I couldn't believe it."

"Incredible what happens when you clearly and concisely use your skills of communication to tell someone the truth," he said, dragging me back to Enid.

I sighed. "If she shows that sketchbook to Eris and my brother, I'm dead. Gods. She must think I'm such a creep."

"Maybe she doesn't."

"It doesn't matter," I said, trying to distance myself from her. "She'll turn nineteen, and then she'll find her mate."

"Yeah. Maybe it's you."

"It's not me," I said, shaking my head and pushing my plate away, my appetite suddenly gone. "Why would I be? She's so special, and I'm... just me."

"Enid is just Enid, too, and she craves nothing more than to be seen that way. You already give her that."

"I don't know."

"Would you regret it? Loving her while you had the chance?"

"For the next two weeks?" I asked, lifting my brows.

"Who knows what will happen? Maybe you get to love her for one week, or one month, or one year. Or an entire lifetime."

I swallowed. "I've loved Enid since the day I met her."

He stood. "Just tell her that. I'm going shopping. Clean up the kitchen for me if you're going to hide here all day."

I looked around at the disaster he'd created. "Okay."

Cass went upstairs to gather his clothes, and I got started on the dishes, lost in thought while I washed them. He would leave out the tower window, and I saw the darkness of his shadow fall over the forest when he did.

A few minutes later, the front door opened, and I asked, "What'd you forget?"

A voice that was definitely not Cass said, "Nothing."

I ducked to look under his kitchen cabinets and dropped the dish I was washing. "Enid!"

Chapter Eleven

Enid

I WATCHED THE EMOTIONS roll across Leo's face. Shock. Shame. His cheeks reddened, and he glanced down at my hands, his brows lifting. I held the sketchbook, and I drummed my fingers softly on the leather cover. Last night, I'd looked at every picture.

"You found me," he muttered, shifting on his feet.

"You're not good at hiding." I glanced down at the book in my hands. "Or maybe you are."

Leo was still ducking to look at me under Cass's kitchen cabinets, and he winced, coming around the counter to face me.

"I... uh." He blew out a raspberry. "I know you're probably angry to find that. I'm sorry—"

"Yeah, I'm angry!" I stepped forward and slapped him on the chest with the book. "Of course I'm angry! I want you to explain this to me, Leo." When smoke curled around my fingers, I took a deep breath, not wanting to incinerate the entire book. Or Leo. Not before I heard this explanation, anyway.

He blurted, "You weren't supposed to see it."

"Well, I have, so now you're going to tell me why you've drawn these." I flipped through the pages, like I had done a hundred times since I'd found it. They were beautiful, all of them. I blushed, seeing the picture of me in my swimsuit. Leaving that one open, I looked up at him, arching my brow.

Keeping with his stunned-stupid answers, he said, "I like to draw."

If he was going to make me spell it out, I would. "This is more than an affinity for sketching. There are dozens of them. What are these? I think I deserve an actual answer, don't you?"

I saw the crack in his eyes, the light hazel color shifting as honesty broke through. He ran his hands down his face. "Okay. Okay." His brow furrowed. "Those, Enid, are depictions of what in this world I am most afraid of losing."

I looked down at the soft leather cover, running my finger over the supple texture. "Me?"

He scoffed. "Are you shocked? Really?"

There was an undercurrent of vexation in his tone that made blood rush to my cheeks. "Why shouldn't I be?"

"Why shouldn't you?" He paused and pursed his lips, laced his fingers on top of his head and then threw his hands out to his sides, as if to physically release himself from his tied tongue. "Because it has always been you! You walked into my home four years ago and bewitched me! I was a kid who didn't give a shit about anything that didn't contain a guitar riff, and then you were there, and it was over for me. When would I see you? When could I speak to you? When I might be clever enough to make you laugh so I could see your smile! The songs I write. The drawings. It all became you."

"If that is true, then why, *why*, did you never think to say something?"

His expression softened, and his shoulders dropped. "Because it soon came to worrying about when I would lose you. What if I said something, and it ended our friendship? What if you have a mate?"

It was my own logic being applied, so I shouldn't be angry, but I was. All this time of wondering and waiting, and the answer had been right there, tucked under his mattress.

"I can't believe you thought I wouldn't reciprocate."

"Well, I understand if you don't want to be friends anymore..." he started, and then his eyes widened. "Wait, what?"

"Are you shocked? Really?" I asked, rolling my eyes and tossing the sketchbook to him before turning on my heel.

He fumbled to catch it, yelling at my back, "Well, yes, I am! Where are you going?"

"I am late again for elemental mastery!"

I exited Cass's tower into a torrential downpour. There hadn't even been a cloud in the sky when I'd walked here. It came down with such ferocity that I slogged through quickly forming puddles on the dirt path, uncaring of the water that seeped into my sneakers.

"You can't just say that and walk away!" he said behind me, yelling over the reverberation of the rainfall. "Enid, wait! If you feel that way, then why are you so angry?"

A crack of lightning snapped just overhead, followed by a crashing roll of thunder that vibrated my eardrums. "You should've told me!"

"I could say the same to you! I'm the one who has to watch you date someone else! You think that's easy?"

I pressed the heels of my hands to my temples, and lightning cut across the sky. "I was trying to get over you!"

"Well, how could I have known that?"

"Well, it doesn't matter, does it? You don't fall in love before you find your mate. Everyone knows that. We both know it's dumb, right?" I asked, turning to him. My eyes brimmed with tears, and the rain grew heavier, washing down the trail in a cutting river.

Leo stopped, his chest heaving, and studied my face. "Yes. Everyone knows the rule. It's foolish."

I nodded, turning slowly back toward home as the rain softened to a drizzle.

"But I just have to know one thing."

I opened my mouth to answer, but his warm fingers, dotted with the calluses that came from playing the guitar, closed tightly around my upper arm, stopping me. It was like a dream, blurred by the gentle rain. Our noses touched first, his brushing mine in a quick, subtle seeking of approval. I pressed up on my toes, tilting my head, and felt his hand hold tighter to my arm as our lips met for the first time. His were soft, reminding me of the first snow in winter, and punctuated by the cool press of his lip ring. One small overdue kiss, and he pulled away from me. I didn't open my eyes, staying as I was, with my head tilted and my breath shallow.

His voice was hoarse, and I felt the wind of his breath. "As much as I enjoyed that, I feel really, really shitty about Daro."

My brow furrowed, a small smile curling my lips. "I broke up with Daro days ago. That's why I was in your room, to tell—"

He interrupted me by kissing me again. This time it was much more, his tongue against my lips and his arms wrapping around me, crushing me into an embrace that trapped my curled arms between us. My fingers fisted the soaked material of his shirt, and my mouth opened, welcoming and desperate to taste him. It was maple syrup mixed with the peppermint candy I'd eaten on the walk up here.

Our feelings blossomed together, becoming what seemed to be a dangerous dare. Inviting each other to let go of what we knew—everything we'd ever been taught—and welcome the foolery of this kiss.

Neither of us shied away. His hands slowly found their way to my wet hair, cradling my head. My arms wrapped around his neck, pulling him closer. I felt weightless, like I was floating in water, my brain absent of the worries I had carried for the past four years. I was just Enid then, enjoying a kiss I'd dreamed of often, and delighted to find it was better than I could have ever imagined.

A fluttering between our noses finally stopped us, and I opened my eyes to find the sun beaming through the leaves. A warm wind stirred the forest, sending the colored leaves into their autumnal tumbles, one renegade having landed between us.

Leo plucked one from my hair and looked up at the sky. "The weather is erratic today, isn't it?"

"It's my doing, and I don't understand it. That's why I'm always supposed to be in control." I looked up into his eyes, the soft hazel green bright and burning. "But that can be difficult when I'm around you."

Leo pushed my hair out of my face. "You don't have to be in control around me. I am not afraid of you, Enid." His brow furrowed, and he put his forehead to mine, sighing. "But I don't know what to do now, because I don't think I'll ever be the same after that."

I acknowledged my thundering heart. "Me neither."

I pressed onto my toes and kissed him again, vowing that I would be able to let go if we discovered on my fast-approaching birthday we were not mates.

Half of me believed it, at least.

CHAPTER TWELVE

LEO

AFTER THE KISS—THE KISS, and probably the single greatest moment of my life—Enid had to rush away, trying to get to her elemental practice before it was over. She'd left me in a haze of disbelief, and I had returned to wash the rest of the breakfast dishes for Cass, spending the remainder of the morning smiling down at pots and pans.

It was lunchtime, and I had felt the itch in my head all morning. Someone was trying to communicate with me through my block. Probably Finn or Gideon, wondering why I hadn't come to work this morning. I left the dragon's tower and shuffled down the path, making my way to the dining room. I wasn't the first to arrive. Enid looked up when I walked in, and I saw a flush of pink color her pale cheeks. I supposed we should try to act normal, so I went through the lunch line and took my regular seat next to her, fiercely aware of everywhere our bodies touched. She leaned her leg against mine under the table, and my pulse fluttered.

I linked her. *'Did you make it to practice?'*

'No. They weren't there when I arrived. I'm sure I'll be in heaps of trouble.'

'I'm sorry.'

Her toe tapped mine, and she said, *'I'm not.'*

I smiled down at my food.

"Holy shit." The sharp words snapped me out of the dream, and I looked up at Finn's tight face as he sat across from me, frowning. His eyebrows shot up. "He lives. Nice to see you, Gamma."

I sighed. "What? Did you need something today?"

"Yes, I did. Not that you care about making my life difficult."

I shrugged. "Sorry."

Finn rolled his eyes, his anger not quelled by the lame apology, and he stabbed at the meat on his plate like he was imagining it was my face. The doors opened, and the room quieted like it did whenever Gideon arrived somewhere, the pack noting the Alpha entering. My brows lifted because his expression was tight. Eris was next to him, her lips pursed, and River and Rhia, the witches, stood at their sides. I felt Enid tense, and the air around us grew heavy when the new arrivals came straight to the table instead of the lunch line.

"Enid," Eris said, sitting and threading her fingers in front of her on the table. "River and Rhia have reported to us that you are no longer taking your practice seriously."

Enid shook her head. "That's not true!"

"They say you've been late, often, and that you didn't even show up today." Her tone was curt, like the one she used when reprimanding Henry.

"I-I lost track of time," Enid stuttered, and I swallowed, looking at my older brother, who hadn't sat yet. He frowned down at her, with his arms crossed.

"I think we may need to reconsider your participation in extracurriculars for now," Eris said, sighing when Enid gasped. "No more chess league or art club. Certainly, no more boyfriends."

"What?" Enid flattened her palms on the table. "That's not fair, Eris! I'm going to win the tournament again this spring!"

Gideon shook his head. "That chess tournament means nothing. It's incidental to the real world, and the issues we're all dealing with."

"It means something to me," Enid argued.

"Enid, I need you to snap out of this and come back to reality," River started. "You have a duty. You have a job to do, and if you don't wake up and get serious, we're all going to die. Or worse."

Enid withered like a droughted flower, sinking into her seat under the reprimands of the group, all of them ganging up to chastise her. "I know that."

"Then how can you be so selfish? Do you know what punishment you'd face in a coven for being so lackadaisical about your studies? Other mentors would not be so easy on you. I don't know why the goddess would incarnate you as a wolf. Such emotional, distractible creatures—"

My ears flushed. "Why don't you just leave her alone?"

River, who had a commanding presence, looked as though I'd slapped her, her mouth slightly opened as her sharp eyes flicked to me like she was seeing me for the first time. "Excuse me?"

"I said, why don't you just let her be? I think she gets it. She missed one day. It's not that big of a deal."

Finn scoffed. "Spoken like a true slacker."

I frowned. "Yeah, I am a slacker, Finn. I'll admit it. But Enid isn't, and I don't think it's fair with you all ganging up on her when she's spent almost every day for the last three years training. Not even regular weekends off. She missed only one day in three years!"

River narrowed her eyes, studying me, and then Enid. She tsked her tongue. "You are both too young and naïve to understand. Enid must be ready. It won't be much longer now, and the mundane lives of hormonal teenagers cannot interfere with the future of the entire world."

"Let's go now, then," Enid said, standing. "I'll make up for my absence this morning with an extra hour of work. I promise, River, I will be on time from now on."

River offered a clipped nod and disappeared, flashing away alongside Rhia.

Eris sighed. "Enid, you can stay in chess for now, but you are done with the art club and with the theater. It's obviously too much for you."

Enid swallowed and left the table without a word, hurrying to the door with a sniffle. Eris put her face in her hands, and Gideon patted her shoulder. "She'll be alright. We need her to focus."

Eris muttered into her hands. "I know, but Leo's right, too. She's already given up so much, and here I am taking more from her. Did you see her face?"

Gideon said, "Let's eat in my office today," and helped her from the table.

My eyes flicked to Finn, and his left brow arched.

I asked, "What?" and stabbed at my lunch.

"So, you are nowhere to be found this morning, and Enid misses her training session for the first time ever. Coincidence?"

"Of course it is." I dropped my fork. "I'm not hungry."

"Not hungry? Now I surely know something is up."

I glared at him and stood to leave.

"I want that investment portfolio finished and on my desk by the end of the day."

"Fine. I don't understand why we're so worried about stocks if the end of the world is so near."

"Because hopefully it isn't," he said, standing, so we were eye to eye. "As long as Enid does her job, and no one distracts her from that, we'll be fine. Right, Baby Brother?"

"Yeah."

He narrowed his eyes and nodded. I broke away from the knowing look and hurried to my office, taking my tray with me. I really was hungry. The rest of my afternoon was spent on the stupid portfolio, and by the time I'd finished and tossed it on Finn's desk, the sun was setting.

I rubbed my temples as the elevator took me up a floor to housing. Once in my room, I did what I normally did, showering and then slumping in my gaming chair. A few of my friends were on, and I joined their party. We were in the middle of a game, and I was yelling into the mic about some enemies to the east when the code on my door beeped. It was Enid. Normally, she would sit in the other chair and watch me play, but this time I said, "Bye," into the mic, and reached up to turn off the console before the other guys could answer.

I took my headset off. "Hi."

"I could've waited," she said, waving to the TV.

I looked at the TV and scoffed. As if I'd choose that over her. "I don't want to play if you're here." My cheeks warmed, and a soft smile pulled at her lips. "How was practice? Did River forgive you?"

"Maybe not completely. But she was happy with my progress today. I learned a new skill. It's pretty advanced."

"Oh, cool."

"You wanna see?"

"Yeah."

"It might make a little mess."

"That's okay."

Her brow knit in concentration, and she looked down at her hands. They were at her sides and flexed. The air moved, swirling beneath them, and I grinned when her toes lifted off the floor. The drapes whipped, snapping in the air, and any loose papers I had were thrown into a whirlwind.

Over the wind, I shouted, "No way! You're flying!"

Her feet were a foot off the ground, hovering, and she shifted her hands, pushing the air behind her so she was propelled toward me. I opened my arms and caught her as she slammed into me, sending my wheeled gaming chair soaring back into the edge of my bed. She was laughing, and I turned my eyes up, trying to ignore that my face had just been buried in her chest. I grinned. The papers all settled, floating to resting places around us.

"Sorry to be so rough. It's not completely under control yet."

"It was exceptional," I said, my arms around her, holding her stomach to my chest. She was kneeling on my thighs, but parted her legs, sliding down to straddle my lap. Her pleated skirt crawled up her legs, exposing the creamy skin above her knee-high socks. I kept my hands on her waist but imagined what it would be like to push my fingers up her smooth thighs. It was so different from what we'd been yesterday. The way she looked at me, down through her lashes with flaming green eyes, and how she ran her hands up my chest, lacing her fingers around my neck.

She tilted her head and stared down at my lips. "Thank you for sticking up for me today at lunch."

"Well, I was partially responsible for your absence, so I felt I should. Plus, it was bullshit. You do work hard. Harder than anyone I know. Except maybe Gideon, but that's an impossible bar to overcome. He never stops working. I think he works in his sleep. He must dream of stock portfolios and inter-pack relations."

I was rambling, and she snickered, pressing her lips to mine to shut me up. The shock and hesitation from earlier were nowhere to be found, and this kiss immediately took on a different hunger. She slid her fingers up into my hair, digging her nails into my scalp to pull me closer. Our mouths were locked, opening and closing in sync as our tongues rolled against each other. We fought for breath. That's how it was, so searing and desperate we'd rather kiss than breathe.

I'd been trying to shift my hips back, not wanting her to feel the hard strain of my erection against my zipper, but she dropped her hips, grinding against me. A sharp moan erupted in my throat, and my eyes flew open. My hands tightened on her waist, needing her to do that again, but unsure if she knew that. I yanked her down, using the soft warmth between her legs to find that friction. She whimpered, hugging my nape, and I kissed her cheek and her neck. My heart hammered when my mouth found the spot where her mate would someday mark her. I wanted to bite her. Claim her. I felt the sensitive pang as my fangs elongated, and I pulled my face away, my stomach jumping at the near loss of control.

Bleiz said, *'Easy,'* and chuckled. *'Usually, it is the wolf being unreasonable, not the man.'*

Her fingers were moving beneath my chin, and I only realized she was manipulating the buttons of her blouse when it splayed open. I huffed out an, "Oh, gods," when I looked down and saw her cleavage held in place by a white bra. She wrapped her arms around my head, pushing me toward her chest. I kissed the inner curve of her left breast, stunned by the softness. It was the smoothest skin I'd ever felt. Like white silk, drawn through by the threads of blue veins. When she moaned, I hesitated, but she said, "Keep going. Please."

My breath was shallow. "What are we doing?"

"Stop thinking about it. You think too much."

"Okay."

I kissed again, and again, sucking on the soft skin until she whined, her grip tightening on my neck. When I felt the edge of her bra touch my chin, I reached up and yanked the cup down, feeling the heavy breast drop free of its restraint. I blinked, leaning away a few inches so I could see what I'd dreamed of so many times over the past years. The pale blush pink of her nipple was the same shade as her lips, and wanted as much, it seemed, pert and asking for my attention.

I whispered, "Wow," and closed my eyes, pressing my smiling lips to the bud in a soft kiss. She shifted in my lap, grinding her hips against me again, and I moaned into her flesh, opening my mouth and licking the small peak. Her soft gasp encouraged me, and I did it again, teasing her and myself before I gave in, taking the nipple into the heat of my mouth and sucking until she drew a tight breath, her body tensing. I softened the grip of my lips, rolling my tongue over the bud.

She pushed her hips against me, making me want to explode as the tension in my pants neared painful. I reveled in the taste of her, slightly salty with the sweat she'd expended in training, and then like roses. The chaotic scent of lightning. The drugging aura wrapped around me, warm and inviting, and my hands finally ventured to her thighs. Her skirt was hiked up, pushed back by the grinding.

I slid my fingers beneath it, my hands holding a slight tremble when I found the tight line of her panties tucked into the crease of her thigh and hip. My head buzzed, lost to anything but her and that moment. With my mouth still exploring her breast, my right thumb traced the line of her panties toward her center. Her body quivered, and I froze, not wanting to overstep.

"Enid," I said, my voice nothing but a rasp.

Hers was an octave higher than normal, breezy and beseeching. "Touch me. Touch me, Leo. It feels so good when it's you."

More in sync with my animalistic side than I had ever been, a growl rolled in my chest, and I let my thumb continue its journey. I left the seam of her panties and rolled across the center of her. She moaned, pressing toward the touch, and I did it again, running my thumb up and down the slight depression I could feel thanks to the tight fit of her underwear. When I reached down far enough, my thumb sank into wetness, and I groaned long and deep in my chest when I realized she was so excited she'd soaked through. I didn't stop that up and down motion.

I'd never done anything like this before, so I asked, "Is that good?"

She hummed, "Yes. Gods, yes," and bounced up and down to match my motion.

I pressed harder with my thumb and nearly came at the sound she made. Her breast was in front of my face, inviting me back, so I took it with my mouth again. She would tense and then relax, clinging to me and whimpering in my ear. "Leo. Don't stop! There. There." I moaned, unable to believe what was about to happen, and I knew I couldn't have stopped even if a dragon soared in and landed on the bed.

She let out a sharp cry, then fell silent, her arms squeezing me tight. Where her legs straddled me, I felt them quivering, contracting with each wave of her orgasm. After several long seconds, she sucked in a sharp breath, and reached down, grabbing my wrist to stop me. Enid was giggling, her face flushed and sweat beaded on her forehead. Her body was loose, slumped against me, but I was on fire. Never in my life had I felt that way or needed so badly. I wanted her to reach into my pants and stroke my swollen cock. I wanted her to finish me, but I didn't want to ask outright. My hands clamped on her hips, and I yanked her against me, encouraging her to find that rhythm again.

She gasped, jumping like I'd shocked her, but her lips found mine and she started rolling her hips, grinding up and down the zipper of my pants with her center.

Her lips pulled from mine and went to my ear. "Is this what you want?"

I gripped her hips harder, and my cheeks flushed. "Yes. I'm close... I'm so close. You feel so good."

Her soft moan in my ear, a sound of delight, nearly undid me. She quickened her pace and my world unraveled. I dug my heels into the carpet, pressing my hips up to find maximum friction. My hands stayed anchored on her, and I used her body to chase down my release, grinding and pushing into her. She was more vocal than before, moaning in my ear and saying my name. She kissed my neck, and when she got to my marking spot, she sucked hard on the sensitive flesh.

Without thinking, I blurted, "Ah! I'm coming, *fuck*."

A strike of lightning shot through me, and I surrendered to the explosion of release. I wrapped my arms around Enid to stop her movements, and I moaned into her hair, my cock twitching and spilling into my pants.

My breath stuttered, and I dropped my head back against the chair. With the crystal-clear clarity that finishing brought, my cheeks heated at the realization I'd just come in my pants. The heady scent of both of our releases filled the air, yet I was still coming to grips with what had just happened.

CHAPTER THIRTEEN

ENID

LEO CHUCKLED. "THAT WAS really, really unexpected."

I giggled, and he opened his eyes. I was nodding in agreement, but felt my cheeks flush as I fumbled with the cup of my bra, trying to cover my exposed breast. There was a mark where he had sucked the virgin flesh. Leo sat up, reaching to help me, and the brush of his knuckles against the underside of my breast made me bite my lip. My core ached even though I'd climaxed beautifully. I wanted more but didn't know how to ask for it.

We buttoned my blouse up together, our fingers brushing and sliding over each other. While I fastened the third-highest button, he wrapped his heavy hands around my wrists, holding them. My cheeks warmed again, and I glanced up at him, smiling.

The serious look on his face made my brow knit. "What's wrong?"

"Enid. Are we going to keep doing this?"

"I don't know."

His frown deepened. "We shouldn't. Should we?"

"Do you want to?"

"Do you?"

"I asked first."

"Answer on three?"

"Okay."

Together we counted, "One, two, three," and then both gushed, "Yes!"

We laughed, and he turned me in his lap, so he was cradling me. Leo found his seriousness again and said, "Then we should have some rules."

"Rules?"

"Your birthday is two weeks away. If we were smart, we'd just wait until then to see what happens, but..."

"We aren't," I finished. I leaned up and kissed him to show him I didn't think I could stay away. Even for two weeks.

He kissed me back, pulling me closer, and nodded. "Apparently not. And you just broke up with Daro. I think we should... be subtle."

"Not tell anyone? Is that what you're saying?"

"Absolutely. Even though I think Finn already suspects."

"River does, too," I admitted, knowing she far more than suspected.

Leo ran his hand down his face. "Gideon would kill me for *distracting* you." He used finger quotes around the word distracting. "And for... doing this before we know who our mates are. Then your sister would bring me back from the brink of death and kill me again. More painfully."

"I agree. We shouldn't tell anyone."

"And you can't miss any more practice because of me."

"Right," I said, nodding. "I can't miss any more practice, period."

"We'll both make sure that doesn't happen." He swallowed. "Rule three, I think we should leave our clothes on."

"What?" I blurted, then blushed when he smirked.

"You want to be naked with me that badly?"

My cheeks warmed another degree. "Well, I mean. You pulled my bra down. I was naked."

"No, you weren't. Your bra was still on."

"Now you're arguing semantics."

"The point is, we shouldn't go too far. We should not have sex, Enid. It's not fair, you know, to your future mate. Or mine."

"What if you're my mate?"

"Then we'll have sex soon enough." He said the words, but I understood the tone.

I tensed, sitting up in his lap. "You don't think there's even a chance we are, do you?"

"Why would we be? You're the most beautiful, perfect, powerful being on the planet. And I'm..." He shrugged. "You know."

"I know? I know you're the only person who gets me!"

His brow furrowed. "What about Eris?"

"Eris doesn't get me. She means well, and she loves me, but Eris looks at me and sees a child. But that's not the point." I grabbed his face, squishing his cheeks. "Don't you dare say we won't be mates as if you're not good enough for me. Don't put that energy out into the universe!"

Through puckered lips, he said, "I don't want to upset you. I just feel we should not get naked, or we might, you know, mess up and have sex."

"Mess up?" I repeated, my brows lifting as I dropped my hands.

"You know what I mean. It leads right into rule four."

"And what's that?"

He sobered and ran his thumb over my cheekbone. "No regrets, and no broken hearts."

"I can promise no regrets," I whispered. If Leo wasn't my mate at midnight on Samhain, there would be no quelling my heartbreak. "And I can promise if we're not fated to be together, I'll accept it."

If we weren't mates, there would be a pairing ball in December. Singles from every pack would come together. Matches were often found that way. I couldn't imagine it, Leo and I in our formal wear finding we were destined to be with someone else.

"So will I," he agreed. "Although I hate thinking about it."

"Then let's not."

He took a deep breath. "Okay. What do you want to do?"

"Watch a movie?" We both looked at the unmade bed. We'd laid together countless times, but now the bed looked unnerving. In a good way. I grinned and whispered, "Both of us under the covers?"

He nodded, his face red. "Sounds good, but, uh, I need to change."

I looked down at the dark stain on his black jeans and felt my cheeks flush. We both jumped out of our skin when there was a sharp knock on the door.

"Leo!"

Leo sprang up at the sound of Finn's voice, and I covered my mouth to silence my yelp when he tossed me to the bed. I bounced, holding my hand tight over my mouth to keep my giggles contained. He whispered, "Shit! I panicked! I'm so sorry! Are you okay? You should hide."

I scrambled off the bed and scurried into the bathroom, closing the door so I could still see out the crack.

"Hurry up, I want to go home!" Finn shouted, and Leo looked around, grabbing a towel off the floor and holding it nonchalantly in front of his waist.

Leo yanked the door open. "What?"

There was a pause, and then Finn asked, "Where's Enid?"

I could only see Leo. He shrugged. "She's not here."

"Really?"

"Nope."

"Hm. Weird. Wonder what he wants, then."

I heard the shuffle of Finn's feet, and Hades ran in, going to his spot in the window and sitting. He looked right at me through the crack, and I shook my head at him.

"What do you want, Finn?"

"Gideon wanted me to give you these. What the fuck is this? Are you ditching? Going to college? You want to hang out with humans?"

Finn's tattooed arm appeared, handing Leo a stack of papers while he muttered, "Maybe." He flipped through them, a grin on his face. "He looked at programs for me? Cool."

"I can't believe you want to go to college."

"Jealous?" Leo asked, looking up at his brother.

"Fuck no. School sucks. I don't know why anyone would prolong it."

"I don't know why I'd ever expect you to understand. Anything else?"

"Yeah. One more thing. You smell like sex. Go take a shower, you filthy animal. Both of you."

I saw Leo's face blossom red and felt mine do the same. Finn guffawed and shouted, "Goodnight, Enid!" before Leo slammed the door in his face.

I stepped out of the bathroom and grimaced. "So, Finn knows. So much for subtlety."

"He won't tell," Leo said, sitting back in his chair and leafing through the papers. "He knows he's got something on us now and he loves that."

I walked behind him, looking at a printout detailing the business program at one of the closer human universities to the realm. "You're going to college?" I asked, my heart pinching. Leo had talked about it a lot, but I didn't think Gideon would ever go for it.

"Oh, yeah. I forgot to tell you because of all this! Gideon says I can. I just told him outright I wanted to, and he agreed. I couldn't believe it!" He stood up, spinning around and grinning at me.

I made myself smile. I was happy for him, even if my heart was tripping over itself. "That's amazing!"

He frowned. "What's wrong?"

"Nothing. It's really—I'm glad." I paused, and added, "I'll miss you, that's all."

His face brightened. "You should come too. Wouldn't that be fun? Gods, that would be the best…"

"I can't go. We both know that." I swallowed the tight emotion building in my throat. "I don't get to choose things, Leo. Decisions are made for me, about me, without me, and it is what it is."

"Then I won't go until you can," he said, tossing the papers on his desk. "Easy fix. Let's watch a movie."

"I don't want that."

"Well, I do. I'll wait for you. Always. After the dragons attack and you do your thing, we'll go to college together."

"The dragons might not attack for twenty years."

He shrugged. "Then we'll go to college when we're forty. People do it all the time."

"Leo," I started, and covered my mouth, feeling tears brimming my eyes. I mumbled into my hand, "I'm sorry."

He pushed the chair out of the way and hugged me. "Don't cry, Enid. Please? Unless you want to. Then you can."

"I don't want to," I said, sniffling. I hugged his waist, squeezing myself into his chest. He was always so warm.

"What do you want?"

I looked up at him. "I just want to feel normal for a minute. You're good at that. You make me forget who I am. That's all I want."

Chapter Fourteen

Leo

I STARED OUT OF the skylight. I'd slept well until I hadn't, and now I laid here next to Enid, thinking of how much could change in twenty-four hours and what the future held. Both of us were under the covers, and I felt her legs intertwined with mine as she slept on my chest. My arm was numb, but I'd cut it off before I moved and disturbed her. I looked down, studying the soft curves of her face, relaxed in sleep. My eyes stopped at her lips, marveling to know I could kiss them if I wished to.

'I would give anything to know what happens on Samhain at midnight,' I said to Bleiz, dreading the day, and also wishing it would hurry and get here.

'We won't know until it happens.'

'What if she isn't our mate?'

'Disappointment is a part of life. You must trust in the goddess.'

I swallowed. *'Gods, but what if she is?'*

'That's a much more frightening possibility.'

We weren't even mates, and I already felt an intense need to keep her safe. To protect the woman that I loved. If we were mates, I didn't know how I would handle the things she was supposed to do. Enid would face not one or two, but several dragons and evil witches and who knew what else.

'I should take training more seriously. With the spear.'

'Yes, you should. You are an avoider of problems, Leo, but there comes a time when you have to face reality. Your pack needs you. Your brother—your Alpha—needs you. Like Enid, your path may not be the one you would have chosen, but it's the one you must walk. I know you don't like being Gamma, but you should take it seriously.'

'College was a stupid idea.'

'A weak moment when you couldn't stand seeing Daro have her attention any longer.'

'I should have told her sooner. I was so dumb.'

'Should haves are dumb. The gods guide your fate. Things happen the way they're supposed to. Trust, and try not to overthink things like you always do.'

I sighed, wishing I could be like my wolf and not worry about anything because of faith. My mother was like that. Devout to a point that she never panicked, always leaving it in the hands of the goddess and accepting the results, good or bad.

Enid turned onto her side, and I sighed, able to adjust my arm so it got some new blood flow. I mirrored her movements, spooning her, and put my hand on her stomach, pulling her into my body. It felt so good. So right, like she was meant to be there.

When she cuddled into me, I said to Bleiz, *'I'm going to try really hard not to overthink anything for the next two weeks.'*

Two hours later, the alarm went off, and I reached for my phone, leaning over Enid. She grabbed it first and hit the snooze.

"You'll be late," I mumbled.

"So?"

"You're never late."

Any sleepiness I had disappeared because she pressed her lips to mine.

I was grinning when I got to the training room. Finn and Gideon were the only ones here this early, and Finn looked at the clock, his brows lifting.

"Are you on time, Baby Brother?"

I dropped my bag. "I guess so."

Gideon said, "He's early," and glanced out the window. "Are there pigs flying?"

"I want to train with the spear. I want to get better."

Gideon's brows lifted. "You hate meetings that much, huh?"

"Yes," I said flatly, and looked at Finn, who arched his brow, not buying that. "And I don't want to go to college. Yet."

"Why?" Gideon asked.

"I think it's important that I'm here. Helping with, you know, the dragons and stuff."

Gideon gave a side-eye to Finn, who was chuckling.

I nodded. "I'm serious. I want you to teach me, Gideon. You're the best with the spear."

"Debatable," Finn said, and when Gideon looked over at him, incredulous, Finn clarified, "Eris is the best with the spear."

"She is not."

Finn's brows shot up and his mouth fell open in a wide, grinning "O." "I'm telling her you said that!"

"Don't..." Gideon started. He paused, thinking. "You know what? Tell her. Then she'll want to come in here and fight me." A slight grin turned his lips. "I always like how that ends up."

"Will you teach me?" I asked him, stepping under the ropes.

"Of course! I'm thrilled to," Gideon said, grinning and clapping his hands. "I have been waiting for this day! You are going to be a great warrior, Leo."

'Yes, I am,' I said to Bleiz, who snorted his agreement. *'For Enid. Whether or not she's our mate.'*

It was a tough training session, but at the end, when I was unlacing my shoes, I looked at Gideon and said, "You remind me of Dad. The way you teach."

His brows lifted, and he swallowed, staring down as he unrolled the tape on his hands. "Thank you. That is maybe the finest compliment I've ever received."

I shrugged. He was like Dad. Firm and expectant, but fair. Never hesitating to point out flaws, but equally willing to celebrate improvements.

"Well, you're actually very easy to teach. For someone who cares little for fighting, you're a natural with a weapon in your hand."

I muttered, "Thanks."

"Why, really, Leo, are you doing this?" he asked. "It's a quick change of heart in only a day and a night."

I shrugged again. "I don't know. It just dawned on me that I have a lot to fight for. My family. My friends."

"Well, I'm proud of you," he said, and squeezed my shoulder as he walked past me toward the exit.

Finn was still there, the two of us the last to leave, and he said, "It's like you grew up overnight. Incredible. Wonder what could've been the catalyst. In my experience, a woman is usually involved."

I looked up at him and sighed. "Please don't tell. We aren't..." I dropped my voice to a whisper. "We didn't have sex, okay? We haven't. We're not planning to."

"Right. Sure."

"I swear! And this is rich, coming from you!"

"Yeah, I slept with a lot of women. But, I sure as shit didn't come anywhere close to falling in love with any of them, and they weren't slated to save the world." He raised his brows at me. "That is a big, important difference."

"Finn. Please don't say anything to Gideon."

"I won't tell. Not if this is gonna get you off your ass and motivate you. It's risky, though. What happens if she turns nineteen in a couple of weeks, and she isn't your mate?"

"We decided we're not thinking about that."

"Could get messy," he said.

"I can handle it."

"I'm not worried about you. The entire world doesn't die if you go off on an emotional bender. She, however, needs to be focused. In control. Just one slip up and everything could—"

"She knows that," I snapped. "Better than anyone."

"Alright." He tossed his bag over his shoulder. "See you at lunch."

ENID

I manipulated the flame like we were old friends, and it danced across my fingers, separating into five perfect orbs. I focused on the target, and without thinking, just feeling, I sent them. They shot through their respective holes, not even touching the paper, and I spun to face my teachers. Rhia got to her feet, clapping, and River hurried to hide her stunned expression.

She put her hands out. "Enid. Where has this been? You've gone from a novice to a practiced intermediate overnight."

"I just stopped thinking about it!" I said, throwing my arms out. "It's so simple. Fire is not about thought. It's about this instinct. When I stop thinking and just listen to it, it knows what to do. It's like..." I trailed off, not wanting to finish that thought.

Rhia crossed her arms. "Like what?"

My cheeks flushed. "Like kissing someone you really want to kiss."

Both pairs of the witch's eyebrows lifted. "Really?"

"Yes." I sighed, hugging myself. "Once you obey this instinct, the path forward becomes clear, as if a silent guide whispers the next step. The right thing just happens. Beautifully."

"Right," River said, and I opened my eyes, the blush in my cheeks growing hotter at the amusement shining in her eyes. "Well, I've never read that in fire witch grimoires, but if thinking of fire craft as kissing works for you, please continue to do so."

"Okay."

"Enid?"

The serious shift in her tone made me pause. "Yes, River?"

"I have not been a young girl in a very long time, and I have certainly never been a wolf shifter, so I don't understand your heart. However, I am begging you to mind it. It is a relief to see this improvement, but I am also aware of your upcoming birthday. Should things sour in a way you do not want with the Gamma of this pack, I need your assurance that you will remain composed."

My ears tingled with blush at the first outright acknowledgement of my relationship with Leo. "I assure you I can handle it, River."

"Good. Because I feel the need to remind you that one mis-step—one minor mistake on our part at the wrong time—and all of this hard work is for nothing. We let everyone down in the worst way."

"I know. I haven't forgotten my task."

"Then let us continue."

I nodded, taking position, and called the fire to my hand.

Chapter Fifteen

LEO

WITH THREE DAYS TO go until Samhain, the annual Fall Festival started. It was field day today, a celebration of the end of the harvest. My personal favorite because the farmers honored their crops with incredible food. Corn on the cob, candied apples, chili, smoked turkey legs, barbeque beef and pork. I could go on.

There were games. Competitions. Arts and crafts. The cool air was pleasant, a relief from the humid summer, and I was lining up my shot in the open field. Pumpkin bowling, an invention of Finn's that had quickly become one of the most popular events. I was down three from my middle brother for the win, with four logs left to knock down and one more chance.

"You suck! Boo!" Finn shouted. "You're gonna curve it left like you always do!"

Gideon, who had already been eliminated, cupped his hands around his mouth. "Beat him, Leo, and shut him up!"

There were other cheers from the gathered crowd, and I took a deep breath. I did my normal wind up and let the pumpkin go, watching it roll and leaning on one foot to direct it. "Come on, don't curve!"

I knew I had it when Finn hissed, "Damn it!"

The pumpkin smashed straight through the center of the last group of logs, taking all four, and I put my fists up. "Yes!" The crowd joined me with applause, and Gideon threw back his head and howled, which was echoed a hundred times.

I turned to Finn and flipped him off with both hands. He threw out his arms, "I told you I pulled something earlier in the sack race!"

Gideon brought me first prize—a giant pumpkin roll donated by The Crumble & Flake bakery. It was enormous, weighing at least five pounds. I held it over my head in victory while someone announced that the next event, apple bobbing, was set to start soon. The crowd shuffled toward the pack house to find their seats.

Finn headed that way and called back, "You want me to sign you up?"

I was already focused on Main Street, where the booths were lined up. "No, thanks. I'm going to get my face painted."

He rolled his eyes and went on his way, and I moved in a different direction through the crowd. Kat and Enid were at the face painting booth. I stepped aside as a young girl with a butterfly face ran past me to her mother, grinning and giggling. Enid was pretty good, but Kat could do some exceptional work. I got into Enid's line, waiting my turn and cradling my pumpkin roll like a baby.

Enid glanced up and saw me, giving me a wave of her fingers. Her face was painted like a lion, and when I sat in the chair for my turn, she brushed my hair out of my face and asked, "What can I do for you?"

We were supposed to be subtle, but it was harder all the time to be normal around each other. Other than times we had to be apart for work or practice, we'd spent every second together for the last eleven days.

"I won the pumpkin bowling," I said, holding up my prize.

Enid's brows lifted, and she patted the solid roll, giggling.

Kat laughed from her side of the booth. "Oh, no, how's Finn holding up?"

"He's blaming a sack race injury for the loss."

"Sounds about right."

"How much longer are you here?" I asked Enid. "The apple bobbing is about to start. I thought you signed up."

"Yes! I did."

"You can go, Enid," Kat said. "I'll handle these last few."

We meandered toward the pack house lawn, our hands knocking together as we walked. I wanted to lace our fingers, but that might raise some eyebrows. We got on a secluded path, and I noticed no one else was around—okay, maybe I chose this path so no one would be around—and I snaked my arm around Enid's waist, stepping into her until her back was pressed to a tree and her front was molded to mine.

"Hurry and bob some apples so we can go for a walk or something," I said, and leaned down, kissing her neck.

"Why would we do that?" she teased, running her fingers up my nape and into my hair.

"Well, we haven't kissed in, like, six hours."

"Why don't you kiss me now?"

I leaned back, finding it hard to take her seriously. "It might give us away if your whiskers are smeared all over my lips."

She reached up and touched her face, remembering she had paint on, and giggled. "At least it'll wash off while I'm bobbing for apples."

"A lion?" I asked, arching my brow.

"I like lions."

"Really?"

She reached up, toying with the collar of my t-shirt. "Yes. They're handsome creatures."

"If you say so."

"I do."

I grinned, and I leaned into her neck, kissing her marking spot again. My pulse quickened anytime I did. Her scent was so intoxicating there. She took the lobe of my ear between her teeth, nipping it hard enough to make me suck in a sharp breath. A soft growl rumbled in my chest, and I stepped closer, pinning her with my weight. I pressed my teeth to her marking spot, and she gasped, digging her nails into my back. I would never mark her, of course, unless she was my mate and asked me to, but the game was fun. A flush of scent graced my nose, her arousal, and I knew she liked it, too.

Voices down the path pulled us apart, and we stared at each other, both of us caught in this whirlwind of what we felt. What we wanted.

The voices grew closer, and we started up the path to avoid an encounter.

I kept my voice low. "We need to behave."

"You're the one who pinned me to the tree."

"You bit me."

She snickered. "You wanted to bite me."

"You liked it."

"Who says?"

I smirked. "My nose knows."

She smacked my shoulder with the back of her hand and looked out at the forest to hide her grin and blushing cheeks.

We made it just in time for Enid to join the competition. I ordered an apple cider and looked for a spot in the crowd. It was packed, so there were no good seats left. I had to stand where I was looking at the competitors' backs, but soon understood it wasn't so bad when it was Enid's turn. From here, when she was bending over the barrel, her pleated skirt was lifting just enough to see the bottom half of her thighs above her knee-high socks.

"Hey."

I jumped at the voice, lost to the show, and wondered if my mouth had been hanging open.

"Hey. Daro. What's up?" I answered, trying to be normal. I hadn't talked to him since he and Enid broke up, and I sensed he'd been avoiding me.

"Not much. Fun day. Nice roll."

"Yeah. I won the pumpkin bowling."

"Is Finn devastated?"

"Yep. That's the best part."

Daro chuckled, and an awkward silence fell between us. I sipped my cider, looking for an escape.

He sighed, and seeming to get his nerve, asked, "How's Enid?"

I looked over at him, trying to decide if he was asking in the capacity that I was her friend or if he knew we'd been fooling around the last couple weeks.

"She's good."

"Did she say anything? About me? When we broke up?"

"Oh." I paused and took another drink. "Not too much. Just worried you were gonna hate her. That you are angry."

"I'm not angry. I love her."

"Oh," I said again, heat crawling up my neck. "Uh. She'll be glad you're not angry."

"Can I ask you something?"

"Okay."

He leaned closer. "Do you think I can get her back?"

"Uh." I felt like I'd entered the twilight zone. "I don't know, man. Her birthday is coming up, so."

"I know. But look at you. You haven't found your mate, and it's been months since your birthday, so if she doesn't, she'd still be open to dating, right?"

I bit my cheek to stop from saying, *yeah me*, and said, "I don't know. Just have to see what happens at midnight on Saturday, I guess."

"Yeah," he said, distantly. He was the one staring now as Enid finished her turn. My neck flushed again, and I wanted to hit him. I wasn't usually so quick to violence and I cleared my throat.

I lied, "Oh, hey, my brother is linking me, so I gotta go."

"Yeah, see you around," he said, his eyes not moving.

Enid finished her turn, and everyone cheered. Eris handed her a towel to wipe up the running face paint. She got third and was awarded a gallon of apple cider. With Gideon and Eris around, we had to be careful not to tip them off.

We went through the dinner line together, deciding we'd sit apart, but she whispered, "I'll meet you in the top garden. Forty-five minutes?"

I turned away and nearly fumbled my plate when I ran into Christine.

She smiled and put her hand on my arm. "I've been trying to find you."

"Oh," I said, looking over my shoulder for Enid. She was sitting by some other girls she knew and watching, her expression curious. "I've been busy."

"You were great at pumpkin bowling."

"Thanks."

"Do you want to go out? To a movie? Maybe tonight?" she asked, pressing closer to my side.

I sighed and found Christine's eyes with mine. "No. I don't want to."

She gasped. "What?"

"I'm sorry. I don't want to. I also don't want to hurt your feelings, but I'm not interested in you that way."

"You kissed me!" she hissed, her cheeks flooding a dark scarlet.

I felt my face warm, too. "I shouldn't have led you on like that. I'm sorry. It didn't mean anything to me. You're really nice, and it's not you. I just... We should just wait for our mates. Please stop texting me and stuff."

Her expression soured with such hatred that I winced, having never seen Christine so bitter. She pushed past me, hurrying toward the path that led back down into town.

I sighed, feeling sort of bad, but relieved, and I took the open seat by Finn. Kat joined, and the kids were running wild, excited by every single thing that was happening. Absolute bedlam.

I checked my phone every three minutes until forty had passed. The rambunctious kids made it easy to slip away unnoticed, and I took the eastern path up to the top garden. I beat Enid there and sat on our bench, placing the pumpkin roll next to me. A minute later, gravel crunched on the southern path, and I grinned.

She held up her cider. "Would you like a drink?"

"Sure. We can have it with a bite of pumpkin roll."

She plopped the gallon down by the bench and straddled my lap. Both of us had moved past any shyness, and I ran my hands up her thighs, under her skirt, and around to cup the tight cheeks of her bottom, squeezing until she made a small sound in her throat. I sharpened my ears, trying to keep some consciousness toward the paths. People rarely came all the way up here, but you never knew. That effort failed when she pulled her sweater off over her head.

"What are you doing?" I asked, unable to stop my hands from moving to her naked waist. "You're breaking the rules."

"I'm tired of the rules," she whispered, and her hand trailed behind her back. I heard the soft click of her bra, and then it fell forward, dropping between us.

My hands covered her breasts as soon as they were free, and I moaned low in my throat, looking up at her face. Tiny flecks of paint still stuck like multi-colored freckles, but she was more beautiful than I'd ever seen her, her green eyes snapping like lightning. A warm breeze had picked up, pushing her platinum hair around her face like a sunny frame, and her lips were parted, glossy as if she'd wetted them in anticipation of my kiss.

She said, "I always follow the rules. This time I'd just like to follow my heart."

Her hands were at my sides, gripping my shirt and trying to take it off. I asked, "Are you sure?"

When she said, "Yes. No regrets," without hesitation, I lifted my arms, and she slid the shirt over my head. Topless, we embraced, feeling bare skin to bare skin for the first time, and our lips met with a moan from both of us.

Lost in ourselves, we didn't notice that Enid had been followed. I didn't hear the gravel crunch when that person spun on their heel and jogged back down the path.

Chapter Sixteen

Enid

MY STOMACH STIRRED WITH a thousand butterflies, feeling more like dragons in size than insects. We both knew the rules, and now we were breaking them, but I didn't care. I wanted to break the rules. All I had ever done was follow them. Be a good girl. In control. Steady, level-headed Enid. Follow your brain, not your heart. It never mattered what I wanted, just what I was supposed to do.

Now, I was going to take what I wanted. I had loved Leo since the moment I met him, and these past days together had made me hunger for a future with him. I even entertained taboo thoughts, like that I would reject my mate if it was anyone else. Blasphemy. If he had marked me earlier on the path against that tree, I would've been happy, and that went against everything I had ever known. Maybe it was the witch in me, more selfish than the part of me that was the wolf. Maybe I just was a witch and didn't have a wolf.

He understood what I wanted—sex—and broke our kiss. "Is this wrong?"

I had been the aggressor in this entire affair, aside from that first kiss. Leo was trying hard to stick to what we had been raised to believe. You don't fall in love before you find your mate. You don't disrespect other wolves by having what's not yours.

"True love is never wrong, is it?"

He paused at my words. "You love me, Enid?"

"Yes. Yes." I kissed him, and my throat tightened. "I do. Isn't it something special that in a world where we wait for fate to tell us who to love, that we have found it for ourselves?"

"It's something," he said, pushing the hair out of my face. "Some might say foolish."

"So? Is it wrong to be a fool if we're fools in love?"

His brow pinched. "Fools in love can easily become victims of their own hearts."

I put my hands on his cheeks. "I never get to decide anything of my own volition. Even the mate bond determines our fate with no regard to our desires. You may be the only choice I ever get to make, Leo. To love. To be together before Saturday dictates our future. I want you."

He grabbed my face and kissed me roughly, saying between my lips, "I love you, too. I love you, Enid. I always have."

Our lips locked until we needed air, and we broke apart, sharing a gasp. He was kissing down my neck, nipping at my pounding pulse. My body quivered, and I could hear the rattle in his breath. I wrapped my arms around his head, begging him to give attention to my breasts. I ached all over, feeling a desperate madness as the tugging coil in my core tightened.

His mouth was searing on my nipple, his rolling tongue winding me tighter, offering relief and torture at the same time. I ran my hands over his shoulders, down his arms, feeling the muscles move beneath his skin. My own sexuality shocked me when I imagined running my tongue over him instead.

"Leo," I moaned, deep and low in my chest, and reached between us, my hands on his belt buckle.

After some fumbling, I opened it and instantly felt a flush in my face. I hadn't touched him past his underwear yet. He stood without warning, holding me, and we switched spots. He kneeled between my legs, pulling me to the edge of the seat. I watched him line the bulge of his boxers with the apex of my thighs and moaned when he pressed forward, creating a sweet friction that sent a shot of lightning to the top of my head and the bottom of my toes.

"That should work," he said, and looked up at me, his brow knitting. "I am horrified to hurt you."

I was aware of the coming pain, and I wouldn't have my wolf to heal me, but I shook my head. "I'm not afraid. I'll be okay."

He sighed, but I leaned forward and grabbed him, smiling and pulling on his shoulders to bring him back to me.

Movement at the top of the path dragged a shriek from my gut, and I clung to Leo to hide my nakedness. My breath was shallow, rapid pants in his ear, and a small sob bubbled in my throat. All the warm feelings sank with an anchor of humiliation.

Leo had gone still. "Oh, gods. Who is it?"

My eyes were squeezed shut, but I'd seen who it was. Gideon was already walking away. He called over his shoulder, "Leo. My office. Now."

Leo's head dropped against my shoulder. "Well, shit."

I looked again, confirming Gideon had gone, but swallowed because Eris stood there with her mouth hanging open and tears in her eyes. Leo was shoving my sweater into my arms, and I watched Eris' face shift from horror to rage. Her teeth were gritted, and she clenched her fists at her sides. She was going to hit him, I realized, and I shouted, "Stop it! Eris!"

She didn't listen, and I screamed when she grabbed Leo by the shoulder and slapped him hard across the face. When she looked down and saw his open zipper, her mouth fell open, and she raised her hand again. "How *could* you?"

"I'm sorry. I don't know what I was thinking. I-I'm sorry," Leo sputtered, and put his hands up to defend himself.

I stood and grabbed her shoulder. "Eris! Stop it! Leave him alone!"

Lightning cracked across the sky, followed by deafening thunder, and the wind swirled around us, whipping the fallen autumn leaves.

She turned to me, and the disappointment was etched in every line of her face. "Let's go! What are you thinking? You weren't raised like this, Enid! How could you?" She grabbed my wrist, pulling me toward the path, and it all erupted. Years of resentment that I always kept buried.

"Get off of me!" I screeched, and I pushed her hand away. "I'm not going anywhere with you! I HATE you!"

"Enid!" Her face had slackened into a pale mask, tears brimming her eyes. "I just want what's best for you."

"No, you don't!" I sobbed, and the rain started falling, coming down in a flood while lightning lit up the sky. "You just want to keep me! That's all you've ever done! Lock me away! In the cabin! In the pack house! In this little box of what you expect me to be! I'm not a child! You can't stop me from growing up!"

"I know that," she said, and I could feel the edge of her anger soften.

Mine did not. "No, you don't! You don't have any idea what it is to be treated like a-a tool! Like a key that must be kept safe, looped around your neck all the time!" I clutched my sweater to my chest. "I am a person! I try to be perfect like you all want—I try to be the Green Witch—but I am Enid, too. I want things! I make mistakes. I have a heart and soul, and I am someone besides who I am destined to be!" I sobbed and sniffled, pulling my shirt on over my head. "Not that you care!"

She reached for me again. "Of course I care!"

"Don't TOUCH me!" I grabbed her wrist to push her away, and she yelped, recoiling away.

Eris looked at her wrist and gasped. My angry red hand mark was burned into her skin. Her eyes met mine, flooded with watery disbelief.

Leo put his hands up, his palms out in front of him. "It's okay, Enid."

I looked at him, but he was staring at my hands. When I glanced down, I saw flames coiled around my wrists like cobras waiting to strike. My face tightened with a sob, the humiliation of this entire moment bubbling to the surface. I just wanted this one thing for myself—to feel normal with Leo—and they wouldn't even let me have that. My hands grew hotter. I didn't want to hurt anyone more than I had, so I spun on my heel, slipping down the soaked path and into the trees.

Chapter Seventeen

Leo

MY SNEAKERS SQUELCHED, FULL of water from the torrential down-pour that had started outside. Eris and I had an awkward walk back to the pack house together, with her crying soft tears the entire way. I had never seen Enid be so angry, especially towards Eris. The lightning was so powerful it shook the windows of the pack house in the foyer. We rode in the elevator in tight silence, and I stared at my reflection in the metal door to keep from looking at her. There was a lot of guilt and embarrassment staring back at me.

I plopped into a chair in Gideon's office and looked at Finn, whose mouth dipped in a sympathetic half-frown. My eldest brother looked up from some paper he was signing and shoved it away. We held eye contact for several long seconds. I knew he wanted an apology from me, but I refused to give one.

"So this is why you decided not to go to college?"

"Yes."

"Leo. What are you thinking?" he asked and leaned back in his chair, scrubbing his hands down his face.

"I don't understand why this is such a big deal! She dated Daro for months, and no one batted an eye!"

"Oh, we batted several eyes," he said, looking at Eris, "but decided it was ultimately unfair to prevent Enid from dating Daro if she wished to. We ask a lot of her, and we know that. Besides, that relationship didn't present the same problems."

"Problems?" I asked, looking between Finn and Gideon as they both cleared their throats. "What's that supposed to mean?"

"Well, one, you should both be waiting for your mates," Gideon scolded, trying to shame me.

"We don't care about that."

His eyes bulged. "Don't care about that? That is a foundational principle of shifter society! It's selfish; an insult to your future mates not to wait."

I felt a pang of guilt, but asked, "Oh, like you both did?"

"We both regret our decisions. We've told you that many times. I'm disappointed that it seems to have gone over your head."

"I would never regret anything with Enid."

"Have you had sex with her? How many times?"

I wrinkled my face, glaring at him. "That's none of your business. Gods!"

"It is our business."

Finn interjected, "He said he wouldn't." He looked at me, widening his eyes. "He *promised* me."

I couldn't hold his eye contact and looked down at my hands.

"You knew?" Gideon asked, drawing my eyes back up.

"I don't know how you didn't," Finn muttered, leaning against the bureau on the wall. "Gods, Gideon, wake up. You think an eighteen-year-old and nineteen-year-old spending the night together is innocent?"

"They've always been good friends. I just expected they were making good choices. Respecting their future mates," he said, glaring at me. "It'll break Mom's heart if she finds out about this."

My heart dropped. "What? Don't tell Mom!" I looked at both of them and shook my head. "What is the difference between Enid being with me and her being with Daro? They could've had sex. Why do you care so much?"

Gideon cleared his throat. He was uncomfortable, I realized, something that he hardly ever was. I narrowed my eyes. "Just say it. What is this really about?"

He looked at Eris like she might help him, but when she said nothing, he blurted, "Unicorns and wolf shifters can't crossbreed, so there was no concern with Daro. It was a relief, actually, when she was with him because we knew we didn't have to worry about that."

My face flushed. "W-what?"

Finn ran his hand down his face, looking ill, and I glanced over at Eris, who stared off into space.

I realized I had heard what I thought, and shouted, "What is wrong with you people?"

Gideon put his hand out to placate me. "I know it sounds bad—gods, I don't want to be thinking of it—but I have to because I'm Alpha. If Enid falls pregnant, it makes her vulnerable! Having small children makes her vulnerable. She just... can't."

"Have you discussed this with her? That she isn't allowed to have a family until you say so."

"That's not..." Gideon sat back in his chair. "Until it's safe. She tried the conception control elixir three months ago to prepare for her nineteenth birthday, as many people do, and it interfered with her magic. So that's not an option either."

My mouth was hanging open, and I had a new sense of horror for Enid. I knew her life was always under the microscope, but this was beyond anything I would've ever guessed. They were micromanaging her fertility.

"Gods. I don't even know what to say," I said, shaking my head. "Can I go? I suddenly need to vomit."

Gideon sighed, running his hand through his hair. "I know it seems abhorrent to you, but I—we—are focused on the bigger picture, Leo. The safety of the pack. Of the world!"

"I'm sure glad I'm not Alpha," I snapped.

He matched my tone. "You should be. It's certainly not easy or fun."

"We haven't had sex. Okay? Satisfied?"

"Yes." I stood to leave, and he said, "No more of whatever that was back there in the garden. She doesn't need distractions. Got it? I could Alpha command you, but I don't like to. Don't make me regret it. No more sleepovers."

"What if she finds her mate on Samhain?"

"Then myself, the Luna, Enid, and her mate will have a discussion about moving forward and family planning."

"Such a hands-on Alpha," I patronized, and he sighed.

I opened the door and said, "You know, you people should try talking to Enid like an adult. That might work." I slammed the door behind me, which I knew he hated, and asked the empty hallway, "What the fuck?"

The rainstorm had quieted outside, and I linked Enid, *'Are you okay?'*

'Are you in trouble?'

'Not really. I'm supposed to stop seeing you, though.'

'Did they say why?'

'They don't want you distracted. But mostly, they don't want you pregnant. I'm pretty sure he'll use an Alpha command if he catches us alone again.'

'Oh,' she said, and I could tell she was hurt, but not surprised. *'I'm sorry, Leo. That was really humiliating.'*

'I know. I'm sorry, too.'

'What do we do?'

'I think it's best if we just wait to see what happens on your birthday. We shouldn't do something we might regret with only two days to go.'

'The only regret I might have is not loving you when I had the chance.'

I stood there with my finger above the elevator button, unsure how to answer that. I wanted her. More than anything. But I was afraid, too. The deeper we fell into this love affair, the harder it was going to be to accept if things didn't turn in our favor. If we made love and then she found her mate on Saturday, and she was suddenly smitten with another. Sharing her body and soul with him. How would I survive the heartbreak?

She didn't give me a chance to answer, adding, *'I need to find Eris. I was awful to her... I hurt her.'*

I winced at the despair in those last words. *'She's okay. She is with my brother in his office. Don't worry. She'll forgive you.'*

'I know.'

There was a pause, and I asked, *'See you tomorrow at breakfast?'*

'I don't know.'

Chapter Eighteen

Enid

I DID NOT GO to Gideon's office and find my sister, even though I perhaps should have. Leo wanted to wait until my birthday, and the thought made tears brim my lashes again. Maybe it was silly, but I'd wanted that moment. I'd wanted to own that decision as all mine. To share my heart and my body with him without permission from my horde of elders that dictated my every move.

Alas, nothing would ever be my choice; not even in love. Droplets started tapping my shoulders, and I took a leveling breath, trying to calm my emotions before another storm swelled.

I was partially successful, but a deep root of indignation remained coiled in my chest. I stopped, picking up a fallen leaf. It was golden, with little brown dots. The tree above me had once been its home, tall and silent. I pressed my forehead to the rough bark and focused, letting the energy of the forest bring my mind to peace. If a tree could let go of its precious leaf, I could let go of the anger in my heart.

The rain tapered away, and I found myself at the old watchtower, knocking on the thick wooden door. Cass's footfalls echoed on the other side, and he answered the door with a cup of tea in his hand. His giant hand dwarfed the petite cup, and the spicy aroma that curled up as steam tickled my nose. Citrus and a hint of spice.

"Little Witch? Why are you out walking in the rain?"

"Can I come in?"

"Of course," he said, and stepped aside. "Do you want some tea?"

"Yes." I shivered, sitting at his small kitchen table. When he brought it, I wrapped my hands around the cup. The heat seeped into my skin, warming my frozen fingers.

He sat in the other chair, his long legs crowding under the squatty table. "What's wrong?"

"I've been seeing Leo."

He showed not a hint of surprise. "And it's not gone well?"

I sighed and sipped my tea, letting the cinnamon spice coat my tongue. "It's gone too well, maybe."

"How so?"

"Because Enid *can't* do that."

"Enid can't do what? Fall in love?"

I shook my head. "I can do nothing, Cass, except be a good, obedient girl. Practice my magic for this dark day that looms ahead. I shouldn't dare consider any other aspect of life aside from the fight."

"It is important. But too much working and not enough fun poisons the soul."

"No one else thinks so." I stared down at the cloudy brown liquid in my cup, watching the steam curl. It blurred, my eyes filling with tears.

"Cass?"

"What happened, Little Witch? What's wrong?"

"I don't want to be this person." A tear rolled down my cheek, and I wiped it with the back of my hand. "I don't want to be the Green Witch." I looked up into his sad blue eyes. "I would give anything to be anyone else. To be normal, and to shed the burden of the world. Anything."

"Enid," he said, his tone soft, "you're the most powerful being on the planet."

I thought of the burn on Eris' arm. The way she looked at me. My voice was barely a whisper. "I'm a freak."

He gasped. "You are not! You're just a wonderful girl who happens to harbor immense power. You're special."

"This power shackles me, holding me hostage while happiness runs free with the average people! I do not want it."

His brows lifted. "That's probably why you have it."

"What do you mean?"

"To not want it is why you have it. Because I *want* it," he said, his lips curling as his eyes flashed like a predator. "Do you understand, Enid, what someone like me would do with that power?"

I shook my head, my brow knitting.

He chuckled, a dark sound, and wiped his upper lip with his finger. "If I were as powerful as you, a wake of destruction would attend my path. I would take a revenge tour around this earth, finding every single person who's ever caused me pain and giving it back to them tenfold."

"Like who?"

"It doesn't matter," he said, leaning forward. "The point is, it takes a special person to hold such power. So many would corrupt it, but your heart is so pure and lovely that evil doesn't have a chance to infect it. I am sure that's why the powers that be chose you. Even your sister, Gideon, and the others. Could they possess such power and not let it blacken their hearts? Those who seek power rarely deserve it, and those who don't want it wield it wisest."

I swallowed and shook my head, looking down into my cup. "I'm just tired of being coddled like a child. Or treated like some weapon... some object without feelings."

"Then do not let them." My eyes rose to meet his again, and the sapphire blues were shining. "Who are they to make you bend the knee?"

"Gideon is my Alpha. Eris is my-my guardian. River, my goddess-chosen mentor."

"They only hold power over you for as long as you allow it."

"You are a bad influence, Cass," I said, my lips curling.

"Yes, I am, but I'm also right."

I shook my head. "I-I don't know."

"Hello?" he teased, knocking on my forehead. "Is there a fire witch in there? Because I've never known one that didn't host a natural spark of rebellion. If you grow tired of being objectified, then stand up for yourself. Simple. No one can stop you from doing anything. Once you realize that, you're no longer chained."

"I kind of did today." I sighed, shaking my head. "But I hurt Eris with the awful things I said. I-I burned her on accident."

Cass snickered, and I gave him a stern look that sobered his humor. He lifted his shoulder in a half shrug. "I'm not telling you to be vindictive. I'm advising you to advocate for yourself." He paused, as if he might not say what he wanted, and then finished the thought. "You've let them get to you, you know? To cow you and bring you under control. When we first met, you had a way about you, Enid. A presence. Find that again. You are the Green Witch. No one else is you. Act like it."

My brows knit, and I looked out the window at the fiery fall landscape.

"As a matter of fact," he continued, "why don't you link them and tell them you're taking some time off?"

My mouth dropped open. "What?"

"You look like you need a break. Stay here and take one."

"Really?"

He nodded and went to the sink, washing his cup.

I dropped my block. *'Eris?'*

Her worried voice rushed into my head. *'Enid? Where are you? Come home and we'll talk about this.'*

'I'm very sorry for losing my temper and hurting you. And for the things I said. But I'm not coming home tonight. I'm at Cass's and I'd like to be left alone here for a couple of days.'

'What? What about practice? You need to—'

'I'm taking two days off to get my mind straight. I'm sure you will all understand. I'll be home for Samhain. I love you, Eris.'

'Oh. I love you too, but Enid, we really should talk.'

'We will.'

I put up the block and took a deep breath, tracing my fingers over the wooden table.

Cass asked, "Would you like me to go get Leo? I will."

It was a long moment before I answered. "He's gotten into enough trouble because of me today."

Cass scoffed. "Leo doesn't care. He is a natural rebel."

"I know." I sighed. "I've put a lot of pressure on him to turn his back on what we've always been told is right and wrong. He thinks it's best if we wait to see what happens on my birthday, and I should respect that. Maybe he's right. Maybe this is all just a recipe for heartbreak."

Cass was leaning against the kitchen counter drying his hands slowly by running the towel over each finger. "Heartbreak is bearable. It's regret that never stops stinging."

LEO

I sat at the lunch table. The seat next to me was noticeably empty again.

'Enid?'

She was still blocked. She had been ever since the incident in the garden. Panic crept into my chest, and I wondered if I'd ever kiss her again. Was that interrupted moment the last time my hands would be on her? I sighed, struck by the realization. I should have chased her. Why didn't I go after her? Should I now?

"You will survive this, Leo," Gideon said, sitting across from me with his tray and reading my grim expression.

My ears grew hot at being called out. Everyone was here except the kids, who had primary lessons today. I looked up at him, annoyed with his flippant, almost amused, attitude.

"You don't know what you're talking about."

"This isn't exactly uncommon. Many before you have suffered the same fate. Falling in love before your mate. It's just..."

"Foolish. Not done," I snapped. "You act like I have a choice."

"You act like you don't."

I swallowed, pushing my tray away. "Excuse me."

"He's spoiled," Finn said to Gideon, and my neck flushed with heat. "He's always gotten everything he wants. Our baby brother has never worked hard at anything a day in his life. He thinks he just gets this, too, even though it's stupid and selfish. He cares about no one but himself."

The table grew quiet, and Mom said, "Finn!"

I looked past Kat at him. He was still eating, and glanced up at me, arching his brow.

"Why don't you shut up, Finn?"

"Or what, Leo? You won't do anything."

"Fuck you," I muttered, standing and turning to leave, my tray in my hands. My palms were slick with sweat, and my ears felt like they were tinged with flame.

Finn laughed. "That's what I thought."

Bleiz growled in my head. *'I am so tired of this humiliation. Aren't you?'*

'He'll win.'

'Who cares? Just make him bleed.'

Finn, noticing I'd paused, said, "Dad would kick your ass for being such a coward. You really think the Goddess would trust you with someone like Enid?"

A red mist clouded my vision, and I gritted my teeth. Gideon was saying something. A reprimand, but it sounded like I was listening through water.

I took the pot pie in its little metal tin and turned, chucking it as hard as I could at Finn. It narrowly missed Kat and splattered on his shoulder. He looked down at the chicken, white gravy, and vegetables pooling in his lap.

The dining hall fell silent, and I followed the pot pie projectile, stalking toward my brother. He was pissed, his face flushing red, and grabbed Kat under her arms, lifting her out of the way.

The distraction went in my favor, and I grabbed her tray from the table, smashing it over the side of Finn's head. His hands fisted the front of my shirt, and he shoved me back, following with a compact cross jab. I'd never actually been hit. I'd practiced being hit, but I'd never been in a fight. His fist cracked across my jaw, making my ears ring, but I didn't feel any pain.

He grabbed my shirt again, and I threw my head forward, smashing into his face with the top of my skull. We stumbled together, falling onto the table, and it fractured under our weight. I landed on top of Finn, and I had about a fifty-pound advantage. I threw two good punches, one to his nose and one to his mouth, before he got his position fixed, kicking me in the gut and off of him.

We rolled around in the mess of food. I was bigger, but he was better trained. Things got bloody, my ears ringing every time he managed to hit me. I had him now, my arm around his throat, but he pulled a reversal that I couldn't counter fast enough. He was choking and coughing, but he wrapped his elbow under my chin and squeezed.

I clawed at his arm and elbowed him in the ribs until I felt them crack, but he had me in a vice. Blackness dropped like a sheet over my vision, and the next thing I knew I was sucking in a sharp breath. Gideon had me by the front of the shirt, pulling me to my feet.

He was grinning. "You alright? That was pretty good for your first fight."

I shoved his hands off and looked over my shoulder. The table was wrecked, with food strewn everywhere. Finn was crouched there and smiled at me, reaching up and pulling one of his teeth out of his mouth. He stuck it back into its socket so it would heal. His teeth and face were covered in blood, and one of his eyes was nearly swollen shut. I could tell mine was similar, and I knew I had some broken ribs.

I pushed Gideon out of my way. Anyone else in my path quickly sidestepped, letting me pass.

Gideon said, "Alright, you got what you wanted, Finn. Now clean this up."

Finn's words were wet with blood. "What? Come on."

"You started it."

I went out through the garage, grabbed my guitar from my car, and then trudged up to the garden. Half of me expected Enid to be there, but it was empty.

I sighed and sat, strumming the chords mindlessly while the food dried like glue to my clothes. Gravel crunched on the path, and I held the strings to quiet them, listening. The footfalls were feminine.

My cheeks warmed. It was not who I had hoped. "Mom?"

"Leo," she said gently, sitting next to me. She started fussing, touching my face where Bleiz was healing me. As my adrenaline quieted, the pain increased.

I moved her hand away. "I'm okay. I'm sorry, Mom. About the table and stuff."

"Oh." She waved her hand and sat back, smoothing her powder-blue skirt. "Finn deserved it."

"All he does is pick at me."

"He wants you to stand up for yourself. Today you did."

I sighed.

"Now what is all this business, Leo? With Enid."

I slouched on the bench so I could lay my head back. "I don't know."

"Yes, you do. Don't lie to your mother."

I shook my head and put my hands on my face, then winced when I remembered it was sore. "I'm in love with her. I'm sorry, Mom. I know I'm supposed to wait for my mate. I know it's dumb. Unreasonable. And I know Finn's right. The goddess would never pair us."

"How does Enid feel?"

"She..." I trailed off, my cheeks flushing while I searched for the right words to describe this to my mother. Enid had been more aggressive than I had for the most part. "She likes me, too."

"Have you been seeing her? Romantically?"

My cheeks burned hotter, but I stayed with the truth. "Only for a few days." I sighed. "And it's been the best few days of my life. I've had so little of her, and I fear it's already destroyed me."

"You're nervous? Because of her birthday?"

"I've been dreading her nineteenth birthday for years."

Mom put her hand on my shoulder. "You'll have to let her go if she's destined to be with another."

"I know. But I don't know how I'll handle it... losing her."

"Ah. The price of love, Leo. It cost me my sanity for a while, and not even Eris can mend a broken heart." I looked over at my mother, and her eyes were shining. She patted her chest, then toyed with the pearls of her necklace. "Love always ends in pain, no matter what. Still, people keep accepting it, welcoming it into their lives with open arms. They always have, and they always will. Why?"

I blinked and strummed the chords of my guitar, staring up at the blue sky. "Because it's worth it."

"Hm." She smiled, and hugged herself, rubbing her arms. "I wouldn't trade one kiss, one smile, or one touch of your father's hand for an eternity without this pain. This broken heart is my privilege of having been loved by him."

I took my mother's hand and squeezed it. She stood, kissing me on top of the head. "I'm going to make an offering to the goddess that this all turns out in your favor. You are no coward, Leo. What is courage, if it is not loving someone with no guarantees?"

I listened to Mom's footfalls trail away and stood, deciding I would go to Cass's now. That's where Enid had to be, and if not, maybe he knew where I could find her.

I'd only taken three steps when Gideon's voice shattered my plans.

'Leo, there's been an unprecedented vampire breach at Emerald. You and I are leaving within the hour for a meeting.'

'What? When will we be back?'

'Tomorrow.'

I sighed aloud. From his serious tone, I knew there would be no arguing. I glanced over at Cass's tower peeking over the trees and then trudged down the path back to the pack house.

Chapter Nineteen

Enid

I TOYED WITH THE rough chiffon of my skirt. Cinderella was my chosen costume this year, from the Grimm fairytale. My gown glimmered in gold and silver, complete with a full skirt and delicate lace detailing.

The ballroom was bedecked for Samhain, featuring carved pumpkins and twisted gourds, animal skulls and shed antlers, and garlands woven from wheat stalks and autumn leaves. Every corner of the room flickered, lit by the glow of black wax candles. The air was alive with the rhythms of ancient drums and the melodic whispers of our ancestral flutes. People danced. Many donned masks with their costumes. The room shimmered with mystery, like anything might happen on this hallowed night.

My eyes scanned the crowd, looking for Leo. He would be here, but he might be late. I sat with Eris, my hand on her arm, and we ate yet another harvest feast laid before us.

Gideon was late too, both he and Leo having to attend a last-minute meeting in our neighboring pack of Ruby Moon. More than one hundred vampires had crossed into Union territory on the Emerald Moon border with the Dark Kingdom. The threat had been quelled, but Gideon and Alpha Owen were coordinating to send warriors to help Emerald Moon keep their boundary.

I looked at my sister. Eris wore traditional Samhain attire, as any Luna would: a flowing black dress with a shawl crafted of crow and raven feathers. It glinted green and black whenever she moved. The more serious Samhain ceremony had been earlier today, all conducted by her, as was custom. A stag was sacrificed, its blood drained into large bowls, and the first drink taken by the Luna. The blood was then shared with everyone in the pack. Each person, from elders to children, took a small sip to celebrate the end of the harvest and thank the gods for our bounty. The stag's antlers were mounted on a feather headdress, which Eris now wore. Her makeup was dark and heavy, and she drank her mead from a stocky golden goblet.

Her honey eyes turned to me, and a smile curled her black lips. "What?"

"You look like you're from another time tonight."

"As do you, fairytale princess."

"I am sorry, Eris, for the things I said in the garden. And for hurting you." I rubbed her arm where the burn had been. It was long healed, but it frightened me that I'd done that to someone I loved.

Her brow arched, and she paused before she answered, "I am sorry for suffocating you. My heart couldn't bear to lose you, and because of that, I may cling tightly. Can you forgive me?"

"Yes."

"I have been counseled to talk to you like an adult about things, and I will try."

"Okay. Am I not *allowed* to have children?"

She swallowed and looked at her hand, toying with the gems inlaid in her goblet. "We hope very much that you will wait." She steeled herself to find my eyes again. "Until after we've defeated our enemies."

"Why have you not spoken to me about it?"

"When you were with Daro, it wasn't a worry, although I did not like it." Her brow knit. "I expected you to wait for your mate before exploring intimacy. That's how we were raised, Enid."

"I know," I whispered, wondering if my mother and father could feel disappointed on the other side of death.

"Encountering you in the garden with Leo was not only a shock, but it also scared us. Pregnancy is a vulnerable position, and we do not want that for you. The dragons exploited that weakness four years ago when they attacked Diamond Moon days before I was due with the twins."

My brow furrowed, and I curtly pointed out, "I want you to know I have done nothing with Daro that would upset my future mate." The relief on Eris' face made me more indignant. "And I do not wish to have children for many years. So you don't have to worry."

"I am glad to hear you haven't disrespected your future mate, but I am concerned you were about to on Thursday. And you did not appear worried about pregnancy then either."

I frowned and looked away, scanning the crowd again for Leo. "I am aware of where I am in my cycle, if you are so concerned."

She giggled into her cup before she took a sip. "Don't be a fool, my naïve sister, like I was. That doesn't always work." She pointed to where several children played in a circle, Henry leading the game effortlessly despite his young age. "The evidence is there." Eris leaned closer and whispered, "There is a reason that alphas like these Greenwood men have such strong bloodlines. Hm?"

Heat rushed to my cheeks. "I should have been smarter."

She nodded, satisfied. "You turn nineteen in a few short hours, anyway, so I guess we will see what happens."

"And what if Leo is my mate?"

Her lips curled. "I would be very happy for you."

"If he isn't, and it is no one else either, I would still like to see him."

"I would like for you to wait for your mate." She swirled her finger around the rim of her cup. "But as an adult, you can choose for yourself. I will not stop you from seeing Leo, and neither will my husband." A smile spread across my face, and she looked over at me. "I would heavily suggest condoms, however."

My smile shrunk to sheepish, and I nodded.

"So, we are fine? You don't hate me?"

"No!" I hugged her. "And I never have, I promise. I love you."

"I love you endlessly," she said, and kissed the top of my head.

She gasped, and I pushed away from her. "What?"

"Cass has arrived."

I found him easily in the crowd, with the single or otherwise unsat-isfied women all looking his way. I tilted my head, taking him in. "He's a hot dog?"

Cass was in costume, complete with a line of mustard up his body, the bottom of the hotdog jutting out aggressively between his legs.

"A big wiener, I imagine, if you asked him," Eris said, and we laughed.

The band kicked into a song that made us look at each other, our lips curling as we both remembered the days of our childhood.

Eris squeezed my arm. "Go dance! You love this one!"

I ran around the table and hurried to where the circles formed. Two people made room, parting and giving me their hands with wide grins under their masks. The song started slowly, as did the turns of our circles, each one moving opposite of the one in front of it. At the center, two people began to dance, twirling together. There was a count to the steps, and I clicked the heels of my shoes into the wooden floor with everyone else. Someone had taught it to me a long time ago, before I could remember things. My mother, I expected, or maybe my father.

We all capered to the beat, those at the center moving toward the outer rings and us on the far rings moving in. I held the hands of two different pack members now, sharing smiles with them as our feet tapped in sync.

We shifted spots again, and I felt a tickle up my spine. Someone was watching me, with intentions that made my cheeks flare. I took the hands of the next two people but didn't look to share smiles with them. Across from me, in the same circle, Leo danced to the song, his feet moving with everyone else. I'd never seen him dance before, and the side of his mouth lifted in a small smile when he recognized my surprise. I couldn't help the grin that spread across my face. We hadn't shared our costume ideas this year, but I recognized him immediately as a character from a game I'd watched him play. His hair was swept back, cascading over his shoulders as he moved to the rhythm, while his long blue suede overcoat swayed and twisted in time with the music.

On the next shift, I timed my steps, getting into the correct spot that would bring us together in the middle, and he did the same. We were directly across from each other as our small circle of six turned to the music. Our eyes never parted, lit by the flickering candles. The dance became faster as the song went on, and I knew by the tempo it was nearly at its end. On the next shift, I lunged into the center to meet him, and he caught my arm with his calloused fingers. The world around us melted into the golden hue of Samhain, and I smiled up at him, holding my skirt with one hand while our feet moved together.

His eyes roamed down my body. "Grimm's Cinderella."

"Mr. Dorian." I turned with the music, so his hands were on my waist, and mine on his shoulders. He nodded, pleased that I recognized the character.

Leo stepped closer. "I missed you, Enid. My heart ached for you." He paused, his eyes taking on a heat that had nothing to do with candles. "My hands ached for you. To hold you."

I looked at the grand clock that dominated the wall of the ballroom. "In just a few short hours, we'll know."

"Know what?" he asked, though I knew he was aware of what I meant.

"Whether we're destined to be mates or star-crossed lovers."

The emotions playing in my heart flashed in his eyes; fear and excitement moving together.

"Either way, I'll never leave you, Enid. I'll always be here for you, even if we aren't fated for romantic love. I promise."

The song played its last chord, drawing to a close, and the dance floor cheered. We didn't let go, his hands sliding to my lower back, and mine around his nape.

He squeezed my waist. "I've thought about what you said, about not wanting the regret of not being together when we had the chance."

My brows lifted, not expecting to hear those words. I was content to dance with him all night and then go hide in his room until midnight. "And what did you decide?"

"That it's foolish and selfish."

My heart sank, but I nodded, trying to swallow my disappointment. I'd been ready to run out of here, his hand in mine, and bid adieu to shifter customs on our way out. Sorry, Mom and Dad.

Leo came closer, putting his cheek to mine, and whispered, "But I don't care. I will not be discouraged from loving you."

"Neither will I."

"Then if we are fools in love, let us do something foolish."

"What about the potential for heartbreak?"

"I am far past sparing myself that. It would be an honor to have my heart broken by you."

My heart fluttered, stunned by such grim, beautiful words. I leaned closer to his ear, so my lips brushed his skin. "Then what should we do with these last, few, short hours?"

I felt him inhale, smelling me where my pulse raced. His lips brushed my cheek, and I turned into him. The dance floor moved around us, couples spinning to the next beat, but we stood still, our lips nearly touching.

"I'd like to kiss you," he said.

"Then kiss me."

Our lips came together with the ease of familiarity. My hand pushed into his hair, pulling him closer, and I stepped onto his boots to better even our height. There were some giggles around us, and Leo tensed. He broke the kiss and whispered, "I'm being warned by my brother that this is very inappropriate."

Leo glanced at the Alpha table, where Gideon must now sit with my sister, but I didn't look. I asked, "Are you ready to run with me?"

His lips curled. "Yes. I am."

I took a deep breath and closed my eyes, focusing on the flickering presence of every burning candle in the room. When I knew the fire would listen to my call, I brought up my hand and closed it in a tight fist. The flames all snuffed out with a collective hiss, casting the room into blackness.

Chapter Twenty

Leo

Enid put the lights out with the close of her hand. The music cut off, and the crowd erupted into puzzled chatter while everyone tried to understand what had happened. Enid was giggling. She laced her fingers with mine, and we weaved through the crowd towards the patio doors. They led out into the crisp night, where the party had spilled onto the veranda.

When we got to the edge of the garden path, Enid whispered, "Hold on."

I stopped with her, watching her. The moon was bright tonight, its silver glow illuminating her face as she closed her eyes and gently bit her lip. She lifted her hand and opened it as if she was releasing a butterfly. The candles inside the ballroom sparked back to life, returning the pack house to its orange Samhain glow.

"That was incredible," I whispered, putting my block up so my brother couldn't interfere.

She put her hand on my cheek and grinned. "I guess it was worth it to learn fire, after all."

In her costume, she shone like the sun and the moon, all golden and silver, radiant and ethereal. But it wasn't the gown that made her beautiful. It was the light within her, the brilliance of her spirit, that stole my breath. Her grin didn't fade, and she took my hand, pulling me up the path. We passed the bench where we'd been caught on Thursday.

She said, "Let them try to find us this time," and giggled again, ducking into the forest. We'd been told our entire lives that what we were about to do was wrong, but I could do nothing but follow, my fingers entwined with hers and her pale dress shining as it shifted in the starlight.

We ran until we hit a wall of wild rose bushes. Enid took a deep breath and lifted her hand. The thorny branches parted, curling away to give us a path. As they did, they bloomed a delicate blushing pink, the leaves greening and unfurling. The rose patch stretched endlessly, erupting in a shock of color. I looked back as we walked through, watching the limbs close behind us. The world fell silent in their embrace.

We traveled deeper until we came to a clearing. Enid lifted her hands, and the entire glade answered her silent call, rising from its near-winter sleep.

I sucked in a deep breath, smelling the scent of summer, and took her hand. "I really don't know what I did to deserve to stand in the presence of such magic."

Her free hand absentmindedly floated to her chest, where her heart beat. "You saw me past the magic."

I smiled and twirled her as if we were dancing. The newly awakened forest was so thick here that it blocked out the moonlight. I peered at her, wishing my night vision was sharper. I wanted to see her. To witness her beauty.

Enid lifted both hands, and small buds of fire erupted at her fingers. She sent them in several directions, where they hovered below the trees like flickering stars, casting us in golden light.

I put my hands up to hers and flattened our palms. Her hands were so small and delicate compared to mine, barely reaching past my second knuckle. The tips of her fingers were still hot from the flame.

I asked, "Are you reading minds now?"

She laced our fingers. "Why?"

"I was just thinking I wanted more light to see you by."

"Maybe I wished the same."

I chuckled. "Because I am so beautiful?"

In all seriousness, she answered, "Yes," and kissed the line of my jaw.

I leaned back to study her. Her lips. Then the electric green of her eyes, flickering in the firelight. Then her lips again. Her eyes. And finally, when I could bear it no more, I asked, "Enid, are you sure about this?"

She ran her hand over the soft suede of my vest, and up around my nape. I stepped closer, so our chests met, and when she tilted her face up to mine, the ends of our noses brushed. Our mouths opened in anticipation, and she kissed my bottom lip. "I have never been more sure."

My hand captured her head, my palm on her cheek, and I kissed her roughly, pushing her lips open. She matched my desperation, her tongue meeting mine halfway.

We were starved for this kiss, needing each other, after only two days of absence. I said to my wolf, *'She must be. She must be ours. How can it be like this if she isn't?'*

'I pray to the goddess you are right for the sake of your foolish heart.'

If he said anything else, I did not hear it. Enid pushed the jacket off my shoulders, and the heavy suede collapsed in a puddle around my feet.

"May I take this beautiful dress off?" I asked, my hands already searching for the zipper.

"Yes. Yes." Her breath was shallow, and her hands trembled as they unbuttoned my vest and then my shirt.

I found the tiny teardrop zipper on her back, and slid it down, listening to the quiet hum as it moved unhindered. A clasp at the top was the only thing stopping me now, and I flicked it between my fingers. The tight bodice gave, the back opening, and Enid took a sharp breath like she'd been waiting for the opportunity. Together, we shoved the material down her body. It stopped at her thighs, the thick skirt ballooning around her. I grabbed her waist and lifted her into my arms. Her legs encircled me, and my pulse quickened when I felt her silky breasts press into my bare chest. My hands enveloped her firm bottom, and I couldn't help but give a squeeze. She gasped, breaking the lock of our kiss to nip at my lips with hers. I did the same to her, nipping her lips and then the line of her jaw while my fingers traced the ridge of fine lace that bordered her panties.

Her pulse hammered beneath her skin. I could feel it when I kissed her marking spot, and her scent was dizzying, its unrepentant femininity trying to drown me.

Her breath hitched, and she whispered, "I've had the most illicit thoughts... that I wouldn't have minded if you sank your teeth into me on the trail up to the house the other day."

Forbidden arousal snapped through me. My eyes opened at her admission, my breath choppy against her neck. "You'd take my mark before you have your wolf?" My heart thudded at the dangerous territory we'd entered.

"It's wrong," she said, her words wispy as I nipped the tendon of her neck. "But I would."

I shouldn't feel this way. It was *very* wrong, but a thick heat flooded my veins, gathering in my shaft. "Why?"

"Because it makes me truly sick to imagine belonging to another."

I leaned away to study her face. My brother would banish me for marking her early. After the unheeded lectures I'd received in the car to Ruby Moon and back, I knew winning his forgiveness for what I was doing now would be a task.

"I'm not asking you to! Oh, they'd have our heads," she blurted, her cheeks staining a dark red. "I just wanted you to know that I would."

I dropped to my knees and sat back on my feet, keeping her in my lap. Pressing my forehead to hers, I confessed, "I've wondered a million times since my birthday if I would reject my true mate in favor of you."

With a soft sigh, Enid melted into my arms, taking my lips with hers again. She shifted in my lap, and I groaned at the heated friction, flexing my hips to maximize it.

When her head kicked back, I lowered her down onto the chiffon cushion of her skirt. It fluffed around her like a cloud, sparkling in the firelight. I had to pause. To drink her in. She wore only a pair of sheer white panties and matching thigh-high nylons. My hands rested on her knees and slowly urged them apart, opening her legs. Her entire body flushed with color, and I felt her hold her breath. I held mine.

I pulled her closer to me, so her knees straddled my hips, and I slid my hands up her thighs. She pushed up to her elbows and made a small, delicious sound as she bit her lip, staring up at me.

"Are you sure you want to do this?" I asked.

She rolled her eyes and huffed, "Yes. That answer won't change," and reached for my belt buckle.

I caught her wrist and used it to ease her back. "I've never seen you so impatient."

"Well, you're being thick! I don't know how much more direct I could be. I'm lying here naked beneath you!"

"I'm trying to be a gentleman!"

She laughed, saying, "Well, stop it," and her breasts bobbed, her nipples like perfect precious gems.

"Fine." My head dipped, and I captured one of those sensual rubies with my mouth.

My name whispered through her lips, and her legs wrapped around my body, holding me there like she worried I might resort back to chivalry. I scraped my teeth over the bud of her breast. Her hips lifted under me when I did, so I did it again. My shaft throbbed with the awareness that I would finally know how it felt to be inside her.

I refused to hurry even if she wished me to. Beauty like Enid's was meant to be savored; lingered over, traced with my longing. I spent ample time at her breasts, kissing and sucking, not leaning away until both of her nipples were shining in the firelight, glossy from my attention.

She shuddered when I licked up her throat to her ear. "You are mine, Enid. For these next few sweet, stolen moments, you belong to me."

Despite the cool night, our bodies were hot, pressing together. Her hand was in my hair, holding me in the crook of her neck, and she whispered, her lips on my ear, "Don't you ever listen to anything I say? I've been yours since the day we met."

The fire of desire still burned hot, but it shifted to something more tender. I drew back enough to meet her gaze. My world was held there.

She was everything that meant anything to me. We rubbed our noses together, smiles breaking free on both our faces, and we kissed. Gentle this time. Sweetened with the love that only we seemed to understand.

"Then if you are mine, as you claim, I'm going to taste you."

Her eyes flew open, and her entire body flushed pink again. "Y-you are?"

My fingers hooked her panties at her hips, and I said, "I am."

Chapter Twenty-One

Enid

L EO KEPT HIS MOUTH on my body as he moved lower, pulling the velvety white panties down my legs as he did. His lips trailed like flame across my skin, branding me in heat and hunger, leaving me breathless. He paused at my twitching stomach and traced his tongue around my navel.

When I felt the brush of his chin lower, the coil of excitement in my stomach spun, and he took a deep breath.

"Gods, I have to confess I've thought about this often. I want to make you feel good. Better than I ever have."

He hadn't seen me naked yet, though he'd felt me underneath my clothes. I squeezed my eyes shut, gasping when he kissed the seam of my thigh, so close to my center. My knees trembled, unsteady beneath the weight of vulnerability.

There was a long pause, and I peeked one eye open, seeing that he was staring between my legs, his eyebrows lifted and his mouth slightly ajar.

"Gods," I whispered, snapping my eyes shut again.

His hands squeezed my thighs. "Relax. You are beautiful, I promise. Better than anything my mind could've ever conceived. For a moment, I couldn't think at all."

I giggled, slackening my iron grip on the chiffon, only to immediately take it back up when his thumb ran up my center.

He made a deep sound in his chest and pressed the bud of nerves he'd spent these last two weeks pleasuring. I moaned in return, a soft keening hum, and he said, "You are the finest instrument I've ever laid my hands on. Every gasp, every sigh. When I find the right chords, the sounds you make—gods, it's the sweetest music."

He didn't give me a chance to answer. Both of his hands gripped my hips and lifted me to his mouth. Any thoughts I was having shattered to pieces, lost as a pit of pleasure swallowed me whole. I expected the slow exploration we'd shared in the past days, both of us learning together what worked. This was not that. The new, raw sensations consumed me all at once, his confidence and aggression unraveling me with firm strokes of his tongue.

My back arched, trying to relieve the building heat in my core, and his hands clamped on my hips, holding me there. Holding me hostage in this unexpected barrage of sensuality. I felt his tongue slip inside me, and I cried out, his lips still moving against me. The fierce tightening built to unbearable, and when I felt the graze of his teeth against that sensitive bud, it peaked. Everything stopped and then tumbled into bliss, the waves rolling through me with unmatched intensity. I was consumed, lost in satin-wrapped strikes of pleasure. When they finally dulled, I listened to my wild cries echo into the surrounding forest.

My eyelids fluttered open. There he was, resting his chin on my lower stomach, a boyish grin teasing his lips. I immediately snapped my eyes shut again and covered my mouth, trying to suppress a giggle.

Leo laughed, framing my head with his elbows and laying his body over mine.

He smoothed my wild hair. "You're simply glowing."

I mumbled, "That was really wonderful. Thank you."

"My pleasure. Seriously. Are you ready? If not, I am certainly willing to do that again if you'd like."

"I'm nearly ready," I whispered, and this time when my hands drifted down between us, he let me.

Our breaths were heavy, mixing between us as I contended with the cool metal of his belt buckle. I felt his shifting feet. He was kicking off his boots. My cheeks flushed with the awareness we were both about to be naked except for a pair of thigh-high nylons.

His pants went down, his boxers with them. My cheeks blossomed with heat when I felt the weight and length of him fall against my lower stomach. His breath was choppier, and he kissed me while he kicked the pants off his feet. I ran my hands over his chest, feeling the soft brushing of hair that trailed down to his navel, and lower. I hadn't touched him yet, under his clothes, but I was emboldened by his earlier fearlessness.

"I'd like to touch you first."

He kissed my cheek and whispered, "I'm dying for your touch." My heart surged, wild and wanting.

I closed my eyes, unsure why I did, and moved my hands to where I felt the weight against my belly. They both wrapped around him, and my eyebrows lifted, surprised by what I felt and unsure of what I expected. The smoothness of his velvet skin made it easy to run my hands up and down, stroking him, and his head dropped against my shoulder with a sigh.

"Is that okay?" I asked.

"Yes, just like that." His breath caught as a tight chuckle against my neck. "Everything you do feels right."

I tightened my grip and felt his body flex, the chiffon of my dress whispering as he clenched tighter to the material. He was moving with me, thrusting his hips to my hands, and the tight coil in my core was back, recovered from my first climax and begging for more.

"Are you ready?" I whispered.

"Gods yes, but only if you are."

"I am," I said, deciding the first time couldn't be more perfect than here in a rose garden in the firelight with the only man I could ever imagine loving. "No regrets."

He slid down, away from the grip of my hands so I could feel his hard weight against my thigh. I swallowed, my mouth suddenly dry. He lifted my body and slid his cool vest under my bottom—to protect my dress, I realized. My body was hyperaware, feeling every brush of his skin. I wrapped my legs around his waist, inviting him to continue. The dancing sensation in my core promised pleasure.

His hand was between us, and I closed my eyes, taking deep breaths when I felt him at my slick entrance, and then his body rocked forward. The pressure shocked me, and I flattened my hands on his chest.

His voice was ragged. "Do you want me to stop?"

I shook my head, and put my hands on his shoulders, moving my hips to a different angle. "Keep going."

He didn't move quickly, but he was steady, flexing his hips forward. My mouth dropped open, and I lost my voice as the pressure turned to an unbearably sharp pinch.

He blew out a clipped breath. "Wow. You are so tight."

"Is that it?" That was intense, but not so bad.

"Uh... no."

My eyes flew open. There was *more?* I almost asked how much more but decided I didn't want to know.

My hands tightened on his shoulders. "Keep going."

He rocked back and then forward. Something inside me gave, and his weight dropped forward, pushing deeper than I understood was possible. I couldn't stop the small cry that parted my lips. It was too much all at once, and I squeezed my eyes shut, two tears trailing down my temples into the lace and chiffon.

He moaned into my neck. "Oh, my gods. Are you okay?"

I nodded.

"Enid?" he said, his voice laced with concern.

"Just hold on."

"Okay. I'm going to come in, like, five seconds anyway if I move."

I was trying to adjust my hips, beckoning the hot coil of desire to come back. The traitor did not return. I was horribly uncomfortable, but I definitely didn't want to stop. I don't know how long we stayed like that, unmoving, my body trying to harmonize with the overwhelming presence of his.

"Can I kiss you?" he asked, and I whimpered at the sweet suggestion, turning my face to meet him.

We kissed while he slowly rocked his hips, and I focused on the kiss, and how warm his skin felt beneath my hands, and the way his weight pushed me into the dress. His lips left mine, and the brush of his kiss against my marking spot sent a tiny swirl of pleasure down my body. I held him there, and he understood, sucking the sensitive flesh into his mouth. The pain subsided into an intense feeling of discomfort.

I listened to his breathing change as his pace quickened. I was clinging to his shoulders, and I gasped when he suddenly pulled away from me, ripping from my grasp.

His soft moan, followed by the spill of heat on my stomach, and I blurted, "Oh!"

He grabbed his vest, trying to clean me up with it. "Sorry! Gods, sorry. I just had a last moment thought that maybe I shouldn't, you know... inside you. Gideon is already going to kill me for this."

I shook my head. "No! I'm glad one of us was thinking! I just told Eris I'd be smarter."

I giggled sheepishly as he tossed the vest and collapsed with his cheek on my chest, lacing his arms beneath me and hugging me. Soreness echoed between my legs, but I kept my smile, playing with his long, soft hair, and watching my little fire candles dance above us. They'd stayed the whole time, and I smirked, impressed by my improvement in the craft.

Leo said, "Sorry if that was quick. And if it sucked."

"It didn't suck. And if I'm being very honest, I'm glad it was quick."

He winced. "Did it hurt that bad? I'm so sorry."

"No. It didn't."

Leo looked up at me and lifted his brow, easily able to tell when I was lying.

"Well. My body was quite unsure what to do with you. But I'm not hurt. It was perfect."

He put his chin on my chest and grinned up at me. "Promise? You're okay?"

"Didn't you think it was perfect?"

His grin dipped, so it was sheepish, and he said, "Well, *yeah*, of course I did, but..."

"But what?"

He frowned at my teasing, and his fingers moved to my ribs, tickling me. "But I wasn't in any—and I mean *any*—pain! That was the opposite of pain for me."

I was ticklish, and I cackled, trying to grab his hands. He held my wrists, pinning my hands between us, and leaned up to my face. I could feel his breath on my lips when he asked, "Are you okay?"

"Yes. I am." My brows lifted when I felt that very distinct weight on my belly, and I added, "I don't know about *that* okay!"

His cheeks reddened, and he put his face in my neck. "I know! I know that's not happening. I mean, I would. I want to. I can't help it! You're naked. Beneath me. You feel *so* good. If you had your wolf, and you were healed, it'd be a different story."

I gasped. "What time is it? It's got to be close."

He dug around in his jacket and pulled out his phone, turning it to me. "Midnight is almost here, Cinderella."

"An hour," I whispered, and then winced. "Twenty missed calls from Gideon?"

"Yeah. And ten from Finn, but what're they gonna do about it now?"

I shrugged. "Make you attend more meetings?"

He scoffed. "Worth it. One thousand percent worth it." I laughed, and he asked, "What do you want to do now?"

"Sneak back to your room and wait until midnight together."

He nodded and stood, pulling me to my feet. I winced at the tenderness between my legs and glanced down. There were a couple of swipes of blood on my inner thighs, and probably on Leo, but he was already pulling his boxers up and handing me my panties. He helped me get back into my dress first, and then put his own clothes back on, except the vest, of course.

His arms wrapped around me, and he picked me up, cradling me.

I giggled. "What are you doing?"

"I want to carry you."

"I'm okay, I promise."

"I know that," he said but didn't put me down.

I snuffed my flames and restored the forest to its autumnal slumber as he carried me out. We took a different path, which led us away from the party and to the front doors.

Leo peeked in first and then nodded. "It's dead quiet."

"We lucked out." I laid my head on his shoulder, listening to the whir of the elevator after we boarded.

When the doors opened, I said, "You've got to drop me off at my room."

"Why?"

"I need my toothbrush and a change of clothes."

"You can wear my clothes. I like when you do. You're very pretty in just my t-shirt."

"Just my toothbrush then," I said, blushing.

He set me down. "Do you want me to wait?"

"Do you want to shower?"

"Yeah, I probably will—" He stopped mid-sentence, his brows lifting. "Wait. You mean... together?"

"Yes."

He stepped closer, grabbing my waist and pulling me into him. "If we discover we're mates in the shower, I promise it will be much better than what we just did out there in that forest."

"I can't wait," I said, refusing to accept any other scenario.

"I'll go start the water."

"Okay." I grabbed his collar and pushed onto my tiptoes, pressing my lips to his. "I love you, Leo. I mean it. Even if everyone else thinks this is just two silly kids making an age-old mistake. I know it's more than that between us."

His hand cupped my cheek. "I love you, Enid. Always."

"I'll hurry."

He nodded, and I stepped inside my room, clicking the door shut behind me.

Hades stood in the window, yawning. He hadn't wanted to attend the party, hating being the black cat on Samhain.

"Oh, Hades, I had the most magical night."

He meowed, coming to me and rubbing against my ankles. I bent and ran my hand over his back. "Can you stay here for a minute?"

He chortled at me, and I said, "Well, Leo and I are gonna," I cupped my hand around my mouth and whispered, "shower together."

He trotted back to his windowsill with no more questions and settled in his spot. I hurried for my toothbrush, and then jumped on the bed, leaning over and resting my head on Hades' belly.

He licked my ear, making me giggle, and I said, "I love you too, sweet boy. I'll be back in a few minutes to get you."

With that, I left him on the windowsill and hurried down the hall, where Leo's door sat ajar, waiting for me.

Chapter Twenty-Two

Leo

I LEFT THE DOOR cracked behind me and went to the bathroom to crank the shower on. Smiling dumbly, I put my hand under the stream of water. That had hurt her, I knew, but she felt so good, the way her sheath had tightened on me and gripped me. I groaned deep in my chest just thinking of it, and I was desperate for midnight to arrive. Her wolf could heal her, and we could do it again. This time, I was determined she would enjoy it as much as I had.

If she was my mate, I would give her my teeth this time, too.

When I returned to my room, I sighed, annoyed with the itching in my brain. Someone was repeatedly trying to link me. Figuring I could face the music a little, and get some peace from it, I opened the block.

'What?'

'Leo, gods damn you!'

Finn's voice was wrought with panic, and I said, *'We're fine!'*

'You're with Enid?'

'She's in her room, yeah.'

'We may need her out here. There are two dragons in the woods by Cass's tower! And like five hundred vamps!'

'What? We'll be right there!'

'Send her! You stay there and protect the artifact. I smell something fishy.'

My door creaked, and I spun on my heel to apprise Enid of the situation. Except it wasn't her.

"Christine?" I sighed and rolled my eyes. "I don't have time for this. Excuse me."

She lifted her hand and blew on her palm. A sparkling red powder erupted into my face, and I coughed, rubbing at my eyes. "What was that? Christine?"

I couldn't say anything else. My body went almost numb, like I couldn't move. Except my eyes. They darted around the room while the rest of my body stood limp, my hands hanging at my sides. My nose burned with the smell of strong, dark magic.

Christine cooed, "Oh, now you'll finally listen, you big stupid oaf." My eyes widened, and she said, "Cluck like a chicken. Do it."

I tried to link Finn, but the channel was fuzzy, like the static on a bad television.

My brain fought, but my body bent my elbows, hands in my armpits, and I flapped them while shouting, "Bawk, bawk, bawk!"

Christine cackled with delight, holding her stomach, and said, "Okay, stop. That was perfect! Now." She approached me, walking her fingers up my chest. "Kiss me. Kiss me like you do her—Enid—like you love me."

I grunted in my throat, trying to pull away, but my body didn't listen. I squeezed my eyes shut, fighting, but couldn't stop myself from taking her in my arms and kissing her. Her tongue was in my mouth, her hand in my hair, and I thought I might vomit. A quiet gasp yanked my eyes open, and I saw Enid looking through the crack in my door. Her face slackened and then screwed up into a sob. She turned with a swish of her dress and fled.

'Enid!' I shouted in the link, but I couldn't get through.

Christine kept me in the lip lock for several more seconds before finally letting go. She adjusted her lipstick and grinned.

"There, was that so hard? Am I so undesirable?"

I didn't answer, just stared down at her, unable to believe she was this desperate. She giggled again, and I watched her eyes shift from brown to a light gray.

Bleiz said, *'This isn't Christine! We've been fooled!'*

"Now, you stubborn idiot, you're going to take me to the artifact, and fast. Let's go! Act normal if we meet anyone on the way."

She shoved me, and I couldn't stop myself from listening. It was only to the elevator, and then to the office floor one level down, which would be dead at this hour. My eyes stared at Enid's door, begging her to come back out. The entire house was like a ghost town. We didn't see a single soul on our short walk. Children and civilians would be hunkering down, and the fighting wolves were out facing the dragons, unaware that the real threat was inside.

'Gideon! Gideon!' I screamed into the link, but the words just bounced around in my skull, going nowhere.

'We must fight!' Bleiz said, his voice strained as he tried to pry away from this spell she'd put us under.

We stepped off the elevator, and two warriors guarded Gideon's office door. Imposter Christine whispered, "Get rid of them," in my ear.

They put their fists over their hearts in a salute, and one said, "Gamma Leo."

I returned the salute. "Alpha sent me to guard the artifact. You should both go help out there."

Their brows knit and they looked at each other, then at imposter Christine behind me. I begged them with my eyes to catch on.

"Gamma? Are you—"

"Go!" I shouted, my voice booming in the empty hall.

Their eyes widened, and they scurried past us to catch the elevator without another word.

Wolves. Fierce, obedient, loyal, and sometimes idiots.

Once inside Gideon's office, I opened the compartment on the wall and typed in the code that only my brothers and I knew. A secret door opened in the floor. It revealed a long, spiraling staircase that went through the entire house and into the basement. I walked in front of imposter Christine, and I could hear her shallow, shaky breaths.

She prodded my back. "Hurry up!"

I went faster, reaching the first of three doors. Gideon had gone to exceptional measures to keep the artifact safe. The first door was a thumbprint scanner, and I pressed my finger to it, praying to the Goddess for a red light. It blinked green, and the door slid open. The next scanned my eye, with the same results, and the final pricked my finger, taking and analyzing my blood. Only Finn, Gideon and I could open these doors. The last one slid open, and on a pedestal in the center of a small, well-lit room sat the unassuming artifact. It was an athame, a witch's knife, dull and dingy.

I held my breath, hoping imposter Christine would step into the room. River and Rhia had cast a magical ward that would trap a thief. It was our last and best guard, preventing even my brothers and me from taking the artifact. One of the witches had to be here to touch it.

"Okay, okay," Christine said, her voice shaking. She took a pouch off her waist and stepped in front of me. Her hands trembled, and she lit a black candle, holding it out. The flame burned dark green. Out of the pouch next came something that made my pulse flutter. A soul stone. Evil magic. I could smell its acrid scent saturating the room. Someone's soul was contained inside the dark gem. I could see it shining, flitting around like it wanted out. Christine held it in her hand, and took a deep breath, then removed a paper with writing from the pouch.

Out loud, she read,

"Any spell of here be gone!
Take your disaster back to your caster.
I bid thee to flee and return the malice in a fold of three!"

The soul stone in her hand hummed louder with each word, and I saw her shoulders tense, like she wanted to drop it. When she completed the spell, a shockwave blasted from the gem, so powerful I stumbled away. Christine gasped and let it go, where it bounced on the concrete floor. The light that had shone inside it was gone. It skidded to a stop, appearing to be a normal scarlet garnet. She laughed under her breath and looked at the candle. The flame had lost its green hue and burned an average orange.

"That's it," she whispered. "I've done it!" She hesitated and grabbed my arm, pulling me forward. "You get it for me. Go. Get the artifact and bring it to me."

My dumb body shuffled over as Bleiz and I both fought with every fiber of our souls. We grabbed the athame, feeling the hum of its powerful magic, and handed it to a grinning Christine.

She sheathed it on her belt and patted my cheek. "You were so good. Now, sit here on the floor and wait for your shame. Tell your brother and his whore Luna that Sophia says hello."

I sat and said, *'Oh, my gods,'* to my wolf, listening to her heels click away. *'We've done it. We've ruined everything!'* I searched for the pack link, trying to dig it out of the static in my brain. *'GIDEON! Please! Answer me! Enid! Anybody!'*

CHAPTER TWENTY-THREE

ENID

I RAN DOWN THE stairs, tears rolling over my cheeks. A violent sob bubbled in my chest, breaking through the tight grip that shock held on my lungs. How could I have seen what I just had? Christine and Leo kissing so passionately. I burst through the foyer doors, running toward the south, and smashed into someone.

Daro said, "Enid? Are you all right?"

I couldn't answer, and shoved him away, taking off in a sprint to the forest. There was an acre of trees between here and the lake, and I wanted to get to the water. It beckoned me tonight.

"Enid!" he called behind me, but I didn't have the wits to listen. "Stop! You can't go! Haven't you heard what's happening?"

"Leave me alone!" I ducked into the treeline. The naked fall branches whipped my face and tore at my ball gown like they, too, wanted to stop me. I said, "Out of my way!" pushing with my hands so the forest bent away from me.

Leo. Leo. How could he?

He'd known that I was coming to his room. He had known I would see that. Was that his plan? But then, why would we do what we did earlier in the rose patch? It didn't make sense. I thought of their kiss, and the wild look in his eyes when he noticed me. Chest heaving, I ground to a halt.

"It doesn't make sense," I said to the trees, who whispered back with a gentle wind. "It doesn't—"

On the breeze, I smelled it. Magic. Acrid. Dark. I whipped around, squinting into the night. It was nearly a full moon, but the forest was thick here. I lit a flame in my hand and jogged deeper into the trees, following my nose. When I jumped a tiny stream, my dress shoes slipped on a wet log, and I fell. My flame snuffed and my hands tore as they slid across the forest floor, but I barely felt the sting.

The smell was strong here, and I looked around, my eyes catching on the rotting log. It had broken with my weight, and inside, a pale face looked out, its expression frozen in wide-mouthed, perpetual horror.

I screamed. She was decaying, so it was hard to tell from the face who she was, but the necklace left no doubts. It was the locket her grandfather had given her on her seventh birthday. She never took it off.

I covered my mouth, muffling my exclamation of, "Christine!" Had I noticed the locket on her these past months? I tried to remember, but my thoughts shifted. "Leo!" I shouted, scrambling to my feet. "Oh, gods!" Whoever was in the house with him wasn't Christine.

'Eris!' I called into the link, gasping when it went nowhere.

"My, my, my," a froggy voice crooned behind me. "Are we really so fortunate?"

Dark giggles echoed in the trees, and I spun on my heel. I'd never met her before, but she needed no introduction.

"Morga," I whispered, taking a step back.

The old crone was just as River described her, stooped at the shoulders and white in the eyes. I was to run if I ever saw her, and if I couldn't run, fight. Morga lit a fire in her hand, and I swallowed, repulsed by her hollow, decaying smile as the flame shifted over her features. The few teeth that were left were black, hanging by shreds of gum, and her hair was long and stringy, looking as though it had never known soap. The flame danced, illuminating her eyes. They were milky white, but

I knew she had no trouble seeing. We weren't alone either. The forest assured me that others lurked in the shadows.

'Eris?' I tried again, and Morga cackled.

"Help! Help!" She mocked me. "Sorry, you filthy dog, I can't let you call the pack. Now, why don't we just do this the easy way? Come on over here, and we'll get on back to the masters."

I kicked my shoes off and dug my toes into the dirt. "I will die before I go with you."

"So be it!" she crowed and shot the fireball toward me with a squeal.

I pulled up a piece of earth and used it to shield myself from the flame. My own fire wouldn't burn me, but another witch's would. I tried to run, only to be tripped by roots that crawled from the earth and wrapped my ankles.

"Capture her! Don't kill her!" Morga screeched.

A blast of wind crushed me, sending me flying into a tree, and the air left my lungs. Three witches: earth, fire, and wind. I huffed, sucking in a breath, and let my emotions go, sending a torrent of fire into the forest. It lit up the clearing, and I was able to see the other two women slinking around. Morga's daughters, I suspected. Calling to the tree next to one of them, I used a massive branch to slap her, sending her tumbling heels-over-head.

"Careful, Una!" Morga said. "Careful now, she's no slump!"

Fire burned toward me, roaring through the clearing, and I rolled, pulling the moss blanket of the forest floor over me. I scrambled from beneath its smoldering form and focused on the large rock next to me, picking it up and sending it toward Morga. She didn't even flinch, and one of her daughters blasted my projectile with air, sending it clattering into the trees. I gritted my teeth, determined to end this. Morga was a key player, and if I killed her, it would be a dire blow to the dragon enemy.

I took a deep breath, rolling my shoulders, and let go. For one of the few times in my life, I did not have to be in control. If people got hurt—good. I looked down at my hands and watched the purple veins beneath my skin grow dark, lit by the iridescent glow of my eyes. An alarmed cluck gave me a target, and I pulled at the forest, bidding it to crush that bug. The trees collapsed on her, rushing to listen.

The woman screamed, and more fire soared at me as Morga uttered a curse. I used air, a current of it, to hold the torrent of flame at bay. I could see her in the glow, her nasty teeth gritted as she tried to overpower me, adding a second hand to her casting. My air pushed back, taking ground, and I watched her eyes grow wide.

Cass's words echoed in my head, and I shouted, "Who are *you* to bid *me* to bend the knee?" My voice was distorted by the magic that coursed through my veins, deeper than normal as it reverberated in my chest. "Do you forget who I am?"

My hair and skirts whipped around me, and I turned the air current down, using it to push myself across the clearing in a lengthy jump. I landed behind her and lifted roots from the earth, wrapping her wrists and then trying to wrap her hands. She shrieked and burned them away, turning on me with alarming speed for such an old woman. I'd already made my next move, pulling a tidal wave of mud from the damp forest floor where the tiny stream ran. It drenched her, and I unleashed flames, intent on hardening the clay and cooking her alive.

"Mother!" a voice squealed behind me, and I looked over my shoulder and screamed.

Another witch and the imposter Christine emerged from the trees. It wasn't they who tore the shriek from me, but what they dragged with them. A unicorn burned to bone in some places and quivering as they pulled his raw body over the forest floor.

"Let her go!" the young witch said. Taking a silver blade from her waist, she leaped upon Daro and put it to his throat. "I'll kill him! Don't make no mistake, I know where to cut him to bleed him out!" Her eyes were wild, and her body twitchy, like she had too much energy trapped inside her. But her words did not falter, and I felt them to be true.

"Daro," I whispered.

The hardened mud in front of me shattered, spraying shrapnel, and Morga hissed at me, spitting and wiping her face. Her sour expression lifted. "Ah. Sara, my good girl. What have you found?"

The young witch jumped at the praise, inclining her head. "A unicorn, Mother. Nice horn on him. Thought you'd harvest it and his soul since we spent one. This dumb wench left your soul stone behind, though."

Morga glared at imposter Christine, who said, "What? I was focused on this."

My stomach rolled when she lifted the athame from her belt. The artifact!

The old crone shuffled over. "Give it. Give it now!" The imposter handed the athame to Morga, who cooed like she held a newborn baby, running her finger down the blade. She tucked it in her robe and grinned her gap-toothed smile at Christine. "That's good, girly. Master will be very pleased. He'll have a treat for you for being such a good dog."

Christine's smile faded, and I moved toward them, but Sara shouted, "Hey!" and pressed the blade to Daro's neck. He whinnied softly.

I dropped my hands. "Don't harm him. Please."

"We won't," Morga said, "if you come with us. No fight." A wolf's howl sounded in the distance. "Time's up. What say you, girl? Him or you."

Daro shifted back to human form, and his breaths were ragged, rattling through his scorched lungs. His body shook, and he turned his eyes up at me. The pale blue of his irises were bordered with bloodshot red, his voice a rough rasp. "Don't you dare, Enid."

"Me," I said, barely acknowledging it was a decision.

Morga was drawing her symbol in the air. It stayed lit, like the path of a sparkler that never faded. A glowing red fire symbol with her own personal flair. Her signature. "No fight, you'll come with us, and I'll spare the crispy unicorn."

I lifted my finger and copied her movement, drawing my own intricate symbol that featured all four elements, and I felt the binding force of the witch's contract sink into my bones. "Agreed."

"Now! Hurry!" she hissed. "Una, bring Cora!" The air witch limped out of the woods with the bleeding earth witch against her shoulder.

Christine stomped her foot. "Wait! I don't want to be in this body anymore!"

Morga sighed and took a runestone out of her pocket, carved of bone. She crushed it into dust in her hand and whispered to it, letting it go in the breeze.

Christine sucked in a sharp breath and doubled over. I watched with my mouth open as she went through a shift similar to that of human to wolf and became a more mature woman. I glanced over and watched the real body of Christine go through months of decay in seconds, becoming nothing more than a skeleton stuffed in that log.

My heart sank. "Sophia?" Of all the people I expected to see, it was not Gideon's former fiancée. Eris had given her leniency, and this was how she used it.

"Surprise!" Sophia said, giggling, and she took Sara's hand as we all formed a circle.

Morga was digging into her robes, eyeing me. "No offense, but I'm going to be cautious with you." She blew black powder into my face, and I inhaled out of instinct. Her rotten smile spread across her face. "It looks like the ball is over, Cinderella."

"She's a pumpkin!" Sara squealed, giggling with delight.

Unable to do anything else, I sent one last message through the link, unsure if it would even get through. *Leo? They've got me. Daro needs medical help in the Southern Peninsula. I'm sorry. I love you.*

My knees wobbled, collapsing. Sara and Morga held my upper arms, and I felt the magic of the flash as my vision faded.

CHAPTER TWENTY-FOUR

LEO

I STARED AT MY finger resting on my knee. It was twitching when I commanded it to move.

'Gideon? Are you there?'

Come on, you worthless finger, move!

'Gideon! Please!'

In the prison of my unheeding body, I begged my finger to move and my brother to answer as the seconds ticked into long minutes. The athame was lost. I was sure of it, but I had to keep trying. My eyes widened. The finger! It swept across my kneecap. I moved it again, and my lips curled at the edges. A smile! I clenched my hand into a fist.

'Gideon!'

'Leo! What is it? Where are you? Where is Enid?'

'No time! The athame. It's lost. I was tricked!'

'Impossible!'

'I'm down in the vault.'

He didn't answer.

'Enid? Please,' I linked, finding her blocked.

It was several more agonizing minutes before I heard clattering on the stairs and shouting. "No! It's open! Leo!"

I still couldn't call out, so I sat and waited, tapping my finger on my knee.

Gideon ran right past me. "No! No, no, no!" He slid his hands over the smooth pedestal and looked under the lip like the athame might be hiding. "What happened?" He stalked over to me, picking me up by the front of my shirt and snarling in my face. His eyes were the golden hue of his wolf. My mouth opened, but my throat still refused to work and make words. He sniffed, and his brow knit. His eyes faded back to hazel green. With a different insistence, he asked, "Leo? Answer me? Are you hurt?"

I'm cursed. I can't move!'

"Smell that?" Finn kicked the empty garnet. "Fucking dark magic."

Eris picked it up. "A soul stone."

Gideon said, "Leo needs help! Find River!"

Finn shouted up the stairs, and the earth witch appeared in my face. She had soot on her cheek, and I could smell that she was bleeding. Her finger slid down my cheek, and she sniffed it. "Yes. Hm. Living catatonia. I've got some cleansing water." She rifled through her robe and removed a small green vial, tipping it into my mouth. I expected it to taste like water, but it was filled with oils and herbs. It rushed down my throat, and as soon as it hit my stomach, I sat forward, coughing.

I started sputtering before anyone could ask, "The-the girl. Christine. It wasn't Christine! She was an impostor, and she blew this powder in my face. I'm sorry, Gideon! I led her down here."

"He wouldn't have been able to control it," River said, helping me stand.

"She had the soul stone and used a spell to break the one that River and Rhia set in place. Then she took the artifact."

"Morga," River said. "Only her enchantment could carry enough power."

"Finn, send warriors in every direction. They need to search the packlands for Christine Griner. Find her!" Gideon scrubbed his hand down his face, his brows knit. "How could I have missed this? A witch in my pack?"

"Not a witch," I said, and cleared my throat. "She, uh, said to tell you and Eris that Sophia says hello."

My brother's eyes drifted closed, and he took a deep breath, while Eris cursed and smacked the wall, pressing her forehead to it.

"Well, so much for that, then," River said, straightening her robe. "The athame is gone. War it is. I need to speak to Enid."

"Where is Enid?" Eris asked, turning to me.

"She's in her room. That girl, Christine, made me kiss her, and Enid saw, and she got upset."

Eris stepped forward. "But she went to her room. You're sure? I can't link her."

"Yes. Well, where else would she go?" I asked, but as I was jogging to leave the vault, a dark feeling sank into my gut.

We all took the stairs, thundering up them like a herd of buffalo. When I stepped into the resident hallway, I heard a woeful howl, followed by vicious scratching.

"Enid!" I shouted, breaking her doorknob off when I twisted it too hard.

Hades yowled, sprinting out under my feet toward the stairs.

"Enid?" I called to an obviously empty room. Hades had nearly torn the door apart trying to get out.

River fell into step behind the black cat. "Follow him!"

He led us out into the cold night, and Gideon howled, calling warriors to our sides. We followed River toward the tree line, who trailed Hades into the dark forest. Enid would be out here by the lake, upset with me, but fine. That made sense. She sometimes came to the water when she was upset.

I nearly tripped when she linked me. *Leo? They've got me. Daro needs medical help in the Southern Peninsula. I'm sorry. I love you.*
'Enid!'

She didn't answer, and I felt her absence in the pack link, like she'd moved out of range.

"Oh, gods! Hurry! She says they've got her! Up ahead!"

Eris cried, "Enid!"

Everyone else was silent, moving through the trees after Hades. I was at the front and almost tripped over a burned husk on the ground. I leaped over him, grinding to a halt and kneeling to see who it was. His wide, pastel-blue eyes stared up at me, and I could see places where his bone poked through, the flesh burned away. His chest heaved, every breath sounding like pure agony.

"Oh, my gods," I said, covering my mouth and nose to escape the rancid smell of burned flesh. "Eris! It's Daro!"

She was in the middle of the small clearing, her hands cupped around her mouth. "Enid! Enid!"

Hades was howling these long, deep meows that I'd never heard from him, and River stood in one spot, staring at the ground with her hands on her hips and her shoulders slumped.

"Where's Enid, Daro? Where is she?" I demanded, taking his charred shoulder. The skin sloughed away beneath my fingers, and I winced, yanking my hand back.

He was staring at me, and his mouth kept opening and shutting, but only weak sounds crawled up his raw throat. "G-G-*Gone*."

"Gone?" I put my hand on my shaking head. "No! Enid!" I stood, calling for her, too. "Enid!"

"She's not here," River said to everyone, quieting the group.

"Not here?" Eris threw her arms out. "Well, where? Where is she?"

River reached into her robe and pulled out some kind of powder. She tossed it into the air in front of her, and two symbols lit up the clearing. One was red, a fire rune, slightly different from any I'd seen and incorporating an "M." The other was Enid's. A pastel green featuring all the elemental symbols.

"There was a fight here," River said.

I glanced around the clearing. Broken branches, splintered mud, and smoldering moss.

River reached up, tracing Enid's symbol with her finger. "Foolish girl. It appears Enid gave herself up to the crone, Morga, to save the young unicorn." The symbols began to fade, allowing the darkness to creep back into the forest, and River sighed. "The dragons have her."

"What? What do you mean? Gideon?" Eris sputtered, turning to him. "Gideon?"

My oldest brother stood with his arms crossed, his chin on his chest as he stared at the ground. I followed his eyes and recoiled. A petite skeleton was stuffed into a log, a golden locket glinting in the dying light. He kneeled beside her, gingerly taking the locket and clicking it open with his thumbnail.

"I'm so sorry, Christine," he whispered, gently closing it again.

Finn, who'd run further on, burst back into the clearing and took in the scene. "That's it then, isn't it? They got the artifact, and they got Enid." He laced his fingers behind his head. "We're fucked. We're dead!"

I shook my head. "No! That can't be. She can't be gone."

Daro's hand wrapped around my ankle, squeezing, and I glanced down at him. He nodded the best he could, mostly moving his eyes.

"No," I whispered, shaking my head. My eyes brimmed with tears, and I sniffled, wiping at my nose.

"I told you," Gideon snapped, stepping in front of me. "I tried to tell you she needed to be focused, and now we're here."

My brow knitted, and I looked at Finn, who shook his head, his face pale. "That's..." I wanted to argue, but he was right. If Enid hadn't been so upset over my kissing who she thought was Christine, she wouldn't have left the house. If we hadn't snuck away from the party, we would've known that danger had infiltrated the pack.

Eris wept, her mouth open as deep, near-silent sobs shook her body. She stumbled into Gideon's open arms, and cried into his chest, wailing a broken sound I'd never heard from anyone. I thought I was going to be sick, and I walked to the edge of the clearing, bending and putting my hands on my knees. The shock washed over me in waves, making me feel unsteady.

It was several long seconds, Eris weeping while the rest of us stood around in dumb silence.

Gideon said, "Finn? Call the banners. Call the packs. Get them here with their warriors as soon as possible."

Finn threw his hands out. "We don't even know where we're going! We don't know where this ceremony is supposed to take place. Oh, gods, I can't believe this."

"Then you'll do nothing?" Gideon asked curtly. "River says they need a full moon to conduct the ceremony. That gives us," he looked up at the waxing gibbous and sighed, "three days."

"I'll call the banners," Finn said flatly, walking into the woods toward the pack house.

River just disappeared without a word, flashing away in a blink.

"Eris," Gideon said, taking her shoulders. "Daro is hurting. You need to heal him. As soon as he is able, he needs to contact his grandfather. Then you get Wren and the harpies here. I will speak to the Fae King."

Her black makeup streamed down her cheeks, and she sobbed again, blubbering, "She's with dragons! Do you know what they'll do to her?"

He was gentle, but firm. "That's enough of that. Enid needs you to focus. Let's go."

Eris closed her eyes and steeled her lip, and without looking at me, kneeled next to Daro. She put her hands on him, singing her song, and the white light beneath her palms lit up the clearing.

Gideon turned on his heel, marching back through the woods, and I jogged after him. "Wait! Gideon! What about me? What should I do?"

He stopped so suddenly I nearly ran into him, and he glanced back over his shoulder. "I'll let you know, Leo, if I have a job for you."

"What? Gideon." He kept walking, and my voice broke when I called, "I'm sorry! I didn't think—"

"No, you didn't. For now, you've done enough." He ducked under a branch, letting it swing back to stop my pursuit. "Excuse me, I have to go tell the Griners that their daughter was murdered on my watch."

"Fuck!" I hissed, lacing my fingers in my hair. "Enid." My chest tightened as the weight of reality sank in, constricting my heart so it couldn't beat and my lungs so I couldn't breathe.

A soft brush against my ankles drew my eyes down. "Hades?" He meowed at me, and I asked, "What do we do?"

Hades trotted away, calling back to me. I followed, hurrying behind him until I saw the top of Cass's tower peeking over the treeline.

Author's note: I always see my books like movies in my head, and for this part, I imagine a very clear scene with all three of our leading men. The song "Little Lion Man" by Mumford & Sons plays. Leo runs after Hades through the trees in his Samhain costume, his eyes a little wild. Gideon tells Christine's devastated parents the awful news, returning the locket to them, and then he finds Eris in the corner of Ollie's stall, curled up into a ball. And Finn returns to his office and picks up the phone to call the others, then goes to his room and hugs Kat and his children.

CHAPTER TWENTY-FIVE

LEO

Hades took me straight to Cass's, and he was scratching the door when I caught up with him. I knocked, and Cass yelled, "Come in!"

"Cass?"

"In here, Little Lion."

I followed his voice into the living room and recoiled. "Holy Hades, Cass."

His gut was ripped open, and he had his hand over the wound, holding his entrails in place so it could heal. There was a sheen of sweat over his entire body, and he was paler than I'd ever seen him.

"It will heal. Bring me that," he said, pointing at a bottle of malt whiskey on his counter. "Gods, I hate that bitch."

I brought it to him. "Who?"

"Edana." He spat the name like it tasted bad and pulled the cork from the bottle with his teeth so he could take a swig. There was a hole in his stomach, and he sighed when the liquor leaked out, joining the bloodstain he was creating on the blanket beneath him. "That ruby-red hag."

"Why? Because she ripped your guts out?"

He lay back, closing his eyes. "Because once upon a time she made me believe she loved me."

My brows lifted, and I waited for him to continue, but he left it at that.

"Cass. They got—"

"The artifact, I know. I don't know why you're surprised. I always said they would get it."

"Enid," I interjected, my voice thickening. "They got Enid."

His eyes flew open. "She's dead?"

"No." My heart clenched. "Well, honestly, I don't know. The crone took her. Morga."

"Then my brethren have her, and she's not dead."

My heart relaxed a bit. "How do you know?"

"Because that's no fun. They'll want to play with her first."

"Oh, my gods," I said, sitting heavily in a chair and putting my head in my hands.

When he whispered, "Oh, Little Witch, I'm so sorry," I didn't know whether to weep or vomit.

"What do we do, Cass?"

"No artifact and no Green Witch. Our chances of success just went from about twenty-five percent to about zero."

There was a yowl somewhere farther up in the tower, and Cass asked, "What's that cat doing?"

"Hades?" I called, and he beckoned again.

I shot to my feet, taking the spiral staircase up to the top of the stone tower. Hades was waiting, sitting in front of one of two doors. I glanced in the other entryway as I passed it and saw a bed dressed with black silk sheets. Cass's room.

"You want to go in here?"

He put his paws up on the closed door in front of him, staring up at me.

The hinges were silent as I opened it, and my brows lifted. An office of some kind, with maps covering the walls. They were written on and dotted with little colored tacks and notes. Papers rested in neat stacks on an old oak desk. Behind it, sat a classic executive chair adorned with midnight black leather.

Hades trotted across the royal blue carpet and leaped onto the desk, looking at me.

"I've gone through it all," Cass wheezed behind me, holding the wall for support with one hand, and still containing his guts with the other. "So has Gideon. We've flushed out every lead."

"What is all this?"

"The documents found at Xeron's castle. We've been trying to track down where the ceremony will take place." He sighed. "I've looked at these papers a million times."

Hades laid down on the desk, his tail twitching back and forth like the pendulum of a clock, counting every second we were losing.

"Okay," I said to the cat. "We'll look again."

ENID

The smell of the wet rock, and a deep ache in my shoulders. I tried to move my hands and couldn't. It all flooded back in a rush, my heart thundering to life.

'Stay calm,' a voice said in my head. It was melodic and beautiful, yet commanding, reminding me of a heavy wind chime. *'I am your wolf, anointed hand to the Moon Goddess herself. I am called Skadi.'*

'Skadi,' I repeated. *'We're captured.'*

'Yes.'

'I've ruined everything with my stupidity! I-I should've known that wasn't Christine! They've got the artifact! Gideon and others, they don't even know where the ceremony is taking place!'

'Let us just focus on surviving for now,' she said tenderly.

My chin was resting on my chest, and I cracked my eyes open. I still wore my gown from the Samhain ball, but it was ripped and streaked with dried mud. My feet were clasped in iron cuffs and chained to the cold wall that I was suspended from. Not just cold, but wet. The dampness seeped from the rock into my gown and into my bones. I winced and turned my head, looking up to confirm my hands were also clamped in iron. They were fisted inside the cuffs, and my nails dug into my palms, making me bleed when I tried to move my fingers. With my hands and feet captured in iron, I could use no magic.

'*You're also drugged with wolfsbane to stop you from shifting. If I were a normal wolf, it would stop us from communicating. Be wary, because we aren't alone,*' Skadi said, and I studied the room. My eyes were drawn first to the glaring pile of treasure glittering in the corner. Golden coins and gems and chalices.

'*Dragons,*' I said, knowing that they liked to hoard gold and other pretty things. More than liked. It was a need for them. Even Cass succumbed to it in more ways than one, including his extreme promiscuity. A collector of beautiful women.

On one wall there was an ancient map, yellowed and curling at the corners. Notes and pins littered the old paper, with the focus leading toward Australia.

Below it, making my heart skip a beat, sat the three artifacts. An old chalice, the bell, and the athame. Together they hummed with magic, vibrating the room with their power. It was here that I found the only other person in the room with me. Morga was reading from a leather-bound grimoire, but the way she slumped in the chair suggested she might be sleeping.

The low light in the room came from the opposite wall. A terrarium of some kind, filled with snakes. All kinds of them. Pythons and vipers. Why they didn't attack each other, I couldn't understand. Something seemed wrong about them. The eyes. They didn't seem snake-like at all, and the intelligence they held made the hair on my neck tingle.

Next to the tank, mounted on the wall, were various instruments of torture. Some of them dated back to medieval times, and I recognized the pear of anguish and the heretic's fork. There were also saws, blades, and whips. My mouth was dry, and I wondered if I would be unfortunate enough to face any of them.

'*What do we do?*' I asked Skadi, looking up at my iron-bound hands.

'*We wait for opportunity to present itself. They have to take you off this wall, eventually.*'

There were three doors, and I jumped when one banged open, accompanied by the loud echo of a deep voice. Morga snorted awake and shot to her feet, bowing despite her already hunched back.

The voice belonged to the most beautiful man I'd ever seen. He was flawless, with honey-brown hair that trailed down to his mid-back, a well-defined jaw, and high cheekbones that arched over his Gracian nose and soft, full lips. He looked like a marble sculpture, and his eyes held as much life as one. They were yellow and flat, giving away the predator that hid behind his angelic features.

He smiled and held out his arms. "Oh, my sweet girl. You never disappoint me, darling."

I blinked when I understood he addressed Morga, who grinned, a froggy giggle bubbling from her chapped lips. "All glory to you, Master Nox."

"So, we are ready?" he asked, crossing the room to take her gnarled hand and bring it to his lips. "It's all in place?"

"The ceremony can commence at the next full moon."

"Isn't she invaluable?" he asked, turning to the companions that trailed into the room after him.

"A most dutiful servant," an angelic voice cooed, inflected with an almost unnoticeable Scottish dialect. It was a woman, whose eyes were on me and not Morga. She, like the dragon called Nox, was an ethereal beauty with dead eyes. Her long burgundy hair hung in waves, and she wore a dress of emerald velvet. Her red-stained lips parted in a smile, revealing shining white teeth. The third man who accompanied them slid a chair out from the heavy table for her, and she took the seat.

He, another dragon, wore clothing I associated with western Africa. A billowing robe over a shirt and loose trousers. The material looked light and breathable, colored in a beautiful jade green and adorned with gold stitching. His dark curly hair was cut close to his head. He, too, was flawlessly attractive, with mahogany skin and strong features that melded perfectly.

"Is this really her? The Green Witch?" the woman asked, still studying me. "She's just a wee babe!"

"That child killed your idiot brother, Edana," the third man said, taking his seat and laughing a deep belly rumble. Like his clothing, his dialect hailed from Africa.

She glared at him and hissed, her round pupils shifting to slits.

"Now, now, Tirich, you know she's sensitive about her idiot brother," Nox said, snickering with him.

Morga shifted on her feet, holding the back of her chair for support. "This child is more dangerous than she appears, my lords and lady. Don't underestimate her."

Nox tilted his head, scrutinizing me as he approached. I stared at him from my spot on the wall, trying to keep my breath steady and my knees from trembling.

Skadi said, *'Do not react to anything he does. That's what he wants.'*

"Now, what do we do with you?" he asked. With how I was suspended, we were level in height, and he got uncomfortably close, his nose inches from mine.

His yellow eyes bore into me, searching. For what, I didn't know, but I held the dead stare, refusing to look away.

He suddenly laughed, and I flinched, blinking. Nox glanced over his shoulder, still chuckling low in his chest. "Not your average wolf, that is certain."

The others watched, their eyes sparkling with curiosity. And humor, I realized.

Tirich said, "I think we should feed her to the beast when it wakes. It will be hungry, and she will make a delicious offering."

Nox lifted his finger, pointing it at Tirich. "That is a great idea, my friend." He turned back to me, stepping closer, and nestled his nose into my cleavage, drawing a deep inhale. I gasped when he crouched, grabbing my hips and shoving his face into my crotch.

Skadi hissed, *'Stay calm. He's searching for a reaction.'*

'He's going to hurt me.'

'Yes, probably.'

"You smell like a freshly deflowered virgin!" Nox grinned up at me, and the others erupted with laughter. "Weren't you a naughty wolf for Samhain!"

My cheeks exploded with heat, and I stared at his forehead, trying to be anywhere else in my mind but here.

He clicked his tongue, his tone condescendingly cheerful. "Is he your mate, then? What's he like? No, let me guess! Just perfect for you in every way?"

Edana shifted in her seat, crossing her ankles. "What a bore! To have only one man for your entire life."

Nox nodded, but arched his brow, pushing my hair off my shoulder. "Seems not. Look at that. No mark." I tensed when he touched the spot with his thumb, pressing into the bed of nerves there. "Do you think your lover would be upset if I marked you myself?"

My heart quickened and tears sprang to my eyes as he leaned forward. I saw the glint of his fangs elongating.

"No! Please!" I begged through my grimace, trying to pull away, and I screamed when I felt the pierce of my skin. Pain erupted, searing down to my toes. "No! No!"

Nothing happened. No melding of our souls. He was laughing into my neck, and kissed my cheek.

The sharp pain was still there, and Skadi said, *'Be calm. He's stuck you with his claw, not his teeth.'*

Nox leaned back, watching my face as he dug the claw deeper. The pain was like nothing I'd ever known, every nerve in my body reacting as if it were set aflame. I couldn't close my mouth, but I couldn't draw a breath to form a scream or a word.

Finally, after what felt like hours, but could only be seconds, he withdrew. My body trembled, and a single tear ran down my cheek.

Stepping back, he turned to his companions and strode toward the table. "They are so sensitive about that." He chuckled, adding, "Isn't that right, pet?"

My brow knit. He wasn't talking to me, Morga, or the other dragons. There was movement below the massive oak table, a bare foot slipping back under into the shadows, followed by a whimper. I hadn't even seen her there, her wide gray eyes staring out from the darkness.

Sophia was nude, clinging to the leg of the table. She was caked in blood down her front, and it still seeped slowly from her own marking spot. My stomach rolled. There were other injuries too. Burns on her arms and legs, probably from silver, and I recoiled when I saw one of her fingers was only a bloody stump.

Nox sat in his chair, and I jumped when, for no apparent reason, he lifted his boot and kicked her hard in the face. Sophia crumpled, sobbing quietly and rolling herself into a ball.

'Goddess help us.'

Skadi shifted in my head. *'Indeed.'*

CHAPTER TWENTY-SIX

LEO

C ASS USED THE FRESHLY brewed pot of coffee to refill my cup, and I yawned, rubbing one of my eyes with my fingertips.

I blew on the mug and took a sip. "Thanks."

"You're welcome."

We'd been up for two days with only a couple hours of sleep. He sat down on the chaise lounge and draped his head back over the armrest, dumping the rest of the pot of boiling hot coffee down his throat with one slow turn of his wrist.

I watched the steam roll out of his mouth, and said, "Wow."

"Ah," he sighed, smacking his lips. "That's better. So, where are we?"

I looked around at the stacks of papers and file folders and shook my head. "There's too much. We'll never get through it. I don't know what to do!" I groaned, leaning my head back against the chair. "Gods. Can we turn that off?"

Cass looked at the television. For two days, we'd sat here while nature documentaries droned in the background. "No. It helps me think."

"Can we watch something else?"

"No."

"Well, it's annoying!" I snapped.

"I don't care. It's my TV. *Mine*. And we'll watch what I want."

I sat back reflexively at the growl around the word *mine*, and Bleiz said, *'Maybe we don't poke the dragon when he's lacking sleep.'*

Hades rubbed his cheek on one stack of folders behind me, and it fell in a cascade of papers.

Cass huffed, "Now your cat is making a mess of my office."

I rolled my eyes. "Well, have you heard of a filing cabinet?"

"I don't need one because I'm not a slobbish wolf."

Hades hopped down, ignoring our squabble, and started batting a piece of paper around on the floor, stalking it and pouncing on it like prey.

I narrowed my eyes and stood. "What is it, Hades?"

The paper was small and old. Tall, slanting cursive written on some kind of parchment.

"It's nonsensical poetry," Cass said.

I read it aloud,

"Under the soft blue skies
Lurks a horror that multiplies
Under the soft red rock
Resides a stony lock
Under the soft blue skies."

The hairs on my neck prickled, and I read it one more time.

"It's a clue," I whispered, glancing over the parchment at Hades.

He seemed vexed, his eyes slitted as he angrily chewed his claw. Annoyed, probably, that he had to do all the work.

Cass looked at Hades, then at me. "A clue to what?"

"Where they are? Where the ceremony is?"

"Okay. Then where? Somewhere with blue skies and red rocks?"

"I guess."

"Groundbreaking," he said dryly. "That narrows it down to thousands of places. I'm going to make more coffee."

I sat down at the desk, holding the paper. "Utah? Arizona?"

I read it again.

And again.

And again.

ENID

I craned my neck, trying to turn my head hard enough to reach the wet wall behind me. My mouth was like sandpaper. They'd given me no food or water since I'd arrived here, and telling time was impossible in this windowless stone room. I thought often of that last Samhain feast and how I'd taken it for granted.

The wall was cool on my cheek, and I licked at the stone. It was damp, but it did little to quench my thirst. When the pain in my neck became too much, I relaxed. My shoulders hurt every moment, threatening to pull from their sockets under my constant weight. If Skadi wasn't awake and slowly healing me, I imagined they already would have.

The dragons were eating. A grand-looking meal of lake trout and roast vegetables. All the fixings. Bread and butter. Rice pudding. Wine and honey mead. My mouth watered, and I licked my dry lips.

"She's so thirsty!" Edana cooed from the table, rising from her seat. "Poor girl."

I winced, feeling sorry I'd brought attention to myself. She strutted over with her wine goblet in hand. "Go ahead, open up."

I stared at her, knowing there was no way she was about to give me a drink of that wine.

"I said open," she said, a frown pulling down her ruby lips. "Aren't you thirsty?"

"No, thank you."

The men snickered behind her, and her cheeks flooded with dark red anger. They liked to pick at her, and it was easy to tell she was at the bottom of the pecking order. I was thankful when she was the tormentor. Tirich only liked to watch, it seemed. He never approached, but Nox iced my blood when his attention turned my way. He was scary, his abuse always holding a sexual undertone. Groping me and torturing my marking spot.

A selfish part of me was relieved Sophia was here to share the burden of his predilections. She mostly lived under the table, but sometimes he took her through one of those doors, and I'd listen to her screams for what felt like hours. I suspected I didn't get the same because they were at least a little frightened of me. They acted like they weren't, but they had taken no chance of removing me from this wall.

Edana slapped me. "Open!"

I sighed, tasting a twang of iron, and parted my lips slightly to satisfy her. She dumped the full goblet over my head, and I did my best not to react. I left my mouth open, and some of it ran past my chapped lips, mixing with the blood on my tongue. The small taste was worth it, although it did little to quench my thirst.

"There you go," she said sweetly, patting my cheek.

I dropped my chin to my chest and stayed quiet, hoping to avoid any more of their torment. Edana returned to the table.

'It will be the full moon soon enough,' Skadi said. *'They will have to move us, and that is when we will have the best chance of escape from these shackles.'*

I must've dozed off because the scraping of chairs startled me. They retired, thankfully without looking my way again. The room grew quiet, lit by the glow of the terrarium.

Movement under the table caught my eye, and I watched Sophia claw up the side of the table and snatch Tirich's used plate. She shoveled the half-eaten food into her mouth, hunched over it on the floor like a wild animal, her eyes feral while she watched the door.

"Sophia!" I whispered. This was the first time she and I had been alone together, and she froze, her eyes darting to me. I motioned toward the desk where Morga often sat. "The keys! They're right there!"

The big iron key teased me, resting only a few feet away and promising me freedom from these cuffs.

Sophia was shaking her head, thrashing it back and forth with the force of her fear. She crawled back under the table and clung to the leg, her body trembling.

"Come on, come on!" I snapped, knowing vampires would be in at any time to clear the table. "Sophia!"

Tears streaked the dried blood on her face, and she sobbed, looking back at the door.

I softened my tone. "I can get us out of here. Please. Please, Sophia. You just have to get one of these cuffs off and we can escape. Be brave. You're a wolf, aren't you?"

She rocked back and forth on her heels, another sob wracking her body. I opened my mouth to beseech her again, but she darted from under the table, running across the room.

"Yes! Yes!" I cheered, my heart racing with her.

She was weeping, and snatched the keys, running up the three wide steps to where I hung. Her hands were shaking so badly she dropped the keys, and despite it all, my heart cracked for her.

"It's okay, Sophia. Almost there. You can do it."

She scooped them up and brought them to my right hand. Her poor fingers were so damaged; broken and burned. Her wolf wasn't healing her quickly. Probably drugged with wolfsbane as well.

Sophia groaned low in her chest, trying to make them work and get the key in the lock.

"That's it!" I said when she nearly had it.

The door banged open, and my eyes collided with Sophia's. The fear swimming in hers sent a shiver down my spine.

"Turn the key! Unlock it! Unlock it! Hurry!" I pleaded, but Sophia was frozen.

Morga shuffled in, leering at us. "I knew someone was touching my keys!"

'They're enchanted,' Skadi said.

'How could I have been so foolish?'

'With the artifacts there, it's impossible to sense any other magical energies.'

"I'll handle this," Nox said, pushing past Morga at the door. He was in his nightclothes, tying his robe as he crossed the room.

When she heard him, Sophia wailed like a trapped animal and dropped the keys. She threw her arms around my neck, sobbing into my shoulder.

"It was me! It was me!" I yelled, probably ten times before he got to us. "I made her do it!"

He grabbed her hair, dragging her away from me, and she clung so tightly to my neck that the nails she had left scratched my skin. I fought the restraints, trying to hold on to her.

My dehydrated body somehow found the moisture to create tears, and they flowed down my cheeks. "No! Don't hurt her! It was my fault!"

"I'm sorry. Please. I'm sorry," Sophia said, over and over, her voice already hoarse from all the screaming she'd done.

He laughed harshly, leaning into her face. "I'm stunned. Here I thought I'd broken you." It was said like a jest, but I could feel his rage simmering at her defiance.

Tirich and Edana floated in wearing their night attire, and took their regular seats at the table, smiling pleasantly like it was an after-dinner special. Nox slammed Sophia down so she was lying prone with her upper body on the table, and she stayed there, her back shaking with sobs.

He went to the wall of torture, staring up at the many options like he was deciding at a restaurant.

Edana threw out a suggestion. "Use the bullwhip."

Nox shook his head and grabbed a nasty-looking flail. Edana's brows lifted, and she glanced at Tirich, who tilted his head, their expressions suggesting they didn't expect something so extreme, but they enjoyed the choice.

Nox walked to me, and my knees trembled. I steeled my bottom lip, glad he was leaving Sophia be.

"Do you know what this is?" he asked, holding it up for me to see.

I sniffled, trying to compose myself. "A flail."

"Yes. It's called the cat-o'-nine-tails because it's got nine knotted thongs of cord. Painful already in its original form, but we've modified it for you silver-sensitive folk."

I looked closer. There was silver wire rolled into each cord. He hauled back, whipping it across my bare arm. Pain exploded from the spot, and I yelped, my eyes filling again and my chest heaving. My body reeled, trying to understand what had just happened. I glanced over and saw my flesh was split in several places, the wounds angry and bleeding.

"I just want you to know how it feels," he said, and turned on his heel.

I fought the restraints. "Don't! Please don't. Isn't there anything good in your cold heart?"

Over his shoulder, Nox continued, ignoring my pleas, "Fifteen lashes. You'll count them, Green Witch."

He brought the flail over his head and snapped it across Sophia's back. She wailed, her knuckles white where she held the table. He looked at me, cupping his hand around his ear.

"I won't!" I shouted, a sob bubbling in my throat.

His eyes flashed. "Then we start over, and it's twenty!" He snapped the whip again, this time across her bare behind. She shrieked, and he looked at me, his brows lifting.

"O-one," I said, unable to stop my tears.

"Was that so hard?" he asked and raised the flail again.

When it was over, I'd counted twenty strikes, and Sophia was either dead or unconscious. Her back was a mess, blood rolling down her legs and pooling on the floor. The scent of iron filled the large room, and I could see where white bone stuck out in places along her spine. I was sobbing and sick. Bile churned in my gut, and I would've vomited if I'd had anything to eat. Nox approached, and I steadied my jaw, waiting for my turn.

"I'm not going to hit you again," he said, reading my thoughts. "I know your type. Watching that happen to her was more punishment than this flail could ever deliver upon you."

"I'm going to kill you," I said flatly.

"Really?" He tilted his head like he was trying to understand, then pointed at Sophia. "That woman betrayed you. She infiltrated your pack and stole the artifact, dooming the world as you know it, and she did it for paltry revenge over a broken engagement. Yet here you are, so upset about this misfortune that she's brought upon herself. Why?"

"I do not wish to see her hurt simply because she has hurt me."

Nox tilted his head, and I could tell it wasn't an act. He was truly trying to understand. "Interesting." I thought that would be it, but he said, "I'll make you a deal."

I stared at him, trying to discern his angle.

"Your freedom for her life," he said.

Edana, Tirich, and I all said, "What?" at the same time.

"Tell me you want me to kill her, and I will. Then I'll unshackle you, and you can go free."

Edana stood, hands flat on the table. "Nox?"

He held up his hand to silence her, watching me. "I give you my word, Green Witch. If you ask me to break her neck right now, I will release you."

I believed he would. My eyes flicked to Sophia's bleeding form hunched over the table.

Skadi said, *'It might be a mercy at this point.'*

I shook my head. "I decline."

"Are you sure? Last chance. She's half dead, anyway!"

"No."

"No," he repeated. "If the roles were reversed, she'd beg me to flay the skin from your bones if it meant her freedom. Mere days ago, she held unrelenting contempt for you and everyone you love. How can you choose her over freedom?"

I sighed. "I feel bad for her."

His eyebrows nearly touched his hairline. "Really? Bad for her?"

"She's a selfish fool, but I don't believe she's evil." My brow knit. "There must be something good in her."

Nox shook his head. "I think you're a lost cause, Green Witch. I am thankful the gods incarnated you as such a stupid, emotional creature."

My cheeks burned, but I glared at him. "It is not wrong to feel empathy for those who would harm me."

He laughed, and the others did, too. "Don't you feel empathy for me? You threatened my life mere seconds ago."

"Empathy is not limitless. It's impossible to empathize with evil. You are evil. All of you." I looked at the table where the others sat.

Nox nodded. "That's the only intelligent thing you've said this entire conversation." He turned on his heel, snickering under his breath.

I swallowed. "But you do have my sympathy. I cannot imagine what it must be like to be alive but unable to live."

He stopped, his shoulders tensing.

I stared at the back of his head. "You will never find joy without harming another. You cannot feel love. Or make a true friend. You'll never know sadness. Or heartbreak. The world is dull and listless for you, and I am so sorry. What is immortality if there's no one to share it with? I know you must suffer, wondering what it's like to care and have someone care for you."

Nox pivoted, coming back up the stairs and snarling in my face, "You know nothing!"

I held his glare without flinching and whispered, "Do not worry. I was sent to bring you the ultimate peace. The gods chose me to end your pain."

He drew back, his eyes narrowing. Confusion tinged with fear danced across his face.

From the edge of my vision, I saw the veins on my arms had turned a deep violet, and I knew my eyes were bright. "I promise, Nox. I will end your lonely time on this earth. You will be free."

He snorted and stalked from the room, Tirich and Edana at his heels, whispering to each other. I stared at Sophia until I was able to see the rise and fall of her back. She was breathing, and finally, gingerly, she slid off the table and crawled underneath it, lying flat on her stomach on the cold stone floor.

I opened my mouth but closed it without saying anything. An apology felt absurd. My thoughts trailed to poor Cass, who'd spent over two hundred years in a dungeon with these dragons.

CHAPTER
TWENTY-SEVEN

Leo

"**L**ITTLE LION!"

I jolted awake, snorting. Bright light filtered in through the windows, and my stomach sank. It was day three.

"Cass! Why did you let me fall asleep?" The parchment poem was stuck to my sweaty forehead, and I snatched it.

"Shut up! Look. Look at this!"

He was rewinding his documentary and pressed play. The narrator recited his script. "The black-footed rock wallaby is one of several nocturnal mammals that live in the shadow of Uluru. Classified as endangered, the small mammal feeds on nearby grasslands at night and shelters in the sandstone caves during the day to conserve water."

I stood, crossing the room to take the remote. "Cass! Are you kidding? I don't care! I don't care about some freakin' wallaby!" My eyes filled, and my voice was thick when I yelled, "Enid is going to die, you psycho!"

Cass held the remote out of my reach and clicked rewind. The show went back ten seconds. "That lives in the shadow of Uluru. Classified as endangered, the small mammal—"

He clicked rewind again, and stared at me, his sapphire eyes twinkling as the narrator said, "In the shadow of Uluru."

"Uluru?" The word itched my brain as my eyes dropped to the paper in my hand.

Cass reached over and covered every word with his fingers except the first letter of each verse.

U

L

U

R

U

"Uluru," I said again.

He repeated, "Uluru."

"Uluru!" I shouted.

"Uluru!" he shouted back.

I grabbed his arms, and we started jumping together. "Uluru! Uluru!"

"Cass! You're a genius!"

"Yes! Yes, I know I am! I am the greatest!"

I stopped, my eyes widening. "Oh, shit! How far ahead is Australia? It must already be night there! We're out of time! We need to tell Gideon!"

"Then we better hurry!" he said, laughing and snatching Hades as he ran toward the open balcony, dragging me with him and starting his shift.

"No! No! Cass! I'll just link him!"

He threw me, tossing me like a rag doll over the balcony rail with a grunt. My stomach dropped and then crawled into my throat, blocking the scream that ripped up from my toes.

The ground was fast approaching, and I flailed, trying to grab hold of air. When I concluded death was imminent, the black dragon swooped beneath me, scooping me onto his neck. His wings created a cloud of dust when he flapped to stop our fall, and we climbed rapidly, his belly kissing the top of the pine trees. Hades rode gracefully between the spiky horns on Crux's head, balancing like he was riding a skateboard.

"I hate you!" I yelled and then patted the dragon's neck. We knew where to go. He'd actually figured it out. "And I love you!"

Crux snorted, chuckling low in his barrel chest.

Bleiz said, *'Have faith. The moon goddess is with us. The odds of that particular show being on at that time and Cass catching it are astronomical.'*

'I hope you're right.'

"We're coming, Enid," I said as the pack house came into view, and added, "Woah," when I was able to see the surrounding grounds over the trees.

The fae army was here, their royal purple tents lined up in neat rows with their mermaid banner flying from the tops. Silver armor glinted like lost coins in the morning sun, and I watched many of them stop to shout and point as Cass and I flew over.

Their army bled into ours. Shifters I recognized scurried to get things done for my brother. Beyond them, fading deep into the forest, I could see the camps of each pack, their family crests flapping proudly in the breeze.

At the front of the house, women in black robes mulled around, some sitting at tables drinking tea and talking with their heads together. There was a flash of flame and then a burst of steam. A water witch and a fire witch were sparring off to the side.

I gasped, rubbing my eyes to make sure I was really awake. Flitting amongst the witches were sprites. A child-sized cousin of the fae with wings like dragonflies. I'd never seen one outside of a book.

'Where are you?' I asked Gideon.

'Conference room.'

"Conference room!" I shouted to Crux over the wind, and he tilted his body, gliding down to the respective balcony.

I leaped before he landed, my momentum carrying me in a burst through the doors. All eyes turned, scrutinizing me. Finn and the other Alphas took up most of the seats, but the fae king was also there, sitting next to a heavily wrinkled witch with silver hair. On her other side was a man I recognized. Daro's grandfather, Zekaiel. Their expressions were flat, revealing nothing.

My eldest brother, however, looked less than impressed, his eyes framed by large black bags, and a shadow of unshaven beard on his face. "This better be good, Leo."

"It is. Cass figured it out!" I held up the parchment poem. "I know where to go!"

Gideon's eyes lit up, and a slow smile curled his lips.

ENID

Movement in the room pulled me from a dream where I imagined I was being stretched on the rack, my arms and legs being ripped off. Morga and her daughters were busy, the air buzzing with anticipation as they gathered the artifacts and other various things.

I tried to roll my shoulders and winced. "It's time?"

"Nearly," Morga croaked. "Why? Excited?"

"Honestly, I'd rather be eaten than hang here for another minute."

She chuckled. "We'll get you cleaned up soon." Turning, she regarded me with her milky eyes. "You reek. Not a suitable sacrifice."

"I sure wouldn't want to eat her," Sara agreed, giggling.

I wrinkled my nose. "That's rich coming from you, old woman. You smell like basement dust and cobwebs."

"And still better than you, nasty dog."

I started to sass back, but Una spun, blowing more of that black powder from her hand into my open mouth.

It tasted like vinegar that was far too acidic, and I coughed, trying to spit. A numbness spread through my body, and I fought to keep my eyes from drifting closed.

'So much for plan A,' Skadi said dryly as the world went dark.

CHAPTER
TWENTY-EIGHT

LEO

E VERYONE GATHERED AT THE back of the pack house, sweating in the unusually hot November sun and waiting for further instructions. We were down to the wire on time, with the full moon at midnight less than an hour away in Australia. I stood by Cass, shifting on my feet and petting Hades, who rested on my shoulders.

Gideon approached in his leather battle armor. It was special, made for wolves who fought in both human and shifted form. I wore the same. The breast and back plates would move with the shift to protect the wolf's shoulders, and the leather pteruges served a similar purpose, covering the broad parts of the wolf's hind legs.

Gideon was flanked by River and Rhia, who had just returned from Uluru. They carried battle staves designed to help concentrate and channel their magic. We were waiting for their confirmation that the old poem was pointing us in the right direction.

"You are correct, dragon," River said to Cass, stopping in front of us. "Uluru is the location we have been searching for."

Cass scoffed. "Of course, I am."

Gideon looked at his watch. "We are forty-five minutes from midnight."

"Hello, River!"

A smiling woman approached. A witch, I realized, and felt my brows lift. She was unlike any of the others, dressed head to toe in pink. A bubblegum-hued dress made mostly of tulle, sparkling shoes, and pink and white striped socks. Her hair was a mess of pink curls, and she wore a silver circlet that sparkled in the sun. All of that pink contrasted strikingly against her sepia skin, and even her eyes were altered by magic, her irises a dark fuchsia color. In her hand, she held a diamond-encrusted wand, and on her waist, she wore a leather waterskin, making sure she never ran dry of her element.

River nodded a clipped greeting. "Nadaria. Is everyone in place?"

"Yes, we've positioned ourselves around the group. We just need them to squeeze together a bit." She held up her fingers an inch apart. "High Priestess Xena says we need to be a little closer to cast a stable circle."

"Are you ready, Alpha?" River asked with a nod to Nadaria.

"Get closer!" Gideon yelled. "The witches need us closer together to cast the circle!"

Everyone looked at each other. We were allies, sure, but we weren't really friends.

"Come on, people!" Nadaria sang above the crowd noise. "Act like you like each other!"

The sentiment was echoed by the leaders of each faction, and I looked around. Fae, sprites, unicorns, harpies, wolf shifters, and one dragon all squeezed together, standing like sardines. Over a hundred witches in their black robes formed a circle around us, and I took a deep breath, ready to go.

My brother turned to look at the balcony of his office and lifted his hand. Henry and Ceres waved back, my mother's hands resting on their shoulders.

He cleared his throat and shouted, "The witches will move us now! If you haven't been transported by a witch before, be prepared. It can be unsettling."

Everyone went quiet, a tense anticipation thickening the air.

High Priestess Xena, the silver-haired woman I'd seen in Gideon's office, stood at the center of the circle. She lifted her hands like a conductor, and her voice boomed over the crowd. "Are we ready, sisters?"

The witches started humming in response, all at the same frequency. It reverberated right through my skin to my bones. The surrounding air sparked to life with magical intention, and the trees of the nearby forest quivered. Hades purred softly on my shoulders, matching their tone.

Xena's lyrical voice rose above the noise. "Guardians of the North! We call you beings of Earth, to bless our circle with grounding!"

The witches at the northernmost part of the circle, where River stood, chanted back, "Hail and welcome, Earth Guardians!" and then continued humming.

Xena turned. "Guardians of the East! Come to us, spirits of Air, and bestow our circle with intellect!"

Rhia and the other air witches answered, "Hail and welcome, Air Guardians!"

"Guardians of the south, we summon you, beings of Fire! Bolster our circle with strength!"

"Hail and welcome, Fire Guardians!"

"Guardians of the west, we call on you, spirits of Water! Gift our circle with intuition!"

"Hail and welcome, Water Guardians!"

With the last word of that chant, there was an explosion of magic among the witches, a bright white light erupting between each one and connecting them.

The humming became deafening, and the magic grew so thick in the air that I heard people sneezing to exorcise its irritating presence from their nostrils.

Xena spoke once more.

"Remove the chains of time and space,
And let our spirits soar.
Travel now to our place of choice,
For we've called the elements, four!"

I was blinded by the bright white flash, and I felt I was being pulled at my belly button by a string. The sensation worsened, like I was being torn apart, but by then it was already over. I gasped for air and opened my eyes, blinking away stars from my vision.

Someone next to me doubled over, vomiting, and a collective murmur broke out over the crowd.

The pack house was gone, sitting in our pine forest on the other side of the world. Our army was huddled together in a red desert, with the great rock Uluru towering a couple hundred yards away.

Three dragons flew near it. They were up to something.

I looked at Cass. "What are they doing?"

He was watching, his jaw set, and his brow furrowed.

ENID

The air had changed. Gone was the damp humidity of that rock cave, now replaced with a dry heat. My body wobbled as if I was being pulled in a wagon, and I fought the dark sheet of the drug that held me under.

"You said you know where it is," Nox hissed. "You'd better find it."

I could hear the shuffle of Morga dragging her old feet. "I do, Master. It's here somewhere, but the book says the keyhole will only appear in the illumination of the full moon."

"Well, a lot of good that is. It's overcast!"

"Yes, could be a problem. Might have to wait until the next full moon if we miss it."

His voice was lower. Darker. "You won't survive until the next full moon if we miss this opportunity."

"Yes, Master," she said, and I heard the pages of her old grimoire turning.

We stopped moving, and my eyes cracked open. I could smell untouched, beautiful earth. Beside us, a red sandstone cliff face stood at an incredible height, at least a thousand feet high. I was chained to a dolly of some kind, my hands and feet still locked with iron. My skin felt dry, like I'd been scrubbed too hard with cheap soap. I looked down. My dress was gone, replaced by a white, gauzy smock.

"It should be right here," Morga said, her gnarled hand brushing over the rock, searching. "On the eastern side just below the serpent-shaped cave formation. Look for the keyhole, girls! We must find it." Her daughters started inspecting the rock, and after several long minutes Morga glanced over her shoulder, glaring at the sky. "Blasted moon. Terrible night to be bashful."

Skadi chuckled, and I smirked. Nox asked next to me, "Is there something funny, dog?"

"It appears my goddess disagrees with your plans."

"Well," he said, walking away. "Maybe she can be reasoned with." His voice distorted, and he started his shift, becoming a massive dragon covered in amethyst-colored scales. He called out, and I watched Tirich, the jade dragon, and Edana, the ruby, join him in the sky. I was struck, just as I had been at Diamond Moon, by their intense beauty. Their scales sparkled even in the dark night.

After they'd gained significant altitude, they moved in sync, working together and filling their powerful lungs with deep inhales.

"Keen eyes, girls. Watch for it," Morga croaked, staring at the wall.

The dragons blew all at once, and a tiny spot opened in the cloud cover, allowing a single beam of moonlight to shine through. My eyes snapped back to the wall, and Una called out, "There!"

Where there had been nothing, there was suddenly a keyhole, sparkling with magic as it appeared. Morga lunged forward, shoving a rusty key into the hole before it disappeared again. The rock shifted when she turned it, moving with an earthly groan. The ground shook as the massive slabs of sandstone parted, making the metal of my iron chains chatter. Sandy dust rained down around us until I was forced to squeeze my eyes shut.

'That's a big door,' I told Skadi when I opened them again.

The opening and the corridor beyond it were broad enough for all three dragons to stroll side by side without any difficulty.

I felt air swish next to me, and Nox said, "Hurry! They're here."

"Who, Master?" Morga asked.

He glared at me. "Her friends."

"How many?"

"More than I expected. We can't let them interfere." Addressing Una and Cora, he said, "Go. We need our armies. One of you, retrieve the vampires, and one of you, speak to the dark elf empress."

"Empress Raysan has not committed to our cause," Morga said, her bushy white eyebrows knitting.

"Not yet. Tell her the fae are here, including the king. Dark elves won't pass up an opportunity to kill their bastard cousins."

"Yes, Master," the sisters said, and disappeared.

'They figured it out,' I said to Skadi, my eyes burning with tears. *'They've come!'*

'Praise be to the goddess. We have a chance.'

Chapter Twenty-Nine

Leo

THE RUMBLING OF THE earth stopped. Something big had happened on the other side of Uluru.

Cass looked at Gideon. "I believe they've opened the door."

Finn said, "Uh-oh," when both the green and red dragons turned in the air, screeching and flying in our direction.

"Cass, Finn, Leo," Gideon said, "go stop that ceremony! We'll handle these two!"

Finn looked at the rock, then back at Gideon. "Stop the ceremony? By *ourselves*?"

"Look!" I pointed. Hades was already half the distance to the rock, running at a full sprint. "Enid is there! We've gotta hurry!"

"I'm coming too," Eris said.

Finn took half the arrows from his quiver, those tipped with Dragonsbane, and handed them to Kat. She, too, had a bow, and had become the best markswoman in the pack. With two supernatural souls lending her their talents, her hand-eye speed and coordination were unparalleled.

"Good luck," Kat said, kissing his cheek.

Finn wanted to linger, to stay with her, but Cass was already shifting. Eris and I climbed onto Crux's neck, and I held my hand out to help Finn up.

My brows lifted when I saw he'd taken on a green inflection to his skin.

"Have you flown yet?" I asked as Crux spread his wings.

"Not on a fucking dragon." His nails elongated and dug into the spike he held.

Crux started into a run, and the ride became rough as he bounded into a sprint, then leaped into the air, flapping to gain altitude.

"What about them?" Finn shouted. The red and green dragons targeted us, screeching.

Crux dove straight down to avoid them, and I closed my eyes, my stomach in my chest. Finn bellowed, "Ohhh, shit!"

Wild screeching snapped my eyes open, and I watched Wren and her flock swarm like a murder of crows, attacking the dragons' soft wings. The rubbery flesh shredded like cheese under the powerful claws of the harpies. I winced when one got too close to the red dragon's waiting jaw and was crunched in two.

The distraction was enough, and we rounded the eastern side of Uluru unhindered, coasting down in a spray of red sand to an enormous door.

River, Rhia, and Hades waited.

"Let's go!" I shouted, but River grabbed my shoulder.

"Don't!" I looked at her, and she shook her head. "It's warded by a powerful fire witch."

Rhia picked up a small rock with a gust of air and thrust it down the long corridor. Explosions erupted, fireballs appearing from nowhere and intersecting the rock, blowing it to smithereens in a matter of seconds.

Finn said, "You first, Cass," and Crux grunted, narrowing his blue eyes at him.

I tried the link. *'Enid? Are you okay?'* But she didn't answer.

River reached into her robe and removed a glass ball. It looked like a clear Yule ornament. Some kind of purple moss was nested inside, and it was sealed with black wax, a pentagram charm set into it.

She said,

"Any spell of here be gone!
Take your disaster back to your caster.

I bid thee to flee and return the malice in a fold of three!"

My brows lifted. "That's the same thing Sophia said in the athame chamber."

"Yes," River said, as if she wasn't surprised. "Our mother taught us."

"Your mother..."

"Morga is my twin sister. Now, hush."

I clamped my mouth shut, and she said the spell again, closing her eyes. The moss inside the glass started to glow, and I felt Finn take two steps back.

River tossed the ball into the hallway, and the flames erupted again. I flinched away, holding my arm up to shield my eyes from the bright eruption. The flames didn't incinerate the ball. They were absorbed into it. The orb landed with a heavy thud in the sand and spun like a top, the moss inside glowing with purple flame. It whined, shrieking like a boiling teapot, and I joined Finn, stepping back away from it.

The ball came to a sudden stop, blowing its wax top. With an anticlimactic sputter, a curl of purple smoke rose out of the hole, and the corridor fell quiet and dark.

River was trying to catch her breath, and she nodded. "That should do it."

Finn said again, "You first, Cass," but Hades and I were already in motion, crossing the threshold.

I grimaced, half expecting to be blown to pieces, but the fireballs did not appear.

ENID

I tried again, *'Leo! Anyone! They're warding the door. Be careful!'*

The wolfsbane was still too thick in my blood to establish the link. I watched Morga and Sara finish their spell, and I could feel the malice intent of the magic they'd just cast.

Morga shuffled over to where we waited. "She'll break it, my sister, but it'll buy us time."

"Let's go!" Nox snapped, yanking the chain in his hand. Sophia was almost catatonic on the other end, collared like a dog, and she stumbled forward, nearly falling to her hands and knees. Some of the wounds on her back opened again, seeping with fresh blood.

Sara pushed me on the dolly, jogging to keep up with the dragon. The large corridor opened into an even bigger chamber, indicating a huge portion of this massive rock was hollow. Green flamed torches burned along the walls, and I wondered if they'd stayed lit for thousands of years. Sigils of witchcraft were carved into the stones beneath them, and I swallowed, recognizing several.

Dark. Power. Fear. Death.

In the center of the room there was a dais atop three intersecting flights of stairs. Sara grunted with effort, dragging me up to the top as the dolly bounced on each step, jostling me.

A serpent was carved into the floor at the top, and three pedestals stood around it. At the center sat a table, and on it, a skeleton in iron cuffs that had nearly dissolved to dust. The table had small tracks that appeared to drain into the symbol on the floor.

'A blood sacrifice to close or open the door,' Skadi said.

Morga barked, "Hurry now, Sara. Get her up there. I'll place the artifacts."

Sara was breathing hard, her face sweating as she pushed the old bones off the surface. She tried to blow the black powder in my face, but I was ready this time. I held my breath and turned away. Sara giggled wildly, her eyes wide with fear as she glanced at her mother.

Morga uttered, "Stupid wench. You better figure it out, or we'll just use your blood!"

Sara searched around and picked up a large rock. I said, "Wait!" but she smashed it across the side of my head. Twice. Stars erupted behind my eyes, and I tried to struggle while she moved me. It was useless. I was wrapped tightly in this iron chain that burned my skin everywhere it touched and Sara was stronger than she looked, grunting as she lifted me onto the table.

Morga said, "Your blood, my lord?"

Nox took the athame and slid it across his palm, handing it back to her slicked with his blood. She placed it on its pedestal, and the sigils that ran up its base lit up, glowing iridescent red. Next, she filled the chalice with a clear, blue liquid, and placed it onto its pedestal. The symbols below glowed a brilliant blue. Finally, she muttered an enchantment under her breath over the bell. It started ringing, a soft *bing-bing* that kept a steady rhythm, even after she shuffled away from it.

Nox tied the silver chain around the base of the table, and patted Sophia's head. "It was fun, but I'm bored with you." He retreated down the stairs to watch from a distance.

Using the same key as Morga had on the stone door, Sara unlocked the sacrificial cuffs and placed them around my arms and legs. With a small, sharp knife, she sliced my arm in the soft bend of my elbow. The cut was so deep I felt the blade scrape bone. Hot blood poured from the wound, no doubt filling the sacrificial tracks.

I cried out and said, *'Skadi! What do we do?'*

A roar filled the chamber, and Sara stopped by my head, gasping.

I heard Nox say, "Oh, Cassian."

'Now!' Skadi shouted, and I underwent a partial shift, my teeth elongating. We latched onto Sara's hand that held the key, and she shrieked, dropping it to the floor.

When she pulled away, her hand was gushing blood, and Morga said, "Just go, you dumb girl! Go help the master. I'll finish this!"

Chaos broke out behind me. Growls and magic. The chamber grew hotter, the roar of flame echoing like thunder.

"Enid!"

"Leo!" I yelled back, yanking at my restraints.

Morga stood by my head, one hand holding her grimoire and one extended out by her side. Her voice low and resonant, she said the spell. It was in an unfamiliar language, so I didn't understand it, but the artifacts started to hum.

Nothing happened, although the artifacts kept their buzzing tune.

Morga clicked her tongue. "Gah! More blood!"

She took a knife from her robes, and I gritted my teeth, preparing to be cut again. The blade came for my neck this time and I thrashed my head. Just as I expected to have my throat sliced, a rock smashed into Morga's fingers, making her drop the knife.

"Not today, Morga!"

The old crone gnashed her teeth and glared at the voice. "River! Here to face defeat again?"

I felt the heat of her flame as she retaliated and sighed with relief when she moved away from my head.

A familiar black ball of fur leaped up onto my chest, and I sobbed. "Hades! Oh, I am glad to see you!" He rubbed his face on my chin, purring. "The key," I told him. "It's on the floor somewhere!"

He looked over the edge, but I felt movement by my left hand.

"Sophia!" I shouted when I glanced down. Her bruised face was set with stony determination.

Key in hand, she turned over my wrist and plunged it into the lock. She freed not only the wrist restraint that held me, but the iron cage on my hand. It was then that I saw the skull atop the iron key. I'd read about them—an extraordinarily rare item—a skeleton key capable of opening almost any lock.

"Yes! You did it! You did it, Sophia! We're going to get out of here!"

She looked at me and said, "I *am* a wolf."

A projectile, possibly a rock, came from behind me, thrown with such force it went straight through her chest, leaving a gaping hole where her heart had once been. Her eyes widened, and I screamed.

She was dead before she slumped over me, but I called, "Sophia!" I heard Nox laughing and knew it was his doing.

"Oh, no," I whispered, watching Sophia's blood leak out of her body and flood the tracks beneath me.

'Hurry! Hurry!' Skadi barked, and Hades yowled, looking at the floor.

The artifacts hummed louder, the *bing-bing* of the bell swelling into a hammering tune.

My hand didn't want to open after being clenched for so long, but adrenaline forced my sore fingers to work, and I snatched the key from Sophia's slackened grip.

The chain that wrapped me was my focus. I found the padlock on my stomach, and the skeleton key was a perfect fit.

The tension of the chain slackened just as the ground started shaking, vibrating the layer of dust on the table. My eyes widened when I glanced over the edge. The floor was slowly splitting open beneath me. I held the skeleton key with my teeth and used my free hand to manipulate the stone of the table, breaking the rock around the shackles that held my still caged hand and feet.

'Time to go!' Skadi said, and I threw myself off the table.

The chain was loose, but it was still wrapped around me, hindering my every move. My legs failed to catch me, and I fell flat on my face with a groan. After being hung on that wall for days, my starved, dehydrated body didn't want to cooperate. Hades grabbed the collar of my smock, trying to drag me toward safety as the floor continued opening beneath me. I inched like a worm, barely getting far enough to escape being crushed by the stone table as it tilted, then plummeted down a long tunnel with an ear-splitting crash.

I glanced over my shoulder and watched it disappear into the opening darkness, Sophia's limp body still chained to the base. When I heard it hit the bottom, something answered. A series of squealing shrieks traveled up from the hole, and the sound iced my blood. It didn't sound like a dragon. It didn't sound like anything I'd ever heard. It just sounded big.

"Hurry, hurry," I mumbled around the key I still held in my teeth, crawling and dragging my iron-weighted feet.

The chain was slowly loosening its hold on me, gathering around my waist, and I used my elbows to move faster. I tried to touch the stone, calling to earth to stop its withdrawal, but the iron that restrained me weakened me, and I could not overcome the mechanisms that pulled it.

The floor was carrying me toward the edge, but it retracted faster than I could move. It disappeared beneath me, and I lunged for the ledge. My fingers brushed, but I missed it, and my stomach dropped as I fell, weighted by the chain and the cuffs.

A hand appeared, grabbing my wrist and dragging me up over the edge.

"Leo!" I said around the key, falling into him. He hugged me while I half-laughed and half-cried into his chest.

"Enid, are you okay? Gods, that was close. Almost didn't make it. We need to get this chain..."

His voice trailed away, and I felt his worry. Felt it. My eyes whipped open, and I looked up at him. His pupils were dilated, and his nostrils flared. A slow, broad smile spread across his face.

'Not ideal timing,' Skadi said, *'but this is our mate. Part of you, the witch, has sensed this connection for some time.'*

'That's why I was so—'

'Increasingly aroused and irresponsible in his presence? Yes. Witches tend to be selfish creatures.'

My cheeks flared, and I dropped the key, laughing. I touched his face with trembling fingers, making sure he was real. "Oh, Leo, I knew it!"

He hugged me tight. "I can't believe it!"

We kissed, my freed hand cradling his cheek, but Hades yowled behind us, looking into the hole. He turned to me, chittering, his green eyes wide.

Oh yeah, the world was ending.

"Oh, gods, the key. The monster," I muttered, searching the ground beneath us. "Where did it go?"

Leo said, "We have to hide," and picked me up, shaking off the chain and sliding behind the pillar the bell was perched on.

"Wait! The key!" I said again, holding my cuffed hand up.

"There!" He pointed. It was where we'd just been, sitting close to the edge of the hole. Hades hurried away from the opening, batting it toward us. It landed a couple of yards away, out in the open between this pillar and the next. Hades ducked behind the bell pillar to hide with us as the world started to tremble.

CHAPTER THIRTY

LEO

E NID'S FREE HAND WAS covered in burns from the iron.

'I want them to die,' I said, feeling Bleiz shift in my head. There was an agreed aggression between us that I'd never felt before.

'They will.'

'I can't believe it. She's our mate.'

I felt his hesitation. *'Yes.'*

'What's wrong?'

'Here I have chastised you for deeming yourself unworthy of such a powerful female, and I find myself stunned in the presence of Skadi.'

'Skadi is her wolf? How do you know? You haven't even seen her yet.'

'She speaks to me.'

'What? We haven't completed the bond.'

'She's powerful. The beloved companion of the Moon Goddess herself. She sits beside her throne. The great white wolf.'

The trembling of the ground ended our conversation, and I looked up, watching the ringing bell as it gyrated on its seat atop the pillar.

Something screamed—a shrill screech that cut my eardrums like a knife—and from the hole burst the beast.

"Holy shit." I sandwiched Enid against the pillar to hide her as the room fell into stunned stillness.

"What is it?" she whispered so quietly it was barely a breath.

I expected a dragon. I thought it was going to be a dragon. Cass did, too. Maybe just a huge one.

It wasn't.

The room was clasped in the grip of silence, and I peeked around the pillar, daring a glance.

Perched atop the hole, taking in the room, sat a serpentine monster ripped from the pages of ancient literature. It was enormous, with the tallest of its three triangle-shaped heads halfway to the ceiling of the chamber. Its scales were black, or maybe dark green, but looked different from Cass's. They were softer; more skin-like. More snake-like.

"A hydra," I whispered. "It's huge."

The head closest to us spun on a swivel, eyeing our pillar. I froze, my heart beating in my ears. The key was less than ten feet away, out in the open.

I frowned, keeping my voice low. "How do I get the key?"

"We're supposed to kill *that* ugly bastard?" Finn shouted, and the hydra shifted, the three heads clicking in their throats as they turned to the small group spread out at the bottom of the stairs.

I glanced around the pillar at Finn, and he side-eyed me. He was trying to get it away from us. I nodded.

He waved his hands. "Hey! Here! Here, you ugly prick!"

The hydra roared at him, and he shifted back to his wolf, howling, yipping, and causing a ruckus. I dove out, scrambling for the key. The piece of sandstone it laid on lifted courtesy of Enid, throwing the key to my waiting hand, and I scrambled back behind the pillar.

My shoulder hit the rock with a thud as I slid back, but I made it without being seen, and I slipped the key into the lock on Enid's wrist.

There was a crash, and I winced as the bell tumbled from where it teetered on the pillar, falling and bouncing down each step as if it had the intention of ratting us out.

Enid and I stared at each other, our eyes wide, and I heard Eris yelling, "No! Hey! Here! Over here!"

I smelled the beast first. Musky, wet paper. A clicking sound drew my eyes to the left as the head closest to us leaned around the pillar. Its irises were bright red, and the iridescent color framed black, vertical pupils. It opened its mouth, and a long, forked tongue flicked out, testing the air. I was more worried about the fangs, though. They were curved with a deadly point at the end and measured half the size of my body.

I slid in front of Enid as the disjointed jaw opened further, liquid dripping from the fangs as it readied to strike.

A slab of stone erupted in front of us, blocking the beast as it made its move. It hissed when it crashed, and I turned to find Enid had her other hand free.

"Down!" I yelled. The other head was right behind her.

I grabbed her and pushed her, both of us ducking as it struck. It missed us, but a fang nicked my shoulder.

I shouted a curse, reaching up and touching it. I'd been cut before, but this burned like a thousand wasp stings, ripping down my arm to my fingers and up into my neck. I looked, and watched blackness spiderweb from the cut, following the path of my veins.

I vomited and rolled onto my side. The world spun around me, and my words were slurred, barely understandable. "Gods. Enid?"

'It's a potent venom,' Bleiz said, and my vision went dark.

ENID

"Leo? Leo!" I shouted, trying to rouse him while I unlocked the cuffs from my feet. Leo had rolled to his side away from me, and he lurched onto his back. His eyes were white, turned up into his head, and his body went stiff as a board.

'He's seizing,' Skadi said, and I gasped. *'The beast is venomous.'* Leo shifted before my eyes, becoming Bleiz. *'His wolf believes he can better handle the venom.'*

Bleiz spasmed, rolling from side to side on the stairs, white foam leaking from his mouth. The hydra focused on him, all three heads about to fight over the first bite. I yelped, putting my hand to the ground and smashing one with another rock slab.

Shaw leaped over me, lunging in stride and grabbing hold of one monster's nostril. It shrieked, jerking its head up. He held on, growling.

'It's venomous. Careful!' I linked Finn, relieved to find the link was working.

"Enid! Look out!"

It was Eris behind me, and I looked up. The third head had abandoned eating Leo and now loomed over me. I could smell its breath, hot and musty. My hands flew up to blast fire, but I worried I wouldn't be fast enough.

A deep yowl saved me, and Hades in his shifted form, a black panther, jumped atop its head. He clawed at its eyes, ripping one clean out.

'A little help!' Finn said in the link, and he was being pursued by the other two.

Everything was happening so quickly, I was having trouble deciding what needed attention first.

'There,' Skadi barked, and I looked up. A nasty stalactite hung just above the rightmost head.

Using air and earth, I picked up the pillar next to me. The rock listened, but it was heavy, and I dug deep. The veins on my arms darkened to purple as I sent the pillar flying with a grunt, hoping my timing was correct.

It broke the stalactite, and the heavy, pointed rock fell in slow motion, cutting into the beast's neck and severing it. The decapitated head flopped like a dying fish, its jaws opening and closing. The other two shrieked, stumbling away from us and nearly falling back into the hole.

"Yes," I whispered and scrambled to my feet, running for Bleiz. "Leo! Eris, help!"

She was right by my side and put her hands on him. When she sucked in a sharp breath, I knew it wasn't good.

"I can't cure the venom, but I think it's run its course. I'll fix what it's affected, and hopefully that's enough."

"It was just a tiny nick," I said, parting Bleiz's fur to inspect the wound. It was barely an inch long, but angry and purple, blackness staining around it as the venom ate at his flesh.

"Any more than that and he might not be with us. It's done significant damage to his heart and lungs."

I put my hand on her, offering my strength so she could heal him
quickly. It was like a conduit, my power flowing to her as we sang the
song our mother taught us when we were children.

Finn linked us. *'That was the opposite of help!'*

We both looked up, and my eyes widened. The severed head lay still,
its red eyes distant with death, but the stump left behind had already
sprouted two new heads!

'I didn't think that was possible!' I said, shaking my head.

'It's right there in the story!'

Hercules and his twelve labors. One of which was slaying the Ler-
naean hydra.

'I thought it was just that. A story!'

'Oh, it's pissed now!'

'Run, Finn!'

The hydra reared back, its middle head opening its jaw as if it were
going to spit fire. It rocked forward and spewed not flame, but a green
liquid that coated the stairs, barely missing Shaw as he turned tail and
ran.

The stone smoked, sizzling, and the stench was so vile I gagged.

'It spits acid?' Finn shouted, the words ringing in my head. *'This
just keeps getting better and better! Anyone have Hercules' contact
information?'*

'How'd he do it? Cut a head off and burn the stump, right?'

"Leo should recover," Eris said, sweat on her brow.

Bleiz had stopped seizing, and his breaths were even, but he was not
conscious. I ran my hand over his soft scruff.

Eris gasped. "Enid, look out!"

One head had snuck behind us, and Eris grabbed me, but it was too
late. We both tensed, ready for the bite, but it never came. A deep
feline howl echoed in the chamber.

We both screamed, "Hades!"

The black panther had taken the bite for us. Even with a fang buried
deep in his chest, he fought, trying to scratch its eyes. It chomped him

with a sickening crunch, and I sucked in a sharp breath, unable to find air. It felt like the fang was through my heart instead.

"No!" I wailed, even though he was already dead.

The creature tossed him in the air and swallowed him whole. A high-pitched ring whined in my ears, and my hands grew hot.

CHAPTER THIRTY-ONE

LEO

B LEIZ STARTLED AWAKE, BROUGHT back to consciousness as a terrible pain cracked in his chest.

It was so intense, I asked, *'Are we bitten again?'*

'No,' he said solemnly, getting to his feet. *'That is grief.'*

My mind was fuzzy, and I tried to understand. *'Grief?'*

It was coming from the bond, I realized, and my thoughts went to Eris. Had she been hurt? Killed? But the Luna was suddenly next to me, her cheeks stained with tears. She shoved me down, lying on top of me as a hydra's head passed over us.

'Enid, are you okay?' I asked, finally getting my wits back. At least the link was finally working.

She was a short distance from me, crouched on her knees. Her long platinum hair formed a curtain around her, and her voice was flat. *'Get Cass, Finn, and Eris and run, Leo. Leave this place. It is my destiny to stop this beast, not yours.'*

'What? I'm not leaving you.'

She turned, and I recoiled, barely recognizing her. Her eyes glowed bright fluorescent green, and the veins on her entire body were a dark violet. Every single one, even the tiniest, stood out against her pale skin. I could feel her presence. The air simmered with heat. When she lifted her arms, flames coiled around her wrists like fiery serpents ready to strike.

"Run," she said again, this time aloud. Her voice was distorted into a deep, magical hum. A hydra head was diving to bite her, but she raised her hands and unleashed a torrent of flame so hot my next breath seared my lungs. The beast shrieked, and the skin on its neck and chin bubbled and blistered. It healed faster than Cass, and I watched the wound disappear as quickly as it formed.

"Time to go," Eris said, pulling at Bleiz's scruff. Shaw wasted no time, sprinting past us and dodging a snapping snake head.

'It killed the cat,' Finn said in the link, *'so I'd get the fuck outta the way if I was you.'*

The clawed foot of the hydra descended upon us, so Bleiz opened his stride, running and ducking the massive swipe. Eris shifted to her silver wolf next to me, picking up speed.

The room was emptier than I expected. Cass lay shredded on the floor, having lost his battle to the other dragon. I wasn't surprised. I knew Crux was small for a dragon, but I didn't expect him to be half the size of his opponents. Everyone else was gone. Shaw ran to Cass, nudging him with his nose, and he stirred, somehow still alive.

'Where are the witches?' I asked Finn and Eris.

Eris answered, *'Their fight took them back toward the exit.'*

I skidded to a halt, turning to watch Enid. Atop the dais, she was on her feet, standing and facing the beast in front of her with her hands out at her sides. Wind started to blow, churning the chamber, and the flames slithered over her arms, waiting for their next calling. The hydra heads all moved independently, like four periscoping cobras, flicking their tongues to get a read of her. They seemed warier now after getting torched.

'That's going to make an incredible sketch when this is over.'

'We've all got to survive first,' Bleiz said, his anxiety mixing with mine. *'We cannot just leave her.'*

'What do we do?'

The middle head made the first move, rocking back and opening its maw. A green liquid spewed forward, but Enid ducked, running straight toward the beast. The ground sizzled behind her, the stone melting, and another head dove, going for the bite. She used air, pulling a current down so its mouth slammed shut, and then she jumped atop it.

I took a step forward. *'What's she doing?'*

'Wait,' Finn said. *'Just wait. You'll be nothing but a distraction.'*

I'd never seen Enid in battle. He had.

Through Bleiz's sharp eyes, I watched her manipulate the air, using it and the movements of the beast to jump from head to head. It was so frustrated that it bit itself, two of the heads getting into a hissing squabble.

She leaped from the hydra, jumping and pushing herself with a current of air to a rock ledge. With a slap to the wall, she conjured stairs, running up them to gain higher ground. The beast pursued her, finally leaving its place over the pit, and I could see it had two legs up front, but the lower half of its body was a single tail like a snake.

Enid was hundreds of feet off the floor now, and she pressed her back to the wall. The hydra had her cornered, and my heart hiccupped as it rose on its long tail to an incredible height, clawing up the wall, its four heads fighting to get to her first. It could climb stone.

'Enid! Get outta there!'

She ignored me and reached up, standing on her toes so her fingertips grazed the ceiling. Her eyes glowed bright green, and her chest heaved with the strength of each breath. She bared her teeth, yelling. A war cry.

A loud, deep sound echoed above us, and the stone cracked under her hands, fracturing out like a lightning strike.

'Run!' Finn said, using Shaw to shoulder Bleiz toward the exit. *'She's bringing it down! She's going to collapse this chamber!'*

'I can't just leave her!' I said, taking off toward the dais.

Crux stepped in front of me, healed by Eris. He snagged me, grabbing me like a pup by the scruff. Bleiz was feral, growling and snapping, but only able to get a bite on his chin. It did nothing, his glasslike scales not giving an inch.

We ran as the rumble behind us grew until it was deafening, the rock snapping and groaning. I watched as the ceiling collapsed, shaking the earth with tons upon tons of falling rock. I lost sight of Enid as she buried the shrieking hydra. And herself.

'Enid! Enid! No!'

The tunnel started falling, but I could see the dark hole of the exit ahead. Crux, Calliope, and Shaw dove for freedom, narrowly escaping being crushed as the doorway was filled with heavy stones behind us.

Rain poured from the sky, lightning arching like flashes of a camera in the darkness, and the wind whipped my fur. Puddles pooled everywhere, the dry ground unaccustomed to so much moisture. A distance out in the desert, we saw fire eruptions, and I knew River and Rhia were in a serious confrontation with the crone Morga and her daughter.

Finn asked, *'Should we help them?'*

'No.' I could feel her. She was alive. *'Enid. Are you okay?'*

The weather quieted, with the wind easing and the rain softening to a sorrowful drizzle. Her voice was so calm. *'I'm alive. Meet me at the top of the rubble. I need Crux.'*

After Crux dropped me, I shifted immediately and climbed onto his back. Finn and Eris were right behind me.

"Take us up! We've got to fly over! She's alive."

He didn't hesitate, throwing out his wings and flapping hard to get us in the air. Crux coasted over the top of Uluru toward the section that was now collapsed. The rubble burst like a mushroom releasing its spores, rocks flying in every direction, and Enid climbed out, stalking to the edge of Uluru and looking out over the battlefield.

The clouds drifted, and in the light of the full moon, I could see our army toiling in sloppy mud to fight thousands of vampires. They weren't alone. My eyebrows lifted, and Finn voiced my thoughts.

"Dark elves! They left their mountain. I can't believe it!"

It was the elves, though, with their dark blue skin and black hair. They were engaged in bloody combat with their fae cousins, both races pushing the boundaries of agility. A rivalry that went back millennia. The remaining dragons were out there; the amethyst and jade on the ground, and the ruby in the sky. Three deadly, shining gems that rained down fiery death on enemies and friendlies alike. I looked for Gideon, but it was too vast and too chaotic to tell where he was.

We landed on the rock with a thump and all jogged to Enid. She had her arms out and was manipulating the air to funnel rain into her mouth, drinking like she hadn't seen a drop for days.

Eris and I called out nearly identical sentiments over the downpour. "Enid! Thank the gods you're okay!"

"You squashed it!" Finn said. "That was incredible! So much for these." He held up his quiver of arrows, tipped with Dragonsbane steel.

"We aren't done yet," Enid hissed, malice intent I'd never heard from her coloring the words. She turned to us, and I put my arms out to embrace her, starting to console her about Hades.

"Enid, I'm so sorry..."

She pushed my hands away and strode past me, ripping a single arrow out of Finn's quiver on her way to Crux. The onyx dragon bent down so she could climb on his back, and she leaned up to whisper in his ear.

"I want Nox."

Crux growled deep in his chest and leaped over the edge of Uluru, spreading his wings and coasting into the chaos. Enid turned her hands, and a cyclone of air formed. Crux banked around it, and she and he together added fire to the wind. The flaming tornado ate through a flank of vampires and left a trail of ash in its wake.

I looked at Finn and Eris. Eris was pale, tired from having to heal Cass.

Finn threw out his hands. "Great! They left us on top of a mountain."

"It's a really big rock, actually," I muttered, watching them head for the amethyst dragon.

CHAPTER THIRTY-TWO

ENID

THE GROUP OF FAE and wolves scattered so Cass and I could land on the flooded field in front of Nox, who looked back at Uluru and snorted when he saw it partially collapsed. I slid from Crux's back, my bare feet sinking into the mud.

Nox flashed his teeth, taking two steps back. His head whipped from one side to the other, as if he was looking for someone.

"Your old hag is busy," I said curtly, toying with the sharp tip of the arrow I held, "and so are your friends." I pointed it at him. "You're going to pay for what you did to Sophia." My voice thickened. "You're going to pay for what your beast did to Hades!"

Nox's wings untucked like he might take off, and Crux lunged to stop him, biting at his face. As always, I was impressed with the speed at which the enormous beasts could move. Nox pawed Crux away, shoving him aside and then slashing his wing.

Crux was badly outmatched. Nox towered over him with a growl like a clap of thunder reverberating in his barrel chest. I reached for earth and air and sent a spray of wet sand into his face, aiming for his glowing orange eyes.

My heart ached at the loss of Hades, and I dove deep into those feelings, letting them wash over me. I stomped my foot, cracking the surrounding earth, and lifted the large pieces of rock I'd broken free. With a push of my hands, I sent them soaring at Nox. They hit him, one slamming hard into his skull with a sickening thump. He continued to ignore me, biting Crux on the back of his neck. I heard the shining black scales crack under the immense pressure.

Two flashes appeared, and I sucked air through my teeth, now confronted by Una and Cora. They were younger than Morga, but the dark magic was already taking its toll. Their teeth and lips were blackened, and their empty eyes stared out from dark pits. Una's long hair was ragged, looking like tendrils of oil, and Cora had her head shaved, swollen purple scars running over her scalp.

Nox made a rumbling sound when he saw he had allies, a dragon's laughter, and attacked Crux with new ferocity. I took a deep breath, putting my hands out. Like in the chamber, I called with my heart to the elements.

'Earth, wind, fire, water, come to me. Bless me with your strength.'

The elements complied, rushing to fill my blood with their humming power. Deep in the earth, I could feel what I wanted. The surrounding desert acacias had extensive root systems, and I called on them. They erupted from the ground, as thick as iron chains, and I attacked, searching to restrain the witches.

Una was the oldest of the daughters, an experienced wind witch, and she turned, calling a gale that she sharpened like a blade. It sliced through the roots before they could reach their target. Cora slapped the earth, and it listened, rolling with a shockwave and knocking me unsteady.

I hurried back to my feet, sending pillars of flame in their direction. Una pushed with her air, jumping to an incredible height, while Cora raised an earthen shield to protect herself.

Una whipped a cyclone into a fury, trying to catch me in it, but I turned the wind to my own hand, and added a burst of flame. The storm roared, rattling my eardrums, and Una's mouth dropped open when it grew and whirled toward her, whipping her black dress.

Cora pushed her earthen shield at me, trying to crush me, and I pulled water to my hand. With a turn of my wrist, I turned it into a whip and I snapped it, splitting the oncoming stone in half. The crack was bone-rattling, echoing across the desert and joining the chorus of war.

The earth witch rushed to conjure something else, her eyes widening, and I raised my water whip to strike her.

It felt like a tree trunk smashed into my back, and my feet were suddenly off the ground. I flew, unsure of which direction was up until I hit the ground. My already cracked ribs snapped, and I couldn't find a breath. Skadi rushed to heal me while my head lolled to the side, trying to understand what had happened.

Nox's scales glittered, dancing in the light of the flames I'd lit as he raised his broad tail again, bringing it down to crush me. I opened a crack in the earth beneath me, falling in, and his tail smashed just above me. I called to the acacia roots and bid them to wrap around his feet.

With him distracted and my ribs mostly mended, I scrambled from the crack and turned on Cora. Her nose bled from both nostrils, and her eyes widened. I stomped on the earth, sending a row of sharp spires erupting from the ground. Using the water that collected in a fine layer on the sand, I glided toward her, sending three pillars of flame at Una, who appeared to defend her sister.

I conjured the water whip again and snatched Cora's wrist with it, using it to fling her. Una barely evaded the flame pillars and tried to hit me with a razor-sharp slice of air. I called earth, lifting a wall of rock to intersect it. The elements crashed with an ear-splitting crack like thunder, exploding in dust and debris.

When the red dust settled, Cora lay motionless, face down in the mud. Una floated down, staying suspended in the air, and eyed me. Her chest was heaving, and the right half of her lower body was blistered by burns.

"I could do this all night," I said to Una, calling another cyclone with a whirl of my wrist. "And the wind favors me, don't you think?"

Just as I raised my hand to add fire, she flashed—a skill I had yet to, or maybe never would, acquire. I spun, expecting her to appear behind me, and caught a glimpse of her kneeling by Cora. They both disappeared, choosing freedom and life over capture or death.

'*They are smarter than this arrogant fool,*' Skadi snarled, speaking of Nox. '*Finish him. The moon goddess has delivered us to this moment. We are the hammer of justice.*'

The purple dragon still contended with my roots, and I lifted my hands, calling to the earth. *Give me more. Give me your strongest.* I used them like threads, stitching him to the earth. He blasted flame from his maw, and the wet roots sizzled and smoked. Every one he burned was replaced by three more.

The desert was covered with standing water, and I pulled at it, directing it beneath Nox's feet. It inundated the sand, destabilizing it. He was a gorgeous beast with all of those shining purple scales that sparkled like gems as lightning licked the night sky. As beautiful as they were, they would spell his doom. They were heavy, and he started to sink. I pulled him down into my sand trap, and the roots wrapped his horns, anchoring his massive head to one side. He sank to his belly, and I stopped the water so his heart would stay above ground.

Flame erupted from his maw, but it couldn't save him, blowing pointlessly into unoccupied air. Crux had regained his strength and lunged, sinking his teeth into Nox's wing and tearing it free with a savage growl. Nox erupted with a shrill bellow, thrashing to free himself. His furious roar ended with a soft whine when he realized his anger was not powerful enough to liberate him from my earthen grasp.

I stopped in front of him and crouched down, studying the slit pupil of his massive orange eye. "As big as you are, dragon, the earth is bigger." His heart galloped behind the translucent flesh on his chest. He cried out; a sharp, pitiful sound, begging the others for help.

I looked around and saw no one rushing to aid him. "They do not come. You will die alone."

His chest rumbled, a sound of disbelief.

"Yes, I imagine that as old as you are, death is quite a shock, but a promise is a promise. Your pain will end soon."

He called out again, his visible orange eye a swamp of fear, and Cass, now his human self, laughed behind me. "That is a sweet sound, Nox, to hear you beg for your life."

I ran my hand down the amethyst scales of his neck, and whispered, "I wish there was another way. To slay such elegance feels wrong, but evil wrapped in beauty is still evil."

He started to shift back to human. I tossed the arrow up and caught it by the fletching, bringing it down in the same motion. His yellow eye widened as it sank into the soft flesh of his chest, plunging easily into his heart. The massive organ beat twice more, the shaft of the arrow quivering in my hand with each thump. When it stopped, I ripped it free. His body completed the shift, becoming the vile man who had tormented me.

I stared at his blank eyes until I was sure he was dead, and then, with a push of his shoulder, I shoved him back into the sand pit. The earth churned, swallowing him whole, and then hardened into a sandy tomb.

"One down," I said to Cass, who nodded his agreement and shifted back to his onyx dragon.

A shriek from across the field drew our attention, and I climbed up, watching from Crux's shoulders. A group of water witches, led by one dressed in all pink, froze Tirich's feet to the ground. Fae warriors riding unicorns harassed him on the ground, while harpies and sprites buzzed around his head, slicing at his fleshy wings and eyes with claws and small daggers. He was spraying fire and fighting to free himself, but Kat, from the back of a black unicorn stallion, nocked and released three arrows. Her speed was unmatched, and her precision was deadly.

Tirich was a quick beast and lifted his leg, managing to stop two of the arrows. The third skirted by with mere centimeters to spare. The shining tip hit home, bringing the wailing green dragon to his knees, and then to his side, where he lay dead.

Cheers erupted from that side of the field, and I added to the tally. "Two down. One to—"

Crux grunted and lunged, cutting me off. I nearly lost my footing and had to crouch and grab onto one of his spikes. He charged forward as if he were going to take off, but stopped and snorted. His frame shook with fury as he let out an ear-splitting roar.

The red dragon, Edana, was fleeing. She called back an answer, and Crux rumbled with a low growl, blowing two smoke rings from his nostrils.

"I'm sorry," I said, sensing it was personal. I patted his neck. "But I think that's it."

Scanning the battlefield, I watched wolves herding the last of the blood-crazed vampires into groups, allowing our allied fire witches to incinerate them en masse. The dark elves were gone. There weren't enough dead to equal their original numbers. They must have been flashed away by Una when she sensed defeat. One dark witch could transport many if she burned enough soul stones.

More cheers erupted around us as everyone left on the battlefield slowly realized we'd done it. It was over. Cries of pain and grief bled into the cheers, and I swallowed hard, my eyes sweeping over the wreckage left behind.

Both sides had suffered losses, but at least we seemed to have fared better. The wolves cornered some vampires against the rock wall I'd created during my fight with Una. One was a young woman, her red eyes wild as she snarled and lashed out. She had her nails painted pink, a stark reminder that this was someone's daughter. Someone's friend. A missing human that no one would ever find. Her family would never know what happened to her; that she died twice. Once when they turned her and finally in this desert.

I sighed, rubbing my heavy eyes to stop the tears. I felt like the edge of a well-used dishcloth—frayed and unraveling. My thoughts went to Hades, and disbelief flooded me again.

"Can you take me to Leo, please?"

Crux chortled softly, and I felt his muscles bunch. Before he could jump, a loud rumble echoed over the valley. The cheers quieted, and everyone turned to the source of the sound. Uluru seemed to quiver, and in a burst of stone, the hydra broke free from where I thought I'd buried it for good. It squealed defiantly as gasps and exclaims echoed around me.

"Impossible," I muttered, unable to believe it had broken through all of that rock.

'There is a reason they locked it beneath a magical seal,' Skadi said. *'This creature is close to a god. A beast spawned by the most ancient monsters.'*

Two of the heads flopped uselessly, crushed by rock, and the others attacked them. They chewed them away at the neck, and we all watched as two new heads grew in each place, bringing the total to six.

"That sucks." I sighed. "I should've known it wouldn't be that easy." A fae soldier stood next to me, caked in mud, and I asked, "Can I borrow that?" I pointed at the silver sword in her hand, and she tossed it to me without a question.

My long-foretold destiny awaited.

CHAPTER
THIRTY-THREE

LEO

'*OH, COME ON!*' FINN shouted as we reached the bottom of the trail, only to watch Enid and Crux soar overhead, returning to the top of Uluru.

Based on what we'd heard up there, the hydra was free. Bleiz pivoted, ready to run back up, but Gideon linked me. '*Wait!*'

He approached in his wolf form, flanked by the Fae King Alderan and his guard, as well as Wren, the harpy.

'*I've got to help her,*' I said, shifting to myself and hurrying toward them. "We need to cut its heads off and cauterize the stumps. That's how Hercules did it."

'*Okay,*' Gideon said, but he was interrupted by a chorus of gasps.

"I need to borrow this," I was saying as I unbuckled the Fae King's sword belt. The royal sword was famous, called *Tuilghearr*, or Floodcutter, and probably older than my bloodline. His Majesty lifted his hands, either out of shock or acceptance. I wasn't sure which.

'*Leo!*' Gideon said.

I ignored him, buckling the longsword to my waist. It felt right, the sword, and I prayed to my father for his spiritual guidance. Gooseflesh prickled my skin as I felt the faintest pressure, like an invisible hand on my shoulder, and I knew he was there with me.

I looked at Wren. "Can you give me a lift?"

"Uh…" Her feathery brows lifted, and she looked me up and down. She turned over her shoulder and called, "Hey! Help me!" Another harpy hurried toward us, and Wren flapped, taking my shoulders in her clawed feet. "Hang on!"

I wrapped my hands around her rough ankles. They were scaled like chicken legs. The other harpy grabbed my feet, and up we soared.

ENID

Crux and I landed in the wet sand on top of Uluru. The hydra was near the edge, its six noses up and smelling the air. Their tongues flickered.

'It seeks the sea,' Skadi said.

"You will not leave here!" I yelled, and it whipped around.

Its crimson eyes glowed as the morning sun emerged, rapidly heating the day. Humidity choked the air. The orange sky and the red sand cast everything in an eerie hue, like it was Crux and me with this strange creature on another planet.

All six heads hissed when they saw me, their pupils flexing with recognition.

'I think you've made it angry,' Skadi said, chuckling.

'I could barely catch a breath when it had three heads. It'll be a miracle if I can pull this off!'

'Well, the last one to do it was a demigod, and he had help, so I would agree.'

I looked at the sword in my hand. *'And, unfortunately, I am still better at arithmetic than I am at swordplay.'*

'Lean heavily on your magic.'

I turned to my dragon companion. "If I chop a head off, we've got to burn the stump before it can regenerate."

Crux flexed his claws in the sand, shaking out his scales.

"Otherwise stay back," I said to him. "This is my fight, Cass. I don't want to see you harmed."

He snorted, two smoke rings rising from his nostrils, and growled, pulling his lips back away from his long, sharp teeth.

'Our dragon did not appreciate that wound to his pride,' Skadi said, chuckling.

'I just don't want him harmed.'

Crux faced the hydra, roaring with the bravado of a dragon twice his size. The heads recoiled, looked at each other, and then screamed back. Using its two front legs, the beast rushed us, clawing at the sand while it pushed with its strong tail. My heart skipped a beat. Out here in the open, it moved like an avalanche, bearing down on us with incredible speed.

I looked at Crux, throwing my arms out. "What'd you do that for!"

He bounded forward, blowing a fan of fire to stop its charge. The hydra squealed, rearing back, and I was out of time to think about anything else.

Sword up, dove!

I heard my father's voice as clear as day and gripped the hilt with two sweaty hands, lifting it toward my opponent.

Chaos and survival. Using my sword and all four elements—whips of water, bursts of fire and air, and shields of earth—I deflected the rapid attacks. They came one after another, the heads so desperate to sink their teeth into me that they would have brief squabbles, fighting with each other. I could hear Crux's deep breaths and feel the heat from his fire, but I couldn't get a moment to even see where he was.

A strange, wet gurgle bubbled above me. I glanced up to see a hydra head open its mouth and release a cascade of green acid. Gasping, I threw up a cone of air. The acid diverted, raining in a circle around me and sizzling as it sank into the sand.

A sudden impact sent me flying. It had sideswiped me with its clawed hand, smacking me like a bug. I landed face first in the sand, its rough crystals sliding like emery cloth under my cheeks. Moaning, I rolled over, trying to find my bearings. My eyes opened in time to catch the glint of fangs as a head descended to devour me. I called to the earth for a shield, hoping she would answer in time.

She didn't have to. Leo appeared, dropping from nowhere out of the orange sky. Sword in hand, he cut through the neck of the hydra on his way down, and I barely rolled out of the way so the severed head didn't crush me.

Spinning onto my back, I lifted my hand and cauterized the stump. Leo landed in a crouch and stuck out his hand to help me up. My brows lifted, and I was sure I had fallen a bit more in love with the man. I had certainly fallen a lot more in lust.

His face pinched, and he yelled, "Gross! That stinks so bad!" It smelled like someone was baking a rotting fish.

I nodded and pointed at the smoking stump. "It works though!"

The head had not regenerated.

"Good!" Leo pulled me up to him, wrapping his arm around my waist. "Let's be done with this. We have other things to do."

My cheeks warmed. "Agreed."

The intrusive hydra left no more time for romance, having recovered from its shock at the sudden loss of its head. Leo turned, parrying its bite with a slash of his sword. He sliced across one of its fangs in a clean, swift arc. Unlike the beast's skin, which rippled and mended within seconds, the fang cracked and was left hanging at an odd angle.

A different head came at me, and I sidestepped, spinning on the ball of my foot like my father taught me. Its fang sank into a soft spot in the rock, momentarily locking it in place. Knowing Leo held the one on my other side at bay, I could focus on this kill. I sent a pillar of flame at the next head trying to attack and finished my pivot. Using the strength of air to aid me, I brought the sword down on the stuck one's neck. Fae blades were famously high quality, and this one was no exception. Its razor edge sliced through the hydra's scaly hide and vertebrae with such ease that I was stunned when it struck rock at the bottom.

I spun again and brought up my hand, searing the bleeding stump that was left with a blast of flame. The stench was immediate and unbearable. I gagged and covered my nose and mouth with the crook of my elbow.

A black blur erupted into the fight, Shaw grabbing another head of the hydra by its nostril with a growl. It flung him, and went to eat him like it had Hades, but an arrow soared in, sinking deep into its crimson eye. Turning over my shoulder, I watched a harpy glide into view, its scaly feet grasping Kat by her shoulders. Her bow was drawn, the string still quivering from the arrow she'd just fired.

'*Perhaps we do not need a miracle,*' Skadi said. '*Like Hercules, we only require the aid of our family.*'

Behind me, I heard Crux roar. Gideon wielded his spear, battling the hydra. Eris ran up the spikes of Crux's back and leaped from his head, sword in hand. She turned in the air, slicing through the beast's neck and landing with a perfect roll.

'*Ha! Calliope! Always the exhibitionist,*' Skadi barked.

Crux blasted that stump with flame, and that left three. Above me, the middle head hovered. It was the biggest, and I suspected, the smartest.

When I looked up, it confirmed my suspicions. The red eyes watched me with intelligent consciousness. I lifted my sword, pointing it at my opponent, and it hissed, its broken fang glinting in the morning sun.

Chapter Thirty-Four

Leo

K AT'S ARROW STOPPED SHAW from being eaten, but he was still flung over fifty feet into the air.

"Finn!" I yelled, and winced when Shaw thudded on the rock, unable to get his feet underneath him.

'Ouch. Give me a minute to find all of my ribs.'

The hydra's clawed hand scratched at the arrow stuck in its eye, and I lunged forward, stabbing Tuilghaerr into its lower body. This ancient blade felt not like a weapon, but a living companion. As if it had a soul, and it too, understood the task. The hydra hissed and then made a gurgling sound.

I yelled, "Watch out!" to Finn and Kat, and then lunged forward, getting close enough to the beast I could feel the humid heat from its skin.

Acid erupted from its maw. Kat helped Finn get clear, but a few drops landed on my leather cuirass, burning holes in it. I fumbled with the buckles and ripped it off, tossing it away before the acid could eat through and into my skin. I pivoted, slashing with Tuilghearr across the belly of the beast. The legendary sword was wicked, sharp and heavy, and sliced through like the skin was made of satin.

Blood spurted, and my eyes widened at what was inside the monster. Dozens of jelly-like eggs. One fell out, splatting at my feet before the hydra healed the gaping wound. Inside the translucent red sack, I could see a writhing serpentine mass. A fetus. I recoiled away, and the sack split, collapsing open in the sand. The three-headed baby hydra squealed once, but seemed unable to breathe, its mouth gaping as it flopped around. It quickly perished, going limp at my feet, still covered in a thick red gel.

'*This thing is pregnant,*' I said to Kat and Finn in the link.

Finn was the first to answer. '*We saw. It died almost instantly, though.*'

'*I don't think it could breathe.*'

'*I bet it needs water to survive,*' Kat said. '*Like a tadpole that would eventually become a frog. That's probably why they put this thing out in the middle of the desert. If it were allowed to get to the ocean...*'

'*Dozens of these things!*' I finished for her.

The beast swiped at me, and I ducked the attack. When the clawed hand swung back, I grabbed hold of it, letting it carry me up. It tried to fling me off, and I leaped, using that momentum to propel myself onto its back.

My claws elongated, and I sank them in, coiling and jumping in four long bounds up its neck. I was glad for the practice Crux had given me in riding serpentine beasts. It tried desperately to shake me off, but on my last jump, I raised my sword and brought it down straight into the top of the hydra's skull.

Tuilghearr sank to the hilt, and I felt the beast's neck slacken. I held onto the sword as the head fell to the ground, skidding and throwing a fan of red sand into the air.

The sand hit Kat and Shaw across their chests. They stood slack-jawed, and Kat's mouth opened into a wide grin.

Finn said, '*Who the fuck are you, and what have you done with my baby brother?*'

I ripped the sword free. '*Do you think that will get me out of any future meetings?*'

Shaw snorted a guttural laugh, and we waited, watching to see if the head would recover from a sword through the brain. It did not, and the scream of another hydra head drew our attention. Eris had pinned it to the ground by its bottom jaw with the spear, and Gideon followed up, bringing a sword down through its neck. Crux finished the job, searing the stump left behind so it couldn't regenerate.

My heart clenched. Enid was charging straight toward the middle head, her sword at the ready. The head was low to the ground, hissing and waiting with open jaws.

ENID

'Look out!' Skadi shouted, and I ducked, having to roll away just as I got close enough to cleave the neck.

My brow was covered in sweat, and my arms shook. I groaned, frustrated.

'It's toying with you,' Skadi said.

It was. The beast would bait me by exposing its neck. We'd done it several times, me trying for the kill and it nearly catching me in its trap with a quick bite.

'Then I will play along.'

I charged straight ahead, my sword in front of me. Its eyes flexed with excitement, and it hissed, staying low to the ground just as I'd hoped. Time slowed, my bare feet striking the sand that grew ever hotter in the morning sun. I watched the beast, waiting for the smallest indication of its intent.

There. Its muscles coiled as my foot came down. It lunged for me, and at the same time, I called for a column of rock. The earth erupted next to the beast's head, and I ran up the pillar, using it to vault myself over the snapping jaws and turn in the air. It was so close I felt its breath and the lick of its forked tongue across my thigh. I came down, bringing my sword with me, and cleaved the beast's head from its neck in one cut. When I landed, I turned, blasting the stump with fire.

That was it! My ears were ringing, and my chest swelled around my racing heart. I grinned, turning to find Leo. He was running to me, but his face was contorted, his mouth forming the word "no." My face fell into a frown, and my eyes followed his gaze down.

The sword dropped from my limp fingers. I'd gotten the beast, but it'd gotten me, too. The fang that he'd damaged earlier protruded from my calf, its black venom leaking into my veins. The pain struck suddenly, blazing through my veins like wildfire, and I collapsed, clutching my smock at the chest as my heart twisted in agony.

Leo caught me in his arms before I hit the sand, but his voice sounded far away. "Enid? Enid, no! Stay with me! Eris!"

Something hot rushed up my throat, and I choked, unable to draw a breath and cough it out. I panicked, flailing my arms and trying to find air. Leo took my hand, and I squeezed, tears spilling down my face and pooling in my ears.

'Skadi!'

'We will not survive this injury. I'm sorry,' she said gently, offering me feelings of calm.

We'd won, but I wouldn't live to see it. Leo and I would not have our happily ever after, after all.

"It's not fair," I tried to say, but the sounds I made were nothing like words.

The blurred figure of my sister came into view. I blinked the tears away and her golden eyes came into focus, wide and shining. Her mouth was moving, but I couldn't hear her. Behind Eris stood a tall, shadowy figure in a black robe holding a scythe. I smelled lilies, and the most beautiful purple butterflies fluttered around him. A feeling of calm washed over me, and the need to fight for breath disappeared.

My vision turned black at the edges, and then, all at once, it was gone.

Chapter Thirty-Five

Leo

"Enid! Don't close your eyes," I begged her, ripping the fang from the wound and tossing it. She didn't close them, but they glazed over, staring past Eris at nothing.

Eris was weeping, singing her lullaby. Her hands were glowing, but I felt Enid's heart slowing, choked by the venom. Her hand slackened in mine, and I was shaking my head, the disbelief cold and stark. She'd smiled at me mere seconds ago. Bleiz prayed, his voice echoing in my head, begging the Moon Goddess for a miracle.

"No, no, no! Heal her!" I shouted.

Gideon said something, but I didn't hear it because it was not what I wanted to hear. Eris put her head on Enid's chest and wailed, her knuckles white where she held her arms.

"No," I muttered, and took Enid's head in my hands, running my thumbs over her cheeks. Her green eyes were blank, the swirling magic in them gone. Hot tears streamed down my face as reality struck cold. "Wake up! Please."

"Move! Get outta the way!" Finn shouted, grabbing my shoulders and yanking me away with Cass's help.

I fought them. "No! I promised I'd never leave her!"

Nothing felt real. I turned, lifting my fist to punch someone.

Three unicorns, shining brilliantly black in the morning sun, pushed past me. They dipped their heads, lowering their crystal horns to Enid and pressing them right into the gaping wound on her calf.

Finn was squeezing my shoulder, and we all watched with bated breath, my heart pounding in my ears. Their horns lit like twinkling stars, and I could see the darkness of the poison being pulled into them and then swirling away into nothing.

Daro shifted, dropping to his knees and taking Enid's hand. "Try again, Eris!"

Gideon let Eris go, and she fell forward onto her sister, already singing. I shook Finn's grip away and followed, kneeling and putting my hand on Enid's chest. Closing my eyes, I waited for a heartbeat.

ENID

I was dead. I'd died. It had been cold at first, but now it was warm. Cozy even. My mother sang my lullaby, the sweet tune easing my pain. A soft breeze tickled my nose.

I didn't expect the afterlife to be breezy or painful.

My eyes cracked open to blinding sunlight, and the sudden, panicky need to breathe returned. I tried and gagged. My body flopped involuntarily to my side, and I coughed, spitting a nice mixture of blood and vomit into the sand.

"Enid! She's back!"

There were gasps and cries around me. Someone was brushing my hair out of my face, and I looked up.

"Leo? I'm alive?"

He nodded, too choked up to speak, his hand squeezing my upper arm.

I glanced around. Eris had been the one singing, and she was pale, the bags under her eyes like pits. Blood leaked from both of her nostrils, running over her pale lips, and she sniffled, sobbing and smiling at me. Her hand rubbed my back like she used to when we lived in the cabin and the magic would make me sick. Daro was here, and behind him stood two other unicorns, still shifted to their second forms.

"You saved me," I said, a grin cracking across my face. "That must've been something to see."

He smiled back, but his eyes were sad. "I owed you one."

Beyond him, a crowd was gathering, growing by the second. Finn, Kat, Cass, Gideon. Some harpies, including Wren. Fae soldiers, witches, and our own warriors, all peeking over each other.

"I can stand," I said, my cheeks heating with all the attention. Leo helped me up, brushing the dust off my smock, and I asked, "So, did we win?"

Daro stood too, but Eris stayed on her knees. Gideon bent and scooped her up, holding her in his arms. My brow furrowed, and I reached for her. She took my hand, and around a yawn, said, "I'm okay. Just need sleep." The words had barely left my sister's lips, and her eyes were closed, her breathing even and slow.

"Well, we can all sleep easy now," Gideon said, turning to the crowd, "because we *did* win! Dragons are nothing when we stand together!"

A wild cheer answered, shattering the heavy silence that hung around us. We had actually done it. I smiled. It was over.

"Move! Move! Get out of my way! Where is she?" River shoved her way through the celebrations, her eyes locking on me when she spotted me. I recoiled. Her hair was singed off, her long platinum locks now a burned bob.

"Your hair!"

"To Hades with my hair. Oh, Enid!" She threw her arms around me and squeezed me to her chest. Her familiar scent, like earth and herbs, made the embrace more comforting. Another set of arms wrapped around me, and I could smell the summer breeze. Rhia.

River leaned away, grabbing my cheeks. "I've never been so proud of anyone in all my life. You are a damn fine witch."

I glanced back and forth between them, and my throat thickened. "Hades. He-he..."

She enveloped me in another tight hug, rocking back and forth. Gaon was on my shoulder, caressing my cheek with his buttery soft wing. "We know. He knew his task, and he did what he was sent here to do."

I sobbed, crying into her robes while Rhia rubbed my back. By the time I'd quieted, the crowd was quickly dissipating. I realized many did not come up to see me, but rather to ogle the slain hydra's massive body.

River leaned away from me. "Do not worry. Our Goddess Hecate never leaves a witch without a familiar for long."

"I don't want anyone but him," I said, wiping my eyes.

"Maybe it will be him," Rhia said, squeezing my shoulder. "She'll send who you need. Have faith, and make your desires clear with heavy prayer." She petted the falcon on her shoulder. "Reinier was reincarnated for me once already. He used to be a sparrow."

I nodded, latching onto that hope, and a feeling of calm settled over me. I felt in my heart that it would be okay.

"Now," River said, taking a rag and a vial of liquid from her robes, "let's clean you up a little." She wet the rag and wiped my face. The delicate scent was a sweet embrace. One of my favorites. Rose water. She offered another small bottle. "And now, drink this slowly. It'll help."

I studied the swirling blue liquid before I sipped it. It shimmered, its tiny currents spinning like galaxies in the glass. When I tipped it to my lips, it was like a cold fire. A burning, purifying mint. It was icy in my stomach, making me feel cleansed on the inside, too.

"What was that for?" I asked, handing it back, and expecting an explanation of alchemy.

She smirked. It was a strange look on her normally serious face. "Because I know you're going to go kiss that boy."

My cheeks flared hot. "Oh! Thank you."

River grabbed my face again and kissed my forehead. "It has been my honor, Enid."

"And mine," Rhia said, inclining her head in a small bow.

"Are you leaving me?" I asked, my heart sinking.

"Not permanently, but we will no longer reside at the pack. Call on us if you need us. You know how."

"Will I be able to join your coven?"

"Yes. But later. Now, it is time to rest and celebrate." The side of Rhia's mouth dipped. "And mourn."

River nodded, offering her hand to her wife. They walked away from me together, and I thought they stood taller, as if a heavy weight had lifted from their shoulders.

The grinning pink witch immediately intercepted them. "Hello! Love the edgy new look, River! I wanted to report that I sent others to ward this area and keep any lookie-lou humans away until we get it cleaned up. And we have to put this rock back together! It's sacred to the indigenous people here."

"It's all yours to organize, Nadaria," River said, waving her hand. "We're taking some time off."

She beamed. "Me?"

"I can think of no one more capable."

"Oh." Nadaria scrunched her shoulders, her enormous smile growing somehow wider. "I am honored to have your confidence, River."

River nodded, and she and Rhia disappeared in a flash.

I turned, sighing, and spotted Leo. My brows lifted. He was shirtless, wearing only a leather battle kilt, and speaking to his brothers. Finn was animated, with an expressive smile on his face as he spoke.

'Oh, good,' Skadi said. *'He's already halfway undressed.'*

I grinned, biting my lip.

LEO

I watched Enid speak to River, still trapped speechless in a cage of disbelief. In a matter of hours, she'd been mine, then I'd lost her, and now she was mine again.

'You're sure?' I asked Bleiz. *'She's our mate, you're sure? Like, sure, sure. One hundred percent?'*

'Of course,' he said, chuckling. *'You can rejoice, Leo. It is not a dream this time.'*

'Wow.'

'Indeed. You must've done something good in your past life.'

'Or maybe you did. Skadi, eh?'

He yipped a laugh. *'Yes, Skadi. We have been given the great honor of strong females.'*

Enid was crying now, and I stepped forward to offer my condolences for Hades, but Gideon linked, *'Uh, Leo?'*

'Yeah?' I asked, turning to find him.

He still held Eris, who was asleep in his arms. The Fae King stood next to him, his arms crossed over his chest.

'Can you return the priceless royal heirloom to his majesty before we start another war?'

"Oh, shit." I hurried over, my fingers fumbling with the buckle of the belt. "Sorry! Your Majesty. Just let me—"

The buckle gave, and the sword dropped, falling with a thud into the sand.

My brother sucked in a sharp breath. *'You're giving me all these gray hairs at such a young age, you know?'*

'Sorry,' I said, bending and snatching it up.

I offered the sword to the king with a bow, frowning when I felt an intense need to run away and keep it for myself.

I looked up at him, surprised to find a gentle smile on his face. "Tuilghearr likes you, Gamma. It finds you worthy."

"Really?"

He nodded and took it from me. "That is not a small accolade. You must have a lion's heart."

The greed for it vanished as soon as it was no longer in my hands.

"It's a fine weapon," I said, studying it. The hilt was a piece of art, a beautiful gold and silver inlay, and a pommel set with a giant opal. "The finest thing I've ever wielded."

"Yes. It is."

"Thank you for letting me use it."

"You are most welcome. Don't ever touch it again."

I recoiled, his smile now a tight frown, and nodded that I understood.

"Alpha," he said, turning away from me toward Gideon. He put his fist over his heart.

"Thank you for everything, Your Majesty."

"It was our duty and honor to stand by you in this battle. May the sun warm your path."

"And may the moon light yours," Gideon said, bowing his head.

With that, his majesty left, returning to his guards. A witch waited, flashing the group away as soon as he was ready.

Finn appeared at my side and slapped me on the back. "You should've seen him out there with that sword, Gideon! I was so..." He paused like he couldn't believe he was about to say it. "So proud."

"He'll make a fine Gamma," Gideon said, winking, "when he gets back from college, of course."

Faced with such praise, I was stunned that I didn't search for pockets to shove my hands into. I shrugged. "I did not have my father for long in this life, but I was never lacking in capable teachers."

Their expressions softened, and I felt struck by Gideon's likeness to our father. It was more obvious the older he got.

A quick grin cracked across his face, breaking the resemblance. "Congratulations, Leo. I see the gods have answered many prayers today."

Finn signaled over my shoulder, waggling his brow. "Here she comes."

"Enid," I said, running into her as I spun around. Her feelings were warm in bond, bordering on hot. She grabbed my arms, and sparks flickered everywhere her delicate fingers touched.

We both gasped, then laughed. It was true. The sparks weren't just a part of a story everyone told to promote the mate bond. Something you couldn't really understand until you were feeling them yourself.

I sighed, shaking my head. "You scared me. I don't know if I'll ever..."

"Later," she interrupted, pressing up on her toes. The shape of her lips, soft and open, spelled her intent. My skin felt tighter, suddenly snared like a hare in a lustful trap that I couldn't escape. "All of that sad, serious business can be addressed later."

Bleiz chuckled. *'I must agree.'*

My voice was thicker when I spoke again, rich with his gravelly influence. "What are we addressing now?"

"This," she said, her hands running up my bare chest. Yellow bled into her irises, revealing the wolf inside. The sparks danced at her touch, thrumming the chords of my soul. "This moment we've waited long enough for."

Chapter Thirty-Six

ENID

THE FEELING THAT SWEPT over me was sweet and hot, flowing from him into me through our bond. Our lips met. It was a different kiss now, shared between two people who had grown up so much in the past three days. We'd left a boy and a girl in that rose bramble on the mountain, and here, atop Uluru, stood a man and a woman.

The hunger was unbelievable. Unbearable. His too, and he captured my lips with his, no teasing or coyness, just starvation. I could feel his fangs already tipped, sharpening, and moaned into the kiss. With my wolf now present, his scent deepened, enveloping me in a powerful embrace of raw masculinity. Citrus, spice, and cedar. Heat flooded my stomach, pulsing. Aching. I instinctively reached up and grabbed the collar of my smock, pulling it aside.

I barely heard Finn say, "Well, looks like it's time to hike down this fucking rock for the second time today."

And then Wren. "I'll give you a lift down if you'd like."

"You know, thanks, but I think I'd rather throw myself off the edge."

The sounds faded, and maybe we were alone, and maybe we weren't. I couldn't care less.

"I need you," I breathed, gripping Leo's shoulders, digging my nails in. This heat between us promised to consume me.

He said, "I know," and tossed his leather kilt aside. His hand on my waist lifted me to my toes and then higher, so my feet left the ground. My legs parted, and he guided one of my thighs around his bare waist.

He pressed his hips forward, and with only the gauzy material of my smock between us, the friction was delicious. I answered immediately, without thought, moving against him. Grinding where he strained for me. My head fell back, lost to the pleasure, and I already felt the coil of release tightening.

"Enid. I can't wait any longer." His voice was thick, influenced by his wolf, and I was overcome by his feelings in the bond. Fire and smoke, the flames so strong, they enveloped me. His hand was on my back, and with the help of his claws, he ripped the smock, shredding the light fabric.

The sun sparkled overhead, baking the red desert, and a sheen of sweat quickly formed where our bare skin touched.

"I want you to finish inside me this time," I said, and his head whipped to look at me, his eyes almost black for the size of his pupils. "I want to feel that—us together—for the marking. It should be that way."

I expected an argument, an appeal to my rationale like always. His tongue pushed through his lips, rolling over the bottom one, and he made a low sound of agreement in his chest. He lifted me, and both of my legs wrapped around his waist.

My lips worshiped his marking spot, and my hand tangled in his long hair. He guided me until I felt the head of his length at my slick entrance. If I expected any of the gentleness of the other night, I did not get it. His arm was like steel, anchoring me and pulling me down in one wicked motion.

I was thankful we had not waited for our first time to be this time. The pinching pain I'd endured in the rose briar was a distant memory, appearing and dissipating in a heartbeat. I cried out, holding him. Pressing myself to him.

Leo found my mouth with his again. He said my name into the kiss, "Enid," and the way it sounded sent bumps over my skin; like a prayer, more reverent and devout than the words we'd said to the gods at the Samhain ceremony.

We were moving together. No rhythm, just giving and taking what we needed. The way he held me—standing like this—made my toes curl. He filled me; struck every nerve, and my voice became a mewling hum.

The pressure built with each thrust, with each lash of lightning that coiled in my core, and I said, "Harder. Harder. Don't stop."

I almost regretted saying it because he did stop, freezing like a statue and laughing dryly in my ear. His chest was heaving, and I opened my mouth to say something else, but he lifted me, his hands sliding under my thighs and gripping my bottom so tightly I whimpered.

It stole any control I had, and he held me in a vice, pulling me into him and slamming his hips forward at the same time. I cried out—this broken sound I'd never heard, and he leaned back, looking at me. There was an aggressive question in his gaze, as if asking, "Is that what you want?" He did it again, and again.

LEO

Her voice grew louder, and then disappeared, as if it were stuck in her throat. Sensing she felt no pain, I held her open, making sure I was as deep as possible, pushing her to take all of me.

I watched her face, mesmerized by her expressions that would be alarming in any other setting. Her lips tight, rolled in, and then the next second, her mouth forming a delicate "O" in a soundless cry, her brow knitting. Her eyes had been closed, and they snapped open, staring at me with this sultry, helpless vulnerability that somehow blended beautifully with an expression of shock.

"Fuck," I gritted through my teeth, nearly undone by it.

"Mark me," she gasped. "Oh, gods, do it!"

I groaned low in my chest and buried my face in the soft pillow of her neck, inhaling her sweet scent. I had always liked it, but it was drugging now, the floral scent of roses wrapped in a wild strike of lightning. Kissing the spot first, I took her flesh into my mouth and sucked as hard as I could. My teeth were long and aching, but I didn't want to press them to her. Not yet.

I ripped my face back to stop myself, watching her again. Enid was trying to squirm, but I anchored her with my hands, my fingers digging into her. I kept pushing her closer with longer, harder, and deeper thrusts.

She went slack and, as if apologetic, whined, "I'm coming..."

Her eyes rolled back, and her inner walls clenched, squeezing so tight I nearly joined her.

Not yet, not yet, I begged myself, staring up at the blue sky. I held on, letting the waves pass through her. Only when she stopped and was quivering in my arms did I give her my teeth. I bit her, taking her marking spot as mine while I thrust into her, reigniting that brutal rhythm and stacking her orgasms on top of each other.

Her cry was broken and feral. One of her hands slapped my shoulder with a loud smack, then clenched, her nails ripping at my skin. The salt of her sweat and the sweet tinge of her blood invaded my senses. I felt her walls squeezing me again, and I slowed, releasing one of her legs as the pressure built in my lower stomach.

My hand laced into her hair, probably rougher than I intended, and I pulled her to my neck. Her teeth met my flesh, burying deep, and I dropped to my knees in the warm sand. The sensation ripped through every nerve, as if she were a lightning strike. My cock pulsed inside her. Her soul filled the empty place in my body, belonging there as much as mine did.

I sank down, sitting on my heels and cradling her in my lap. My eyes were closed, and I held her, just trying to catch my breath. Her body was limp against mine, and I ran my hand up and down her back, slick with sweat.

When they finally opened, my eyes caught on something black. My shoulder. "What is that?"

'What?' she asked in the link and giggled breathlessly against me. *'I do not think I can speak yet after that.'*

I smirked and shifted her in my lap so I could get a clearer look. "I've been tattooed."

It was a geometric design, starting at my now-marked neck and rolling down my chest and upper arm. Thorny vines incorporating her elemental signature.

Enid lifted her arm, sporting an identical tattoo. "It's my witch's mark!" She laughed, a deep, sultry chuckle, and walked her fingers up my bare chest. "It looks like you are mine twice over, Leo Greenwood."

Our bodies were still connected, and my shaft started to fill again. She moaned, working me with a roll of her hips, and my hand slid into her hair. I pulled her head back, exposing her neck, and I kissed my mark.

"I'll have you again, Enid. Rougher than that if you can take it."

Her breath was shallow, and I nearly melted into the sand when she ran her hands over her stomach and breasts, gasping, "I'm yours. Have me however you wish."

CHAPTER THIRTY-SEVEN

LEO

WE STOOD IN THE moonlight, nude in the garden. It was a near-winter night, our breaths puffing out in clouds of steam. Goosebumps broke out over my skin, prickling at the cold, and I smelled the first snow falling up higher on the ridge.

"Look," she said, grinning over at me as she stared at the starry sky. "It's the Big Dipper."

I chuckled at the ode to the times when we used the stars as an excuse to lie near each other. "Are you ready?"

It had been a long day. A somber one. The warriors lost at Uluru had been given back to the gods. I could still smell the smoke of their funeral pyres drifting through the pines. It was a great honor for a wolf to die in battle, but that knowledge could only offer their loved ones so much comfort.

"Yes," Enid said, taking a deep breath.

"Go ahead. It's not that bad."

"I'm not afraid," she assured me, smiling.

"I know."

The magic of her first shift inundated the air, and I winced, hearing the crack of bones and rip of skin. The first time was the most painful, but I believed Enid had suffered worse at the hands of her dragon captors. She'd only shared pieces of what happened to her in that subterranean dwelling, but I sensed she was holding back. She'd seen things, I knew, that had taken a part of her. Some of her innocence had died in that den. I didn't pry, though. Part of me didn't want to know details, and if she didn't want to share, I wouldn't ask her to relive any of it.

Enid fell to her hands and knees with a gasp, and in a matter of seconds, the purest white wolf I had ever seen rose in her place. She was smaller than Bleiz, but I had never stood in the presence of anything so elegant. There was a regalness to the way she carried herself on long slender legs, her head the perfect sharp shape of an arrow.

"Skadi," I said, reaching for her. She leaned into my hand. Her fur was like silk, the softest I'd ever felt. "You are breathtaking."

Bleiz pushed me to let him shift, and I didn't argue. We shifted, and I heard Skadi's voice for the first time.

'Let us outrun our grief. Let us play in the pines and meet the first snow of winter as it drops into the valley. I have not seen snow in a long, long time.'

'I heard that,' I said, dumbfounded, and Skadi chuckled.

'Really?' Enid asked, as surprised as I was.

Never had I heard of a wolf able to speak to a human besides their own.

Bleiz only offered, *'She is unique,'* and, slowly, almost shyly, licked her muzzle. Skadi leaned into him, rubbing her head under his chin.

'Come,' she said, yipping aloud, and turned, trotting into the woods.

Bleiz and I followed—in love. So in love.

ENID

In the weeks following Uluru, life had returned to almost normal. *Normal.* I mulled the word in my head because, for the first time, I could apply it to myself. Kind of. People still stared, and I was often sought after like a celebrity, asked to tell again the story of Uluruean Hydra. I always skipped the part where Hades died.

Little Henry especially had become enchanted with the idea of battling the beast. He would beg me to recreate it with the water of the fountain, and would wield a stick like a sword, enlisting Odin and Ceres to be his companions.

But for the first time, I was free. Free to walk my own path. Leo and I had missed the deadline to apply for the winter semester of our chosen university, but Gideon had to pull some strings anyway to get us human transcripts and identities. We would attend in the spring if everything worked out.

In the human world, I would be just a young woman in a biology class who lived in an apartment and worked at the garden center of a major retailer. Most humans did not sense the supernatural. That part of their brains had slowly been shut off in their world of metal and concrete.

'What are you thinking about?' Leo asked, his curiosity piqued by the feelings in the bond.

'How exciting it will be to be nobody.'

We were in the icy garden, lying nude together in a large sleeping bag. I could feel the flowers resting beneath the snow. Our relationship was very much the same as it had been before. We were still the best of friends. Sitting in the garden. Practicing guitar. Playing video games. Now, we just did most of it naked.

"We should head back," he said, holding his hand up to get a read on where the sun was in the sky. "It's getting late, and Daro leaves today."

"We don't want to miss seeing him off. I'm so glad he's..."

I trailed off, sitting up. The sleeping bag slid down, and cold air kissed my naked chest and back.

"He's what? Married already?" Leo asked, chuckling and pushing up on his elbow. "She loves him, too. You can tell by the way she looks at him. Apparently, they've already got a second bride chosen for him when he gets back..."

I reached over, covering his mouth with my hand. "Shh! Did you hear that?"

His eyes moved from side to side, looking, and in the link, he asked, *'Hear what?'*

My heart dropped. It wasn't the first time my mind had played these awful tricks on me in the past weeks.

"I would've sworn it was a... well, never mind."

Just as I accepted it wasn't, I heard it again. A tiny cry. My eyes snapped over to Leo, and he nodded.

"I heard it that time! Over there by the tulips, I think."

I threw the cover off and scrambled to my bare feet. The snow was so cold it was hot as I hurried across the garden. The tulip patch. Hades and I had planted it together our first year in the pack house, him digging the holes and me placing the bulbs.

"Oh. Oh!" I said, my eyes filling. I dropped to my knees, reaching. There, curled in a small empty birdbath, was a tiny black kitten. He was as excited to see me as I was him, springing up and leaping to meet my hands. In the center of his chest was one patch of white fur, exactly where the hydra had bitten him.

"Hades! It is you!" I cried, hugging him to my chest. "Oh, how I've missed you!"

His purr was so loud, vibrating like a tiny motor against my chest, and I stroked his little back with one finger.

Thank you. All glory to your name, Hecate,' I prayed to the Goddess of Witches. At Rhia's suggestion, I'd made offerings at her altar every day for these last few weeks, begging for Hades back just as he had been and promising I would take better care of him this time.

Leo came to stand next to me, shaking his head. "I don't believe it! Hades!"

The kitten meowed, leaning into his hand. Leo had told me, of course, how Hades had lit his path, guiding him and Cass to the right answer about Uluru.

Hades rubbed his cheek across my chin and crawled up under my hair, curling into a ball on my shoulder. His claws flexed, sinking in, and I sighed, elated to feel that familiar sting.

Chapter Thirty-Eight

Enid

W E DRESSED, MAKING IT back to the pack house just in time. Over a dozen unicorns had been staying here while they organized after losing their Alpha equivalent, which they called a Stallion. Daro's grandfather had died on the field of Uluru, killed while engaged in battle with Tirich.

Daro's older brother had taken the title, and Daro had received his own promotion. With it, came a wife. The wedding was immediate, and he was now married to a young unicorn woman named Marna. She fawned over Daro, treating him like a king. It put my guilty heart at ease to know he wasn't lonely anymore.

Today, they were setting off on their journey back home. They lived among the giant sequoias in California, using witches' wards to hide from humans and everyone else. Daro had told me that, even though he wasn't supposed to. It was a sacred secret that, if leaked, could compromise the safety of his entire herd. No one else knew; I hadn't even told Leo.

We held hands and hurried down the steps to where a crowd had gathered to say their goodbyes. Gideon had arranged for cars to take them as far as the California border.

Daro waved when he saw us, coming over to greet us.

"I was afraid I wouldn't see you before we left."

"Wouldn't miss it," I promised. "But we were distracted."

I lifted my hair to reveal the sleeping kitten on my shoulder, and his brows lifted.

"A new kitten?"

"Kind of," I said, grinning.

"Well, I'm glad."

Before the silence grew awkward, Leo said, "It'll be strange without you here."

Daro nodded. "Yeah. We all had a lot of fun together. I hope I'm not too bored back at home."

"Some boredom isn't bad after all this excitement," I said, ready for calmer days.

Leo stuck out his hand. "Well, until next time. I'll never forget what you did on top of Uluru. Thank you." Daro took it, nodding, and Leo said, "Excuse me. I'll be right back."

My brow knitted, and I watched him shuffle through the crowd. Cass was talking to Gideon, standing a few yards away from everyone else. We'd tried several times to visit the dragon these last weeks, but he hadn't been at home in his tower. Or he wouldn't answer the door.

Daro sighed, looking around, and my water witch sensed his stormy feelings.

"Surely you miss home a little?" I asked. "And now you've got a wife. And she's so nice."

I found Marna in the crowd, laughing at something Kat was saying. She was lovely, her white hair twisted in long, tight braids down her back.

"Yeah. She's nice," he mumbled. "I just find it hard to love her when I'm still in love with you."

The words were like a splash of cold water in my face, and I gently closed the bond so Leo wouldn't notice my feelings.

"I'm sorry," I whispered, unsure what to say. "I was never going to be that person for you, even if I never found a mate."

"I know that. But you don't just stop loving someone because they don't love you."

"I do love—"

"Please," he said, putting his hand up. I stopped, and he rubbed the back of his neck. "Don't patronize me, Enid."

My temper flared. "Excuse me? I spent three days chained to a wall in a dragon pit for you! I put the fate of the entire world in jeopardy! Is that not love?"

I crossed my arms, looking around to make sure no one was eaves-dropping. Leo was none the wiser, still speaking to Cass.

"I know. I'm sorry. I am very thankful you didn't let that fire witch harvest me. I am. It's just..." Daro sighed. "You just dumped me and moved on before I could even blink. We went from seeing each other every day to not even talking!"

"I was giving you space to process your feelings."

"You were avoiding me."

"Maybe I was, but it wasn't your fault. I felt guilty. I still do. I feel bad, and unappreciative of how much you loved me, and that I could never return it in the way you wanted."

He sighed. "How much I love you. Still do. Present tense."

My cheeks heated. "I didn't realize you were struggling so badly with this."

"Of course I am!" he whispered hoarsely. "I love you. Love you! The real deal. And you were so..." his jaw tensed, "already ready to fuck Leo after months of telling me you wanted to wait for your mate!"

My mouth dropped open, my cheeks smoldering. No matter what, I knew there was no way Eris and Gideon were airing my business. "How could you know that?"

"I followed you to the garden at the fall festival," he muttered. "I was going to beg you to reconsider our relationship. Of course, I didn't expect Leo to be there. And the way you kissed him and the way you wanted him. I..."

"You tattled on us," I said, glancing around again, and unable to believe the bystanders remained unburned by my flaming cheeks. "You went and told Eris!"

"Yes. I wanted to hurt you because I was hurting." After a pause, he said, "It was wrong. I'm sorry."

I blinked, and we stared at each other until I shook my head. "It's okay. I forgive you."

He frowned and looked away. "I'm just struggling, Enid, to understand how it was so much more for me than it was for you. You were just using me as a distraction from your feelings for Leo. I wanted to love you enough to make you love me, and I couldn't."

"I'm sorry," I said again, unsure what to say because he was right. "I told you over and over not to fall in love with a wolf shifter before their nineteenth birthday."

His brows lifted. "Now you're blaming me?"

"No! It was wrong to do that to you, but I was just dating! Just fun, you know? I didn't realize it was such a commitment for you. If I had known it would lead to such heartbreak for you, I would've never agreed to a date. I'm sorry." I put my hand on his shoulder. "I'm sorry. I don't know how many times I need to say it. I really am. You are so important to me. A dear, dear friend."

We both jumped when his older brother called out, "Are we ready? We need to go."

I glanced up, and my heart hiccupped when Leo was no longer talking to Cass. He was watching us, his hands in his pockets. I opened the bond when I felt him trying to link me.

He asked, *'Do you want me to intervene?'*

'No.'

"I've got to go, Enid," Daro said, watching me look at Leo, and knowing I was talking to him.

"So that's it?" I asked. "This is how we're leaving it? Me with this heavy shroud of guilt on my shoulders and you with a broken heart? What can I say?"

"Nothing. Not everything can be fixed."

I moved to hug him, unsure if he would accept. He did, squeezing me tighter than I expected. Quietly, I said, "Please, Daro, don't let me be responsible for two broken hearts. Move on. Marna loves you. Don't make her feel like you feel right now."

He kissed my cheek, and I tensed. Stepping back, he cleared his throat and fisted his hand over his heart in an official salute. In a detached voice, he said, "Until next time, Enid. It has been a great honor."

I tilted my head, trying to find words. There was nothing to say, and he added, "May the sun warm your path."

Tears brimmed my eyes, and I blinked them away. "And the moon light yours."

He turned on his heel, his steps crisp and hurried. Marna greeted him, talking excitedly about something. She had no idea of the nature of our conversation.

'Even more guilt,' I said to Skadi, watching Daro open the car door for her and then climb in next to her.

'You made a naïve mistake. Everyone errs in life, causing hurt even if they don't intend to. You are allowed to forgive yourself, even if Daro cannot forgive you. He is right about one thing: not everything is mendable. Sometimes things just are what they are. With time, he will move forward.'

LEO

"Cass! Where have you been?" I asked, shouldering up next to him. "We've tried to visit the tower."

"I've been busy," he said, offering a smile. It didn't reach his eyes, and I narrowed my gaze.

"What's going on?"

He and Gideon exchanged glances. Cass said. "We won the battle at Uluru, but there are loose ends that need tying."

"Edana?"

A muscle ticked under his eye. "Yes. And Morga and two of her three daughters escaped capture."

My interest piqued. "We caught one?"

"No. The youngest one was killed by Rhia."

Gideon said, "We don't know what they're plotting. There are other dragon vaults to open. We may see an uptick in vampire turnings in the nearby human cities as they rebuild their army. Who knows what they may do?"

"Well, what can I do to help?"

"Nothing," Cass said, grinning and slapping my shoulder. "You are off to college soon. I want you to enjoy it. You and Enid go have fun, and I know where to find you if I need you." He sighed. "Besides, it could take years to even locate them. We have the information Enid provided about a possible body of water, but there are many lakes and rivers to search in the realm. And searching is hard when the witch is as skilled as Morga."

Gideon said, "Excuse me, I have to see these people off, and they're waiting for me." Cass and I nodded, watching him approach Daro's brother and shake his hand.

I was worried about Cass. I wanted to provide some kind of assurance, but in all honesty, the odds did not appear in our favor.

Bleiz chuckled. *'The odds did not appear to be in our favor when we deciphered the Uluruean poem. The gods have a plan for Cass. He must trust them.'*

"Well, we'll get them, Cass. Have faith in the gods. Don't stress yourself out."

He frowned, shaking his head. "I'm fine."

"Are you sure? I know you and Edana have some—"

"I'm fine," he said again, and looked up, grimacing. "More fine than our little witch is right now."

"What?" I turned over my shoulder, feeling for her in the bond. Enid had blocked me, and I immediately understood why. She looked like she was about to burst into tears at whatever she and Daro were talking about. His shoulders were rigid, his body language tense, and Bleiz shifted in my head, not liking it.

Daro's brother shouted for everyone to get ready to leave. I turned to say my farewell to Cass, but he was gone. My attention went back to Enid and Daro, and I was wrestling with what to do when she looked up at me. Her eyes widened, and her cheeks flushed bright red.

'Do you want me to intervene?' I asked when she opened the bond for me.

'No.'

I watched the rest of the exchange, glad I had such a level-headed wolf when I saw the way he hugged her. Kissed her cheek, lingering there. A wolf like Finn's would be causing a scene. After Daro walked away, I returned, feeling bad I'd left her.

Enid had her arms crossed, and she sniffled, wiping at her nose. "Well, that was awful."

"What happened?"

She shrugged. "He called me out for dating him with no intention of loving him. Like I was using him. And for moving on so quickly to you."

I winced, offering her my arms. She leaned into them, and I rubbed her back. "I'm sorry. I didn't mean to leave you."

"It's okay. He's not wrong about a lot of it. I didn't mean to hurt him, but I did, and there's nothing I can do about it. He had a right to say what he did, and maybe saying it can give him some peace."

I watched the cars leaving, all of them disappearing around the bend of the pack house drive.

"It sucks to have him leave on such a sour note," I said, sighing. It wasn't a surprise to me. He and I had shared several awkward interactions in the last few weeks. Acting like we were good when a giant elephant stood in the room.

She sighed too. "He says he still loves me."

"Of course he does."

Her brow knit. "No jealousy?"

I took her hands. "Just sympathy. How can I be jealous knowing that if I were him, I could've never stopped loving you, either?"

CHAPTER THIRTY-NINE

LEO

MOM WAS FLITTING AROUND my room, shoving random things into my suitcase while I was trying to carry it out.

"You're sure you've packed enough underwear?" she asked, opening that drawer to check how many I'd left behind.

"Yes, Mom. I'm sure they sell them somewhere, too, if I manage to rip them all before we come back for break."

She gave me a stern look. "And pants?"

"Yes, they sell pants, too."

"Did you pack them?"

"Yes. You watched me," I said, laughing.

"Don't laugh at me," she scolded, coming over with her arms out. "I've never sent a son to college."

I accepted her hug, squeezing her tightly and resting my cheek on top of her head. "I'll be okay, Mom."

"You better. I'll make an offering to the Moon Goddess every day when you're gone for your protection. And Enid's, of course."

"Thank you," I said, knowing she wouldn't be talked out of it. If it brought her peace, I wanted her to do it.

I rolled my suitcase into the hall, pleased to see Enid step out with hers at the same time.

We smiled at each other, and I asked, "You ready?"

"Yes!"

We were eating lunch first, so we rode down in the elevator and walked to the dining hall with Mom. When we got inside, a chorus of "Congratulations!" rang out.

Everyone was here, with a banner and cake and everything.

I looked at Mom, who was beaming. "You will find any excuse to plan a party."

Her grin didn't falter. "Of course, I will. Shut up and enjoy it."

I laughed, and we did all the things. Cake and congratulations. Gideon gave me a pair of golden cufflinks, as if I would need to wear a suit, and Finn gave me a finely crafted fae dagger in case I needed to stab a mugger, apparently.

We finally got out to the front of the house where the car waited, and I said, "Alright, thanks everyone!"

Eris hugged Enid, crushing her to her chest, and Enid promised to be careful.

"I'll call often."

Eris nodded. "Text me. Every day. Or I'll text you."

"You better do it, Enid," Kat said, laughing, "or she'll be knocking on your apartment door at midnight."

Finn shoved my shoulder. "Good luck, Baby Brother."

"Don't shove me," I said, pushing him back.

His brows lifted, and he went to shove me again, but I blocked his hands. We wrestled, and he was laughing his antagonist big brother laugh until I broke free.

"Okay, we're going!" I said, unsure if they'd ever let us leave if we didn't pry ourselves away.

Gideon shook my hand, giving me a quick hug. "Learn something useful. We'll be here. Call me if you need anything."

"Thanks."

Enid, Hades, and I finally got into the car, and we both waved in the rearview mirror as we disappeared around the corner.

After we left our packlands, and then crossed the warded barrier of the realm, she rolled down the window and stuck her hand out into the wind, yelling, "We're free!"

The excitement in that tiny cab was palpable. Jittery. We were completely in charge of ourselves for the first time in either of our lives.

I took her hand, resting ours together on the middle console, and grinned at her.

"So, what do you want to do first?"

CHAPTER FORTY

Six Years Later

LEO

I WATCHED HER, AS I always did, and as I always had. Enid was with our nieces and nephews, who had all grown so fast. It felt like I blinked and we were both walking across that stage at the university, accepting our degrees. These kids, who were toddlers when we left, were now children. Sierra was almost in middle school. They still loved Enid and flocked to her whenever she was around. There was just something about her. Children and animals were drawn to the light in her spirit.

They gathered around her while she played a classic game with them at the fountain. Enid brought their imaginations to life with water. The requests were more complicated these days, but she had mastered the element and was putting on quite a show. Several adults had gathered, gasping as she shaped a dragon and flew it around the courtyard.

We'd graduated this spring and decided it was time to return to the pack. One of Enid's botany professors had been so impressed with her they'd come to our apartment and begged her to stay and work at the university in the research department. She had politely declined.

The day we'd left our little apartment had been a sad one, filled with tears. We were both so happy to have experienced so much in that big city. We missed it, just the two of us and Hades, but it was never home. The pack was where we belonged, in the fresh mountain air.

I couldn't say I enjoyed my position as Gamma now, but I resented it less, having gotten to live my life on my terms. I'd played in a band in college, and we'd done pretty well. We even played some festivals and shows, but I could never commit to that dream the way the other guys needed me to, so I'd eventually had to let them move on.

I looked up at the sun as it started its afternoon descent. Soon we would start the more reverent of the Samhain customs, where a stag would be sacrificed by Eris, and the blood shared. Later would be the costume ball, forever my favorite because it took me back to that rose briar. One of the best and worst nights of my life.

Hades was perched on my shoulder watching Enid. Not a big fan of the water, he stayed with me this time. He would never love me as much as he loved her, but I was his second favorite person, and I'd happily take that.

Enid was able to escape when Finn and Kat appeared with candied apples. Kat had the youngest Greenwood in her arms. Callum, or mini-Finn, as I thought of him. A child could not look more like their father. Conceived with the help of a fancy lab in Sweden and an egg donor, Kat had carried him with a healthy pregnancy. He had been Enid's first delivery, right here in the pack house. She'd delivered two more pups in the pack since, having an affinity for it as witches often did.

Enid walked to me and laid easily against my side as I wrapped my arm around her.

"I didn't know if you were ever going to get away," I said, chuckling.

She shook her head. "I had to link Kat to save me, or else I wouldn't have."

"Are you hungry?"

"Yes, I'm starving!"

"I saw you eyeing those turkey legs earlier."

"Ugh, yes, I need one of those. Your child is a meat eater for sure." She laughed and leaned up to kiss me.

Developing pups needed meat. I grinned and placed my hand on her belly. She was only two months away now and was really starting to show.

We walked lazily toward the smell of smoked turkey, stopping every once in a while to look at things. I chuckled when I noticed Eris was already at the booth, grinning widely as the vendor handed her a steaming turkey leg.

She turned and spotted us, the two sisters giggling at each other. Eris was pregnant too. A bit unexpected by the way that my eldest brother told it, but a joyous surprise. Enid had already told me that both babies were girls. She sensed it.

I scanned and found Gideon standing a few feet away. Talking on the phone, of course. The life of an Alpha. He never got any rest.

"Mom, look what I won!"

We all turned to see Henry running towards us with one of those poor goldfish in the little cup that you could win by throwing rings. He handed it to her, beaming.

"Oh, wow, that's great," Eris said as she held up the little cup and grimaced. "Is he alive?" The fish twitched, and she sighed. "Poor thing, we'd better get him into a bigger container. I need to change into my ceremonial dress, anyway."

"I'm going to name him Ares, God of War!"

"Yes, he looks quite menacing," she said, placing her hand on Henry's back and guiding him toward the house.

She waved to us and made a face to show how unexcited she was about the new, scaly addition.

"I need to speak to Gideon about that cruelty. That poor little fish," Enid said, her face pinched as we watched them go.

Death was a part of life, but Enid detested any kind of suffering. Gideon would accommodate her request, no doubt. After the dragon war ended, I'd never seen him say no to her. She got what she wanted whenever she wanted. His way of apologizing, I supposed, for the pressure he'd put her under as a teenage girl.

As I thought of him, my eyes found him again at the edge of the crowd. He watched Eris move away, and he moved too, walking parallel to her while still on the phone. I understood. The instinct to protect your mate was strong, but when she was carrying your child, it was overwhelming.

He made eye contact with me, and I tried to look away, but I was too late. Gideon curled his finger, signaling me over. Sighing, I told Enid, "I will be right back."

ENID

I snacked on the turkey leg and watched Leo talk to Gideon about some matter of pack business. There was a tug on my skirt, and I looked down.

"Hi, Ceres."

She was watching me with those wide yellow eyes, and I could tell she was thinking. Ceres was always that way, watching and thinking.

"May I touch your belly?"

"Yes, thank you for asking."

She put her hands on my belly and smiled up at me. "Our sweet purple flower. She will sing to birds, and they will listen."

The hair on my neck lifted, and I crouched down, sighing from the effort it took. I had told no one besides Leo that this was a girl or what her name would be.

"What does that mean, Ceres?"

"I don't know," she said shyly, her cheeks reddening.

"Did someone tell you that?"

"No."

"Then how do you know?"

Ceres froze, staring at me. She looked over my shoulder and said, "Bye."

"Wait!" I called, but she was already gone, running around a booth and out of sight.

"I'm back," Leo said, helping me stand. He glanced in the direction Ceres had disappeared and asked, "What was that?"

"I'm not sure. She knew I was having a girl."

"She probably guessed. She had a fifty-fifty chance of getting it right."

"She knew her name."

His brows lifted. "Could your mother's bloodline already be showing in her?"

"That must be it." I stared at the corner Ceres had rounded in her retreat, the hair on my neck still prickling, and sighed, making a note to talk to Eris later. "Did you tell Gideon about the fish?"

"Yes, he promises they will all be liberated by the end of the day, and that we'll retire that practice."

I smiled. "Good. Thank you."

Leo laced his fingers with mine, and we walked the garden path up to our bench. Hades hopped down from his shoulders and stretched out on his favorite rock in the sun. I set the turkey leg there, giving him the rest.

Glad to get off my feet, I plopped on the bench. Leo sat next to me, and I lifted my arms, letting him rest his head in my lap. His ear was pressed against my tummy, and I absentmindedly ran my fingers through his hair, listening to the garden. It was a flurry of activity, all the patrons doing their last-minute preparations for winter.

Leo smiled, and I knew he could hear the baby's heartbeat. He loved this, and we soaked up every second. Witches always avoided having two girls, as one always turned dark and one light. No one knew why.

We couldn't risk it, so she was our only. My sweet Sage. A name I'd chosen because I loved the pretty purple flowers of the sacred plant. She was happy now. I could sense it. Maybe because of the turkey leg or the fact that her father was near.

I felt a flutter, and Leo's eyes flew open. "Did you feel that?"

"Of course, I did," I said, laughing. "She's very active when you're around. She knows you."

"Really?"

"Yes."

"That's incredible." He sighed, putting his lips to my belly. "I am going to teach you to play the guitar." When she kicked him again, he chuckled. "Gods! She's gotten so strong."

Sage gave him her best for a few minutes, kicking and shuffling against his cheek. The movements slowed, then stopped, and I told him, "You have worn her out. She's sleeping."

Leo sat up and pulled me to his side, yawning. "A quick nap is not a bad idea."

I nodded and leaned up, kissing him lazily for a few long seconds, and then I settled into him, thankful for his warmth.

I was drifting, and when he thought I was already asleep, Leo kissed the top of my head.

He whispered, "I just love you. Gods, how I love you both." And then, "Thank you. Thank you," to the Goddess.

I smiled, remembering all the way back to when I stood in the shower after that night at the bar and told the Goddess it was him or no one for me.

Thank you for all my blessings.

THE END

546 Years Later

ENID

I stared down at the cup as the leaves seeped into the boiling water. My old bones felt different today. The time had finally come.

I used my magic to pick up the spoon and stir the tea, the gnarled knuckles of my hands too fraught with arthritis to be much good for anything.

'It is time,' Skadi said.

'Yes.'

'Praise be.'

We were both ready. They were all gone now, too long ago. When Eris had been alive, she'd kept the others here. When she made her journey at two hundred and fifty-two years old, everyone else had followed—Gideon that same day. And then Finn and Kat. Leo had held on the longest, but had finally been called home, leaving me here. I'd outlived my entire family. Only one persisted, somewhere far beyond my reach.

I had survived centuries longer than the average wolf, but I still aged faster than most witches. Even though I'd never dabbled in the dark arts, time had taken its physical toll. My bones creaked like this old house.

Everyone was gone, except for the little black dragon. Cass still looked almost exactly like the handsome young man that had landed on Gideon's balcony all those years ago. He came to me twice a week and listened to me talk about Leo, sharing the same stories over and over again because there were no new memories to be made in this lifetime.

My mentors, River and Rhia, I didn't know. They had walked into the forest a long time ago and never returned.

Thinking of Cass, I knew he would be by in the next couple of days. I was sorry for him to have to find me, and I went to the wall, pulling out one of Leo's hundreds of sketchbooks. I used my magic to flip the pages. It was one I hadn't seen in a very long time and, despite it all, my old cheeks flushed. A naked young woman stood atop Uluru, a handsome sword in her hand and the slain body of the hydra behind her. He'd spared no details.

'Was I really so beautiful once?' I asked Skadi. Her memory was better than mine.

'Absolutely.'

I flipped back, finding a different drawing of the same young woman. She was perched on the back of a black dragon, flying over a forgotten battlefield. Liking this one for the task, I picked up a pen and used my magic to write on the back of it.

Cass,

The void calls me now, old friend.

Don't weep for me, as you know I have been ready for a long time. I'll tell the little lion you said hello.

Your treasured friendship has kept Leo and the others alive for me all these years. Thank you for keeping an old woman company.

With great love,

TLW

I ripped the page free and looked around the cabin one last time. Many years ago, when everyone I knew had gone on, I returned here, to the place it all began. The walls were covered with my plants, their tendrils framing sketches and paintings Leo had done. The Dragonsbane spear hung above the fireplace, a reminder of the woman I had been.

Once upon a time, people journeyed for miles to seek the powerful potions I brewed. These gnarled old hands had delivered hundreds of babies into this world. My magic had been legendary, but now no one remembered the old woman in the woods, and I was okay with that, too.

I looked at the bed, which was in the same place it had always been. A dusty memory played in my mind of Gideon ripping the door from its hinges and coming in to find his one true love and unknowingly taking me to mine. It felt as though I'd lived that moment in another life.

I glanced down again at the sketchbook that lay open. It was another sketch of the girl that had been me. She was kneeling on the sidewalk in front of an orange rose with no shoes on. The flower was blooming in her hand. I stared at it, trying to remember the moment but unable to recall.

I shuffled outside, using my magic to bring my cup of tea and the note for Cass. Groaning, I sat on the hard garden bench. It was our bench, mine and Leo's, and I had brought it with me when I left the pack.

I settled in, looking at the companion on my left. I'd brought the guitar out earlier today and set it there, so it was with me. Cass, this guitar, and the sketchbooks kept Leo alive all these years. Without them and Skadi, I would've gone mad long ago.

There was a gravelly meow at my feet. And him, of course. He was asking for a lift.

"Oh, Hades, I believe I can manage it one more time."

I bent with significant effort and scooped him into my lap. He was far too old himself now, a scraggly thing with patchy fur and cloudy eyes.

"Are you ready to go?"

He settled himself and purred softly as I moved my stiff hand across his bony back the best I could.

I sipped my tea and watched my garden, listening to its beauty. The soft whisper of the seedlings as they found their roots; the shuffle of a spider as she weaved her web.

"I will miss you," I told the plants, "but maybe another witch will come along and take this place as hers."

Evening bled into night, but the midsummer air stayed warm. I looked up at the stars and said to the guitar, "Oh, look, Leo, it's the Big Dipper."

An icy gust rustled around me, and I pulled my robes tighter. Cass's note threatened to blow away from the table next to me, so I set my teacup on it. Odd, to feel such a cold wind on a summer night.

I woke up sometime later, gasping as I lifted my head. "It's you."

The God of Death stood before me, his lavender butterflies floating softly around him. He dropped his head in a small nod. "Greetings."

"It's about time you showed up."

"You know I don't decide when," he said, his affect as flat as stone.

"Maybe I will have a stern word with fate."

He might've chuckled. I couldn't tell. His voice was monotonous again when he said, "Your wolf insists on a goodbye, and I was instructed to be accommodating."

Skadi stepped around him, glowing as bright white as the moon.

'This is where we part,' she said, walking up to me.

I put my hand on her head. *'I will miss you.'*

'It was an honor, Enid, to live this life with you.'

'And you. May the moon light your path, Skadi.'

'The moon waits for me,' she said, her wolfish eyes sparkling.

I kissed her soft forehead. *'Then I won't keep you a moment longer.'*

She licked my cheek, and the God of Death raised his scythe, slicing the very fabric of reality. Beyond the cut was another world, and a blast of pine-laden air gushed out. I inhaled the fine scent and watched Skadi leap through before the crack sealed behind her.

When I looked back at my escort, another was there, standing by Death's side in a soft white glow.

"Leo!"

He was so handsome. A boy again, compared to the last time I'd seen him. The young man I'd fallen in love with all those years ago.

He held his hand out to me, and I reached for it, stunned to see that my old, gnarled knuckles were no longer there. My skin was soft and smooth, the beauty of youth returned to it, and I stood easily without aching bones. He pulled me to him, holding me to his chest.

Impatient, I pushed up on my toes. We kissed, and I smiled against his lips. Oh, how I'd missed it.

When we broke apart, I looked up at him. "I've waited a long time for that."

He grinned. "I would've waited forever."

Leo ran his thumb down my cheek, and we stared into each other's eyes. The love between us was unending, unyielding, and unaffected by the time we had been apart.

"Are you ready to go?" he finally asked.

He indicated behind him, and I gasped again. The first face I found was Eris, smiling and waving to me.

On her left stood Gideon, Finn, and Kat. On her right stood two people I hadn't seen in so long I didn't know if I could believe my eyes. My mother and father were there, waiting patiently with my daughter.

Everyone was smiling, calling out to me and waving for me to come with them.

I looked at Leo and nodded. I was more than ready.

"Wait," I said quickly and glanced back, waving with my hand. "Well, come on, then!"

Hades jumped from the bench and ran to me—a spry, beautiful, young cat once again.

I kneeled down and picked him up, helping him wrap around my shoulders. He purred against me as I scratched his head.

Our earthly bodies had disintegrated to dust and were blowing away in the summer breeze. I looked once more at the guitar propped there and said goodbye to my old friend.

Rejuvenated, I was already forgetting the pain of the life I had been living. Pure, bright joy filled my soul.

I turned back to Leo and grabbed his outstretched hand. He squeezed my fingers. I became nothing but peace, walking beside him as he led me toward the real forever.

DRAGON KEEP ME TEASER

Prologue

Cass

I SNIFFLED UP IN the hayloft of the stables, counting the pieces of sharp straw alongside the reasons I hated my father. My mangled hand was stained purple with proof of his loathing. He'd broken every finger, one by one, after I'd spilled a drop of his wine when pouring it tonight.

I stared at my quivering knuckles. With a soft crunch, my first finger corrected itself. One might be thankful to heal so quickly, but I could hardly be. Father's magical blood in my veins was responsible.

Someday, my dragon would wake, and we would fly far, far away from here.

If Father let me live that long. Some days I thought he would just end me, but I was the only child he'd ever been able to sire, and it was with a human woman. He despised me for it. His only son, a half-breed bastard born of the womb of a lowly human. My mother had been a favorite of his. Her coal-black hair and sapphire-blue eyes fit his predilections, holding a beauty not fit for a human, he would say.

Thoughts of Mother brought fresh tears, and I dragged my scratchy sleeve across my face. She'd often spoken of running away to the human world. It was in the chaotic throes of war, the settlers fighting their mother country for their independence, and we could ease in somewhere unnoticed and make a life.

Father had ended that dream sixty-three days ago.

As his aggression toward me grew darker, Mother grew desperate. While Father was sleeping, she plunged a dagger deep into his heart. She didn't understand that it had to be a special blade to take his life. After such an offense, even her rare beauty would not save her.

I pressed my hands against my ears. Dragon flame burned hotter than the fire that warmed the hearth. I could still hear her screams; the sound of her flesh sizzling and popping in the inferno. And the smell. An acrid scent I'd never forget. How he'd sneered into my weeping face afterwards. "Not so lovely now, is she?"

"Cassian?" the sweetest voice called as the ladder to the loft shook.

I sucked in a sharp breath, wiping furiously at the droplets rushing down my cheeks. "Elizabeth? I'm here."

I made room for her, and she cozied up next to me. She'd been working in the kitchen. The herbs from tonight's roast chicken tickled my nose.

I sighed and looked at her, wondering if a young lady would still wed a young man if she'd seen him cry. Someday I would marry her. I had yet to confide that to her, but I planned to do so soon. As soon as I could get my courage up.

As always, she'd attempted to shove her curly black hair underneath her bonnet, but it had escaped in several places. Her wide eyes, russet-brown like the potatoes in the cellar, held a dark sadness.

I sighed again. "You know I detest it when ye pity me."

"Are ye harmed?"

I hid my hand by the side of my leg and grinned. "I shall survive."

Her face pinched, wrinkling the soft dusting of freckles on her nose. "Allow me to see that hand, then."

I shook my head. "Don't fret over it, I beg ye."

"He is a wicked, awful man!" she said, her lip jutting out in defiance.

"Elizabeth! Don't utter such things aloud. If the Master found out…"

I couldn't bear it, the thought of losing her, too.

"Oh, I care little—"

A commotion ripped through the lazy summer silence outside. We glanced at each other and crawled over to the tiny loft window. A group of people, all of them women, approached. I could sense their magic from here.

My brow furrowed. "Witches? Never heard of this many together."

"There must be a hundred of 'em out there," Elizabeth whispered, and the sharp scent of her fear choked the loft.

I took her hand in mine. "It'll be alright. I won't let anyone harm ye."

"Aye, this is it!" one yelled. "Smells like brimstone, doesn't it, sisters?"

They shouted agreements and rushed forward, wielding their staves and their elements to slaughter the vampires that guarded the house. Elizabeth and I watched with bated breath, being sure to keep our heads down.

People started screaming inside as the group invaded the home.

"What is happening?" Elizabeth asked.

I shook my head. A roar that I knew was my father shook the house, and I hunkered down at the familiar sound.

We watched as they dragged him, kicking and yelling, out of the door and down the steps. He was secured with something, a chain of some kind. I expected him to shift and kill them all, but he didn't seem able.

"What is the purpose of this?" he bellowed, his features twisting with blue scales as his dragon tried to break free. The muscles of his arms flexed, trying to grow, but stalled once they encountered the links of chain. His eyes were wild, one orange with a slitted pupil and one white with blindness, a large scar from long ago running through it.

A witch shouted, "Dragons have pushed their will unto others far too long!"

"We're done fearing ye!" another added.

"Monster!"

He fought the chains like a rabid dog. "You will all be dead for this, you wretched whores!"

They cackled in unison, and an earth witch wrapped a root around his face to quiet him. I gasped at their defiance, exchanging a small smile with Elizabeth. Father was being taken away. Forever? Could we be so fortunate?

They were dragging him to a cart when one witch stopped. Her eyes fell on the window that Elizabeth and I watched from, and we ducked, staring at each other.

"Do you sense that?" the witch asked.

There was a beat of silence, and then one answered, "There's another! Another dragon!"

Elizabeth's eyes widened, and she snatched my sleeve. They couldn't mean me! I pulled down the collar of my tunic. My chest glowed orange, unmistakable evidence that I had the heart of a dragon.

The doors of the stables banged open.

"Come out, come out, dragon scum," the witch sang. "Or I'll burn the whole place down to find ye."

I swallowed and looked at Elizabeth. "Ye stay here. Promise?"

"Cassian," she whispered, shaking her head.

My breath was hard to find, but I leaned forward and kissed her soft cheek. Her face flushed a deep red, and mine warmed as I said, "I will be fine."

The familiar rungs of the ladder were slick beneath my hands. A woman waited at the bottom, tapping her booted toe on the floor. She held a flame in her hand and wore long, black robes. Her amber hair was tied in a tight bun, and despite her vile expression, she was lovely.

"He's jus' a boy!" she called. "Too young to even shift yet from the look of 'im." The witch grabbed my hair and yanked me up, sniffing the back of my neck. "Smells human, too. Could be half."

"Bring 'im! They all go!"

I tried to twist away, yelping when she dragged me by my hair with unexpected strength.

"Please! I am human—only a halfblood! Leave me be!"

I kicked her in the stomach, and she doubled over, cursing at me.

I tried to run, but tree roots wrapped around my ankles, tripping me.

"Come now, boy," an older woman said, the earth witch. "Don't make it harder than it need be."

Tears ran down my cheeks, the rocks digging into my hands as I scooted away. I looked at the wagon where they imprisoned my father, nailing him shut in a wooden coffin. "Please, my lady, I'm not like 'im. I'm beggin' ye mercy. I don't want to harm nobody."

"Stop! You leave 'im be!" Elizabeth ran to me and laid her body over mine.

"Don't, Elizabeth! Just run!" I rested my cheek against the top of her head and whispered, "Please."

The witches looked at each other, seemingly at a loss.

"Sorry, boy," the old woman said, her gravelly tone softer. "We 'ave our orders. Move out of the way, girl, we don't want to harm ye."

The fire witch grabbed Elizabeth and flung her aside. She wrinkled her nose, wiping her hand on her robes.

"Yech! The girl's a nulla."

I knew what a nulla was, and I knew that Elizabeth was one. A girl born to a witch who, for some reason, didn't acquire magical powers. Other witches saw them as flawed abominations, but I couldn't care less what she was.

The fire witch kicked Elizabeth hard in the stomach, and she yelped, curling into a ball and sobbing.

"No!" I scrambled to my feet. "I'll come! Just let 'er be, please."

I begged the old woman, and she looked at the other witch.

"Leave the girl alone, we're not here for 'er."

The fire witch hissed at Elizabeth, but walked away.

I stood by the old earth witch, and she wrapped me with the same chain my father wore. It smelled of magic. My skin burned, and it was difficult to find a breath.

"Cassian!" Elizabeth called as they led me away, running after us.

"Don't!" I pleaded. "Jus' stay back!"

Unable to leave it alone, Elizabeth picked up a rock. She threw it, hitting the fire witch in the back.

Flames blazed to life in her hands. "You little nulla wretch!"

I tried to run, to help, screaming, "Elizabeth!"

They stuffed me into my own coffin-shaped box and nailed the lid shut. The carriage lurched, and black powder floated down through the cracks. I inhaled it and felt too tired to keep my eyes open.

Sure I would not survive to sunrise, I shouted, "Elizabeth! I-I love you!" Blackness swarmed my vision, but not before I heard her terrified shriek.

When I woke and got the lid pried up, I found myself locked away in a dungeon deep below the earth. There were others here, including my father.

Six adult dragons, their wicked yellow eyes narrowing on me.

No one to help me.

No escape.

Dragon Keep Me
Teaser

Chapter One

A Couple of Centuries Later

Natalie

I SWIPED AT THE bug that had made it his life's mission to buzz around my face for this entire stupid hike. Digging my phone out of my pocket, I prayed for a signal. No bars. Great.

I had so much work to do, and what does my boss decide is best for me? A team-building weekend just because I fired Greg and told him that a six-year-old could put together a better presentation than he did.

It wasn't a lie. The presentation was flat. I didn't have time for mediocre work, and I didn't have time for a team-building, hand-holding, let's-all-be-friends weekend.

There was a promotion on the table. It was everything I'd worked for. The most important thing in my life.

Kind of the only thing.

I paused, wondering if that should depress me.

With my next step, my shoe slipped on a mossy log, and I kicked it in retaliation. It split open, and a thousand wriggling larvae spilled out onto my shoe. "Oh, ew!" I hopped around, shaking my foot as if it was on fire. "I hate you, Kellen! And I hate you, Greg!"

Thanks to them, I was pretty sure I was lost out here in the dense forest. I smacked at the bug again and groaned as I climbed another steep embankment. This humidity was going to kill me.

How had I gotten separated from the group? One minute we were all together... then they were just gone. I shuddered, reminding myself to remain calm, but the sun was going down. I might be stuck out here all night.

Trying not to think about that, I mocked Kellen's words. "Be nicer. A leader, not a boss." I spent most of my time doing his job and mine, and he had the audacity to tell me I needed to work on my "people skills" after Greg called me a rancid bitch.

Puh-lease. I was the most productive department manager at that place. Kellen could never know what it was like to be a young woman climbing the corporate ladder.

I stopped and turned my ear forward. What was that? There was a buzzing that had nothing to do with my stalker mosquito.

I followed it into an open clearing. In the middle sat a large, square stone. A perfect cube levitating waist-high off the ground. It hummed, and I glanced around, looking for anyone or anything else. The forest was quiet here, the trees tall and silent. Even the birds and insects had quieted. The air was heavy, as if nothing dared to breathe here. My mosquito companion was suddenly absent.

When I got closer to the cube, I noticed small markings all over it. The hair on my arms lifted, pulled towards the stone like static electricity.

"This is weird, right?" I said aloud, glancing around the empty clearing. "Am I dreaming?"

When I focused on the inscribed cube, a trickle of sensation climbed up my spine. I didn't want to touch it, but something deep inside me said that I should. My brain gave me a thousand reasons not to, conjuring up every image from every scary movie I'd ever watched, but my hand floated forward, almost of its own accord.

I stared at my fingertips as they made their way towards the buzzing stone. They were close. I could hear whispers—voices of women, chanting—but I couldn't discern the words.

A sharp pain cut through my forehead, but it was too late. My hand lurched forward. At the brush of my fingers, the stone crackled with electricity.

There was a bright flash.

Then nothing.

Cass

I tightened my grip on her hips, thrusting faster, then forced myself to ease back, remembering to mind my strength. I brushed my fingers down her back. She shuddered and smiled over her shoulder at me.

Good. I had to be careful. Lately, I'd been rougher than usual.

This was how I vented my frustration, and I was truly vexed. I kept running into dead ends in my hunt for the dark witch Morga and her red dragon.

I looked down at my current companion, a fae woman from the nearby city. Pretty. Nice subtle curves. Goddess knows I couldn't remember her name, even if she'd told me five or six times. Daisy? Dahlia? All of these fae women were named after flowers.

My thoughts trailed again. That fucking dream, my last day with Elizabeth, came more often all the time. Others too. The dungeon. Edana and her ruby lips. The beautiful ghosts that haunted me.

The fae girl cried out and dug her nails into my wrist. I'd tightened my grip too much, and I loosened it immediately, grunting, "Sorry."

Careful.

I forced myself to focus, ready to be done. This was one of the rare times things progressed this far. It didn't usually get to sex. I liked to pleasure women—learning what made them unravel—but I didn't particularly enjoy the touch of a woman. Even the gentlest caress dragged me back to that dungeon.

When I finished, I checked her hips, pleased to see I hadn't bruised her when I'd grabbed her too hard.

The woman rolled over, looking at me through her lashes with a cat's smile curling on her lips. She whispered, "Oh, my gods," and then giggled. Relieved I hadn't harmed her, I smiled and patted her thigh.

'It's still early; we can go find another tonight. And another. A pretty bouquet of fae,' Crux, my dragon, suggested, his deep laugh echoing in my head. His tone was both smooth and rough, like the purr of a large cat, and tinged with his avarice.

'You are gluttonous,' I shot back, though temptation stirred. I probably would give in to his whims.

He was persistent. Dragons were greedy. Notoriously so. I hated myself for it, but I had trouble suppressing those urges. To take. To collect. It was a dragon's goal to possess pretty and valuable things. Treasure was the most obvious, and I had plenty of it. Women were pretty, too. Their pleasure was a drug. It satisfied some of his insatiable hunger, and we played off of each other. His need to possess and my need to forget.

He snickered at my thoughts. *'We're the same, you and I, Cassian. You are the dragon.'*

I clenched my teeth, not willing to argue with him. I fought his control, clinging to the shred of humanity I had. Most dragon shifters took their dragon's name when they turned eighteen. I was not willing to give up the name my mother had given me.

The fae girl frowned when she saw I was pulling my pants back on.

Her lip jutted out into a sensual pout. "You're not staying?"

"Oh, uh, no," I said, glancing around for an escape from this dreaded conversation. "That was lovely, though. It's not you."

My phone started ringing in my pocket, saving me. I pulled it out with a sigh.

Staring at the screen, I said, "You can sleep here, and help yourself to anything you need. There is a tub and fresh clothes in the restroom. Excuse me."

I didn't look at her again. My shred of humanity didn't like to see the hurt I caused.

Instead, I stepped out into the hallway, smiling as I answered the phone. "Gideon! You have no idea how well-timed this call is."

He sighed. "I doubt I even want to know, Cass."

Gideon was the Alpha of the nearby wolf shifter pack. He let me stay here in a watchtower on the edge of his pack lands.

We'd been allies last year when the other dragons started a war in an attempt to regain control of the supernatural realms. We'd won, but the evil witch who'd started it all, Morga, had escaped. Along with Edana, the ruby-scaled strumpet who would die by my hand.

"You're probably right," I said to Gideon. "You don't want to know."

"As long as you're staying away from my pack members, I don't care."

I was banned for life from socializing in the pack due to all the trouble I'd caused. Wolf women tended to be possessive. Clingy. I could never love them like they wanted.

"I am. As promised."

"Are you... busy now?" he asked, clearing his throat.

"Not anymore."

"Good. Something is wrong with the ward stone on our border. No one can get in or out of the realm. Can you fly out there and check it? I'm still waiting to hear back from the witches."

"Oh, I do love a mystery," I said, chuckling.

"It's important. If you can't be serious, I'll just go—"

"Relax, grumpy. I'm going."

"Let me know what you find."

"I will."

THANK YOU!

I FYOU HAVE MADE it this far, thank you! I hope you enjoyed The Green Witch Trilogy.

Cass's story, *Dragon Keep Me*, is in the works to make its official debut, and after that, *The Toad Prince*.

Follow me on my socials so you don't miss anything!

Facebook: Lynn B. Romance
Instagram: Lynn Branch @ l.branchromance
TikTok: Lynn Branch @lynnbranchromance

OR

Email me at lynnbranchromance@gmail.com and request to be added to my mailing list.

Peace and blessings,
Lynn B.